# HIGHLAND FLAME

## HIGHLAND OUTCASTS
### BOOK 2

## BY
## ELIZABETH ROSE

## ARE YOU SIGNED UP FOR DRAGONBLADE'S BLOG?

You'll get the latest news and information on exclusive giveaways, exclusive excerpts, coming releases, sales, free books, cover reveals and more.

Check out our complete list of authors, too!

No spam, no junk. That's a promise!

### Sign Up Here

www.dragonbladepublishing.com

*Dearest Reader;*

*Thank you for your support of a small press. At Dragonblade Publishing, we strive to bring you the highest quality Historical Romance from some of the best authors in the business. Without your support, there is no 'us', so we sincerely hope you adore these stories and find some new favorite authors along the way.*

*Happy Reading!*

*CEO, Dragonblade Publishing*

# ADDITIONAL DRAGONBLADE BOOKS BY AUTHOR ELIZABETH ROSE

**Highland Outcasts Series**
Highland Soul (Book 1)
Highland Flame (Book 2)
Highland Sky (Book 3)
Highland Silver (Book 4)

# Author's Note

*(The Highland Outcasts Series features secondary characters from my MacKeefe Clan. The stories about the characters who are making guest appearances can be found in some of my other series, such as **Legacy of the Blade, Madman MacKeefe, Seasons of Fortitude, Legendary Bastards of the Crown, and The Highland Chronicles**, amongst others.)*

Some of the MacKeefe Clan heroes, heroines, and secondary characters seen in this book are:

**Old Callum MacKeefe** (Oldest living man in Scotland)

**Ian MacKeefe** (Callum's son – MacKeefe Clan chieftain)

**Storm MacKeefe** (Ian's son – also a MacKeefe Clan chieftain since they have holdings in both the Highlands and the Lowlands)

**Lord Rook** – (One of the bastard triplets of the king)

*Heroes of the Highland Outcasts Series:*

**Gavin MacKeefe** – hero of *Highland Soul*

**Cam MacKeefe** – hero of *Highland Flame*

**Nash MacKeefe** – hero of *Highland Sky*

**North MacKeefe** – Twin brother of Nash, and hero of *Highland Silver*

✦•◦◇◦•✦

# CHAPTER ONE

*Hermitage, Medieval Scotland*

ER HUSBAND WAS dead and she felt nothing but relief – her only regret being that she was the one who killed him.

Yvaine gripped an iron candle holder in one hand, having used it to protect herself from Dun's usual beatings. Her husband lay sprawled out and dead at her feet on the floor of their chandler's shop. His open eyes still stared up at her in anger.

Dun had always been a mean man, and was the worst excuse for a husband. She'd never loved him, and wished she'd never married him at all. Her family had betrothed her to the town's chandler thinking it would be a good match. He was supposed to take care of her. Their future should have been secure. It was a marriage made with good intent but, unfortunately for her, no one knew of Dun's horrible little secret. Now, they never would.

"God's eyes, what have I done?" Relieved that Dun would never hurt her again, Yvaine still felt terrified for what would happen to her. She stood frozen to the spot in the dimly lit room. Her heart raced and her body trembled. It was an act of self-defense, she told herself. She only did it to stop the madman. To protect herself and her unborn baby. Even so, the fact still remained that she was a murderer now. Yvaine had killed for the first time in her life, and now a shadow darkened her soul.

Her late husband had always taken out his anger on her. He'd even threatened to kill her if she ever revealed his abusive nature to anyone. So, for the last year since they'd wed, Yvaine had remained silent and prayed for an answer of how to escape this life of hell.

Tonight, her prayers were answered. However, it was by a means that she'd never expected. Perhaps she should have been more precise with her prayer for help.

Being in this predicament was going to ruin her life forever. Her heart ached with misery for what she'd become. Once word got out that she'd killed her husband, she'd be locked away and sentenced to death. This wasn't what she wanted at all!

Yvaine had the scars and bruises all over her body to prove what a horrible man Dun really was. Since the day they'd said their vows, she wanted their bloody marriage to be over. Still, she never wanted it to end like this.

The candle holder slipped from her fingers and fell with a thump onto the wooden floor, rolling in a half-circle. Yvaine's hands covered her belly in a form of protection for her unborn child. It should bring her comfort to know that the abuser was dead and could no longer harm them, but an action such as this could never bring her peace of mind.

Murdering one's husband was an offense punishable by death, and Yvaine knew it. Men were allowed to treat their wives badly and even beat them should they decide to do so. Unfortunately, nothing was tolerated when it came to how a woman treated her husband. Part of her regretted her action now, but there was naught she could do to reverse the outcome.

"I – I killed him," she whispered to herself, wondering if this was real or just a bad dream. Her eyes stayed transfixed on the man's lifeless body sprawled out on the ground in a puddle of blood. After she'd hit him on the head, he'd struggled and fallen, grabbing for a nearby table. No table could stop his death, and no one could save her from imminent doom now.

Yvaine's knees buckled, and she grabbed on to the back of a chair to keep from falling. Icy fingers of death as well as the hot flames of hell ran through her body under her thin night shift. She would die now for what she did, and her unborn child would never have the chance to live. Her attempt to protect the baby was done in vain.

There was never any love in this household, even though a loving family was all Yvaine ever longed for. She wanted more than anything to be a good mother, raising a family with a husband who treated her and her children well. All she wanted was a man that she could love.

This chandler's shop was her home, but it was also naught but her prison. Now . . . now she would trade one prison for another, when word got out about what happened here tonight.

Collapsing atop the chair, she broke down and cried. Yvaine didn't cry for her dead husband, because he deserved more than anything to rot in hell. Neither did she cry for herself anymore. No longer caring what happened to her, her only concern was for her innocent little unborn baby.

This was no one's fault but her own. It broke her heart when she realized her child would suffer for it in the end.

"God have mercy," she whispered, realizing just how serious of a situation she was in. Her mind raced wildly, and she knew naught what to do.

There came a small knock at the door and Yvaine froze. Her heart nearly stopped and she found it hard to breathe.

Panic ran through her. All she could think about was Dun coming after her in anger only because their latest batch of candles were ruined by one of his own careless mistakes. He was drunk out of his mind and she couldn't reason with him at all. A bad situation had only turned worse.

"Sister?" came the voice of her brother, Keithen, as he opened the door and stuck his head inside the room. "I saw the candle burnin' in the window and wondered if ye were still awake. Why werena ye and Dun at the weddin' of Gavin MacKeefe and Davita tonight? We had a wonderful time celebratin' at Hermitage Castle."

The whole town had been invited to the Highlander's wedding to the cordwainer's daughter. It was tonight, and took place at Hermitage Castle just outside of town. The castle was owned by the MacKeefe Clan who also had a camp in the Highlands.

"Dun wouldna let me attend," she said softly, her eyes traveling back to her dead husband. "Although . . . now I wish I had."

Keithen's eyes opened wide when he followed her gaze and saw her husband dead on the floor. "God's bones! What happened, Yvaine?" He rushed in, dropping to his knees beside Dun, checking for signs of life but not finding any.

"I killed him," said Yvaine, feeling nothing at all for the man. "I didna mean to do it, of course, but he came at me, tryin' to beat me again."

"Sister?" Keithen stood up, staring at her as she bravely lifted her chin, refusing to seem weak. "Are ye hurt?" When he took her hand in his, he noticed the bruises and welts on her arm. "What's this?" he asked, turning her arm over to inspect it. "Bid the devil, what was goin' on here?" He gently reached out and pushed down her collar, seeing the bruises on her neck and upper chest next. "Yvaine! Ye are covered with bruises. Did this bastard do this to ye?"

"Aye, he did," she said, releasing a deep breath. "Dun always hurt me," she said, staring off into space now, feeling as if this were a nightmare that just wouldn't end.

"By the rood! I canna believe this. If he was hittin' ye, why didna ye tell me?" asked Keithen, in a stern voice. "I would have killed the man myself had I kent what he'd been doin' to ye."

"Dun warned me no' to say a word or he'd kill me, so I stayed silent. Besides, I recently found out I am with child, and I didna want him to hurt the bairn."

"Ye are with child?" asked Keithen in surprise. He flashed a quick smile but then frowned and shook his head. "This is no' guid, Sister," he said, running a hand through his hair and pacing the room. "No one can find out what happened here tonight. We need to –"

"Keithen, are ye comin' back to the tavern?" Both Yvaine's and Keithen's heads snapped around to see the tavern whores, Red and Violet, standing in the doorway waiting for him.

"What are ye doin'?" asked Violet curiously, strolling into the room, rolling her hips seductively as she walked. She stopped in her tracks when she saw Dun's dead body. Her eyes and mouth opened wide.

"Och!" screamed Red from right behind her. She held her hand up to her mouth, looking terrified as well.

"Bid the devil, everyone in town is goin' to hear ye. Haud yer wheesht," snapped Keithen, running over and closing the door behind them.

"How did . . . he die?" asked Red in horror, walking closer to look at the man.

"I killed him." Yvaine turned to face the girls, not even trying to hide what she did.

"Ye killed him?" asked Violet in surprise and confusion. Her eyes swept past Yvaine, then over to Dun and back to Yvaine again.

"Aye," said Yvaine, with no emotion at all in her voice. "I did it to save my life but I see it was all done in vain now. I will end up swingin' from a rope for killin' the bastard who beat me almost every day." She clenched her jaw, feeling more anger than fear.

"H-he did that to ye?" asked Violet, her plucked brows arching. "No lass should be treated like that, no' even a whore."

"Especially no' the man's wife," said Red, laying her hand on Yvaine's arm to comfort her. "I dinna blame ye, lass. If it were me, I would have done it long ago."

"I didna want him to hurt my bairn." Yvaine rubbed her belly.

"Och, ye're with child?" asked Violet.

"That's nice," said Red, sounding like she meant it.

"Lassies, no one can ever find out what happened here tonight." Keithen continued to pace.

"I hardly think we can hide the fact my husband is dead,"

Yvaine told her brother, getting to her feet.

"Nay, but we can tell everyone it was an accident," suggested Red.

"I agree," said Violet. "We'll tell them we were all here and saw the man trip and fall and hit his head . . . on the table. Yes, that is what we will say."

"Nay, I canna endanger any of ye because of my actions."

"Then what do ye suggest?" asked Keithen, stress showing on his face.

"I will just have to tell the truth," said Yvaine, feeling sick to her stomach at the thought of it.

"And risk losin' yer bairn?" gasped Violet. "How could ye?"

"Nay, ye're right. I dinna want to lose my bairn." Tears filled Yvaine's eyes now, as her resolve weakened quickly. "Mayhap they'll let my child be born before they kill me." She looked over at her brother. "Keithen, ye can raise the lad or lassie for me once I'm gone. Either that or ye can bring the babe to our brathair at the priory in England since we dinna have any other family."

"Nay, Sister, I canna raise it." Keithen shook his head. "I'm the owner of a tavern. Do ye want yer bairn growin' up with whores?" He looked over to Red and Violet. "No offense, lassies."

"Humph," mumbled Violet, pulling her shawl around her shoulders tighter.

Red just scowled at him. "I wouldna mind raisin' a child. I wish I had one of my own."

"Ye work for me, and willna get involved with a babe," Keithen said in a low voice.

"What am I to do?" asked Yvaine, feeling as if her life were coming to an end. "Brathair, I am so frightened."

"Quickly, go, pack yer bags," Keithen told her. "We will take care of everythin', but ye need to leave here anon."

"We?" asked Violet, sounding like she didn't want to get involved.

"Aye," said Keithen. "All of us need to help my sister."

"Of course, we will," Red spoke up for the both of them.

"Red, ye go find the undertaker, and bring him here," Keithen commanded. "Violet, ye fetch my wagon and a horse. We'll load Yvaine's belongin's into the wagon tonight."

"Wait!" cried Yvaine. "This is my home. I canna leave here. I have nowhere else to go."

"She's right," said Red. "Ye canna expect her to leave her life behind."

"Yer life as ye ken it, is over," Keithen reminded her, bending down and closing the dead man's eyes.

"The guild will allow me to take over the chandler business since I am now a widow," Yvaine told him. "It is written so in the rules."

"Aye, until the word gets out that ye killed him," snapped Keithen. "Then what do ye think they'll do? Yvaine, ye dinna have a choice. Ye need to leave town and ye need to do it tonight."

"Willna people wonder why I am leavin' before my husband's body is even cold and in the ground?" Yvaine asked him.

"Aye, she's right. That will only raise suspicion," agreed Red.

Keithen let out a deep breath, looking back at the dead man once more. "Then we'll bury his body at first light, but ye will leave right afterwards, Yvaine. We'll tell everyone ye are too distraught to stay."

"Where will I go?" Yvaine felt confused and upset, and so alone.

"Ye will go to Lanercost Priory to stay with our brathair, Gillies," Keithen told her. "Ye will be safe within the priory walls, and yer bairn can be born there. Mayhap after a few years, ye can return once everythin' blows over."

"A few years?" gasped Yvaine. "That is such a long time. Besides, Gillies willna want me there when he finds out I am pregnant, and what I've done."

"Then we willna tell him," said Keithen. "We'll only tell him yer husband died, and that ye need a place to go to mourn."

"I still dinna like this idea."

"Ye dinna have a choice," her brother growled. "It is either that, or stay here and take the chance of being executed for what ye did."

"Nay," said Yvaine. "Never. I will go. For the sake of my unborn child. But what about the business? I canna just leave it."

"Ye willna have to. Ye can take everythin' with ye," said Keithen, grabbing a blanket from the top of a trunk and throwing it over Dun's body. "Ye can continue makin' candles, but ye'll do it at the priory instead."

"I dinna even ken if Gillies will allow that. Or if he will want me there at all."

"He's yer brathair. He'll do it," said Keithen. "I'll send a messenger there this night, tellin' him to expect ye on the morrow. He is a monk and willna turn away anyone, especially no' his own sister."

"Ye'll send a messenger? Who would go across the border to do that?" asked Violet. "We are Scots and no' a one of us is goin' to be anxious to go into English territory."

"I'll go to the castle tonight," said Keithen. "The celebration will just be endin' but everyone will still be awake. Lady Wren and Lady Clarista are both English. They'll ken someone who can take the missive there for us."

"Ye're goin' back to the castle?" asked Red, sounding interested. "Cam is still there. Mayhap I can come with ye, and see him one last time before he leaves for the Highlands."

"Nay," said Keithen. "Lassies, do as I say, and then get back to work."

"Keithen, how will I get there with all my belongin's and all by myself?" asked Yvaine, feeling worried about this plan. It was dangerous, and she was one woman. She couldn't travel or cross the border alone.

"Dinna fash yerself. I'll get ye an escort," promised Keithen, wrapping the blanket around Dun's body. "I'm sure Laird Storm MacKeefe will help us out since he is a fair man. Mayhap some of his warriors can take ye there safely."

"I'm no' sure," said Yvaine. "What will I do there besides make and sell candles?"

"Ye can always take the vows and become a nun," suggested Violet with a snicker.

"True," agreed Keithen. "Perhaps livin' the life of a nun will suit ye and also guarantee that yer bairn is raised well. After all, widows often join the Order, so it is no' an uncommon thing to do."

"Join the Order? Nay! I will never be a nun," spat Yvaine, knowing that choice would mean she could never fall in love and have a big, beautiful family like she always wanted. Her eyes dropped down to Dun, seeing his partially covered face. Suddenly, guilt wracked her body. "However, I will spend my time prayin' for forgiveness for killin' a man." Yvaine dropped to her knees, reaching out one shaking hand to pull the blanket over Dun's face so she wouldn't have to look at it anymore.

"Dinna tell me ye feel sorry for killin' the bastard now," spat Violet. "He deserved it!"

"Mayhap so," mumbled Yvaine, staring at the lump under the blanket. "I may no' have loved him, and we all ken he didna deserve love for what he did to me. But on the other hand, did he really deserve to die? Oh, why couldna he have died drunk in the gutter instead of by my hand? What did I do?"

"Yer only true crime was stayin' with a man who abused ye, when ye should have left him years ago, so dinna start regrettin' yer actions now." Keithen pulled her to her feet. "I've got this handled. Now, all of us in this room must vow to never tell anyone that Yvaine killed her husband." He looked over to the whores. "Is that clear? Do ye promise?"

"If anyone can keep a secret, it's me," said Red.

"I wouldna tell a soul about this if my life depended on it," agreed Violet.

"Guid. Then everyone do as I told ye. At first light, I'll have the undertaker bury the body. Then I'll take Yvaine to the castle."

"Aye. Everythin' will be all right." Yvaine said the words, but far from believed them. Nay, everything was not going to be all right, and she knew it. Even if this crazy plan protected her, it wasn't going to be easy to keep it a secret for the rest of her life. How was she ever going to raise a child by herself in a monastery? And what would happen to her and her child someday if her horrible secret was ever discovered?

━━◆•◦◇◦•◆━━

# CHAPTER TWO

"**W**ELL, WHAT IS my sentence?" asked Cam the next morning, having spent an exciting night with one of the castle's serving girls out in the barn. He smiled at her across the room and winked. Her cheeks blushed and she turned away, heading back to the kitchen.

"Ye are naught but a lustful cur," spat Old Callum MacKeefe, waving his hands in the air like he was crazed. Callum was the oldest man in all of Scotland, although he didn't act like it. Cam had broken some of the man's silly tavern rules when he acted a little too lustful with one of the wenches in the Horn and Hoof Tavern in Glasgow. Then again, Cam liked the lassies and always had one or two hanging on his arms. "Yer sentence is . . ."

"Grandda," shouted Storm MacKeefe, calling the old man over. Storm sat atop his dais chair, as one of the two chieftains of Clan MacKeefe. His father, Ian MacKeefe, sat beside him, as the second ruler. The MacKeefes were a Highland clan, but also gained holdings in the Lowlands when they seized Hermitage Castle from the English years ago. Now they divided their time between living at the castle, and at their Highland camp near Oban. "New happenin's have occurred and we need to discuss matters first," Storm told him.

"All right," grumbled Callum, stomping his newly booted feet across the floor as he made his way over to the others. The boots had been constructed as part of Gavin MacKeefe's punishment for breaking Callum's tavern rules as well. The Horn and Hoof was owned and operated by the old man. Callum was the only man alive who knew how to brew the potent, coveted Mountain Magic whisky. It brought in the main income for the MacKeefes.

"What's goin' on, I wonder?" whispered Nash, Cam's good friend.

"Look!" North, Nash's brother, pointed across the great hall. "Ladies Wren and Clarista are talkin' with Keithen, the tavern owner from town."

North and Nash were twins, but not exactly identical in looks. While they both had long brown hair, North was taller and had more chiseled features than his brother. He was also more serious than the happy-go-lucky Nash. North's eyes were silver while Nash's were hazel.

Lady Clarista was Ian MacKeefe's English wife, and Storm's mother. Lady Wren was English as well, and married to Storm.

"Here comes Gavin," said Cam, seeing their friend whose wedding they'd attended yesterday, as he headed across the hall toward him. Gavin was a big man who looked gruff but had a soft heart with the lassies. His long, black hair lifted slightly around his shoulders as he walked through the hall.

Gavin's new wife, Davita, the cordwainer's daughter, stayed by the women in a huddle. Cam saw a pretty woman with them, but he didn't know who she was.

"Gavin, what's all the commotion about?" asked North.

"It seems the chandler from town died last night," Gavin filled them in. "His widow, who happens to be Keithen's sister, is here."

"Why? What for?" asked Cam, not understanding any of this.

"I'm no' sure, but I think we're about to find out." Gavin nodded at their clan's rulers as Storm looked up at them and waved them over to join him.

"Come on," said Gavin, leading the way with the other men right behind him.

"Chieftain, Cam is ready to hear his punishment now," said

Gavin.

"Thanks, but I can speak for myself," growled Cam.

"Cam, it has been decided that yer punishment will be to act as an escort to Widow Yvaine from the village," Storm announced. He nodded towards the other end of the great hall where the women and Keithen were watching. "Yvaine and Keithen, please approach the dais."

The pretty woman who looked to be in her early twenties slowly walked over to Storm, being escorted by her brother.

"Och, I accept," Cam answered quickly, liking what he saw. The girl was bonnie indeed! She had long, brown hair tied back, and big, brown eyes that he could easily get lost in. She was tall for a woman, and had some delectable curves to her body. Cam was already picturing wrapping his arms around her and tasting her bow-shaped mouth.

"God's teeth, quit smilin'," Gavin warned Cam in a low voice. "The lass has just lost her husband."

"Aye. Right." Cam cleared his throat and his smile disappeared. "I'm so sorry for the loss of yer husband, lass," he told her. "How did he die?"

The woman clung to her brother and hid her face against his shoulder. Cam could hear her crying.

"Guid job, ye fool," Nash leaned over and whispered to Cam.

"Ye always ken what to say to the lassies," remarked North sarcastically.

All three of Cam's friends were scowling at him now.

"I didna mean to be insensitive." Cam looked over to the widow and tried to apologize. "I was just curious, and didna mean to upset ye."

"Her husband tripped and fell, hittin' his head," Keithen spoke for the girl. "My sister is very upset and we'd rather no' hear it mentioned again."

"Aye. Of course," said Cam, thinking the whole situation odd. Why was the girl leaving her home at a time like this? Still, he decided just to remain quiet and try to figure it all out later.

"Yvaine is too upset to stay in town, so she will be goin' to live with another of her brathairs for a while," Ian spoke up.

"I see," said Cam with a nod. "Where is it he lives, and where I will be escorting her?"

"Brathair Gillies lives across the border," said Callum.

Cam thought at first that the old man just meant Gillies was the lass' brother. That is, until he heard the rest of it.

"She will be residin' at Lanercost Priory," Storm finished explaining.

"Lanercost Priory?" Cam's head snapped up in surprise. His eyes roamed back to the girl again. Damn, it figured. She was going to be a nun. Why did he have to be escorting a beautiful woman to a priory, of all places? Just his luck. He realized that, sometimes, this is what a widow did when she couldn't continue on alone after the death of her spouse. Bid the devil, he didn't like this at all.

"I thought Lanercost Priory was in ruins," stated Gavin with a confused look upon his face.

"No' anymore," Storm remarked. "It has been under repair over the past few years, and is now a fully functionin' priory."

"Our brathair, Gillies, is abbot there," Keithen explained. "I thought it best our sister joins him since she is in such mournin'."

"But it's over the border. I dinna think it's safe for just one man to be escortin' the lass," protested Cam. "I mean, with the English right there, ye never ken what will happen."

"We agree," Storm answered. "That is why North, Nash, and Gavin, will be accompanin' ye."

"What?" all three men said at once.

"Me?" Gavin's jaw dropped and he shook his head. "Nay. I just got married, my laird. I also just got accepted back into the clan. I shouldna be away from my bride right now. Or the clan."

"Ye are a Highland warrior, Gavin," Storm pointed out. "Ye are also one of the best with a sword. Ye'll go with them, but to the border only. We've sent a missive to Lord Rook at Naward Castle. He will meet the travelin' party at the border with some of his men to escort them to the priory safely."

"Rook? One of the Legendary Bastards of the Crown?" Cam, as well as everyone else, had heard about this legendary man who was a triplet and a bastard of King Edward III of England.

"That's right," said Storm. "He once lived in the catacombs of Lanercost Priory, but is now laird of Naward Castle where he resides with his wife."

"Well, this shouldna take long then," said Nash, shrugging his shoulders as if it no longer mattered. "North, we'll be back in time for supper."

"I was talkin' about Gavin only," Storm announced.

"Well, what about Nash and me?" asked North. "Do ye want us to go all the way to the priory before we return?"

"Hah!" spat Callum, seeming to enjoy this a little too much. "Nash and North, ye willna be comin' back until Cam's sentence is finished."

"Why no'?" asked Nash, making a face.

"Ye're outcasts of the clan now and canna stay here," Ian reminded them. "Ye are lucky we allowed ye to attend Gavin's weddin'."

"Wait a minute," said Cam, raising a finger in the air. "Do ye mean that I have to stay there? At a priory?" Just the thought of residing within such pious walls was already making Cam feel quite uncomfortable. "With monks and nuns, and prayin' and all?"

"That's right," said Ian. He'd been ill lately, and still looked quite pale. Cam and his friends never did find out exactly what was wrong with him. "Yvaine will be movin' the chandler's business to the priory for now. Cam, ye will help her make candles or soap and whatever else she does. Ye will be her assistant."

"Me?" This sounded horrible to Cam. Next thing he knew, they'd be insisting he join the Order and become a monk while he was there. "I dinna ken how to make candles, and neither do I care."

"Well, I didna ken how to make shoes either, but I learned," remarked Gavin under his breath, speaking of his own past sentence.

"Yvaine will teach ye everythin' ye need to ken," Keithen assured him. "The wagon with all the supplies is waitin' just outside and ready to go."

"How long will I need to be there?" asked Cam, hoping for a short time only. Being away from eligible females for too long would drive him insane.

"Ye'll stay there until ye get a guid report from Brathair Gillies and he tells ye it's time to come back," snapped Callum. "Stayin' a spell away from the women should cure that uncontrollable lust of yers," he said smugly.

"Or make it worse," mumbled Cam under his breath. Running a hand through his long, blond hair, he couldn't even comprehend all this. He'd never been away from women for long, and neither had he ever stepped foot in a priory. Brothels and taverns were where he had spent most of his life. This was truly going to be the worst punishment of all.

"Excuse me," Nash spoke up, taking a step closer to the dais. "Do my brathair and I have to stay at the priory, too?"

"Aye, do we?" piped up North. "After all, this isna our punishment, but Cam's."

"It's that, or stay in the dungeon," Callum told them, stamping his feet like a madman. No one knew why the old man acted the way he did. Perhaps he was just trying out his new boots, or more likely he was going insane.

"B-but we just stayed at town, hashin' out Gavin's punishment with him," complained Nash. "Surely, this isna fair."

Storm, Ian, and Callum spoke in hushed tones, and then Storm gave his answer.

"We agree, it's no' quite fair," he told the brothers. "Therefore, I'll send word to Lord Rook, askin' him if ye two can spend a few days and nights at the end of each week at Naward Castle instead. However, durin' the rest of the week, ye are to spend yer time at the priory, in case yer help is needed in any way."

"Fine," mumbled North, not sounding at all pleased. Then again, at least the brothers didn't have to be there all the time, like Cam did. He figured it was just as bad as staying in the dungeon. The priory would be his new prison now. He longed to go to Naward Castle with his friends and stay with Lord Rook instead.

Lord Rook was a triplet, and triplets were thought to be spawned by the devil and bad luck. When he and his brothers, Rowen and Reed, were born, the king ordered them killed as babies. They were lucky enough to survive, and were raised in Scotland. But when the truth came out about who their father really was and how he'd tried to kill them, the bastard triplets vowed vengeance against Edward. Eventually, they made amends with their father – or at least some of them did. Either way, these three men were legends, and also to be feared. Not many men went up against the king and lived to tell about it.

"Well, when do we leave?" asked Cam impatiently, only wanting to get his sentence over with quickly.

"There is one more issue we must address first," said Storm, looking across the great hall. "This mornin', somethin' was brought to my attention that involves ye, Cam."

"Me? What do ye mean?" asked Cam, hoping whatever it was, it wouldn't lead to a longer sentence. All he wanted was to be accepted back into the clan.

Lady Wren walked forward with a whore who looked familiar to Cam. The woman held the hand of a little girl who seemed to be about four or five years old.

"Cam, this woman is a . . . she is from a neighborin' town," said Storm, not wanting to call her a whore in front of everyone, even though Cam already knew she was.

"Aye." Cam's face lit up in a smile as he remembered the wild night he'd spent with her, even if he couldn't remember her name.

"Give him the girl," Storm commanded the woman, who

brought the little girl over to Cam.

"What?" Cam took a step backward, holding up his palms. "Why are ye givin' me the child?"

"Because she is yer daughter," explained the whore.

"My daughter? Nay," Cam said, shaking his head furiously. "I am no' married. She is no' mine."

"Mayhap ye never wed, but it seems ye have a bastard child to take care of now," spat Old Callum.

"Me? What? Why?" Cam was too much in shock to even speak a full sentence. "How?"

"If ye dinna ken how bairns are made by now, then mayhap ye should stop lyin' with all the lassies," mumbled Nash under his breath.

"Nay," Cam told them. "She's no' mine."

"She is, Cam. She is the daughter of yer favorite whore, Isobel from Perth," explained the whore.

"Perth," he mumbled, his memory coming back to him now. So that's where he'd seen this whore before. And yes, he did have a favorite whore there. "If the girl is Isobel's daughter, then let her raise the child," said Cam.

"She canna."

"Why no'?"

"Because Isobel is dead," answered the whore. "Her dyin' wish was for me to find ye and bring yer daughter to ye."

"Ye'll take the girl with ye to Lanercost Priory," stated Storm.

"As part of yer sentence," added Callum.

Cam glanced down at the little girl who clung to the whore, not even wanting to look at him. She seemed so frightened. "What is her name?"

"It is Avianca," said the whore. "And my name is Lila, since I'm sure ye forgot it already."

"Thank ye, Lila. I'll take the girl to the priory and I'm sure they'll find a suitable family for her in England."

"Nay," spat Lila. "Isobel's wish was for ye to raise her child."

"I canna. I'm a warrior and will be goin' back to the Highlands soon."

Storm cleared his throat, gaining Cam's attention. "If she is yer daughter, then ye are responsible for her."

"But I –"

"Dismissed," said Storm before Cam could object again. "Ye'll leave anon."

"I'm scared," said the little girl as the whore tried to hand her over to Cam.

"Come on, lass," Cam said, blowing air from his mouth. "Hurry up." He impatiently held out his hand but the little girl kept clinging to Lila's skirts, not wanting to go with him.

"Quit scarin' her!" Yvaine rushed over and fell to her knees, taking the little girl's hands in hers. "I'll watch her," she told Lila.

"Guidbye, Avianca . . . and Cam." The whore winked at Cam and left.

"There is naught to be frightened of," Yvaine told Avianca with a smile. "These brave, strong Highlanders will take us to the priory where we'll live with Brathair Gillies."'

"Will there be other children there to play with?" asked the little girl with her big green eyes peeking out at her.

"I'm afraid no'," answered Yvaine softly.

"What will I do there?" asked Avianca.

"I'm sure we'll find somethin' to do." Yvaine glanced over her shoulder looking directly at Cam.

Cam's heart jumped. He could think of several things he'd like to do with Yvaine, but unfortunately that was never going to happen. The little girl, on the other hand, was only going to prove to be a problem. He had no experience at all with children and had no idea how to raise one. God's eyes, why was he saddled with a nun-to-be, and a child that was now his, to make things even more difficult? His life had taken a turn for the worse. This was not the kind of punishment he was hoping for at all.


YVAINE LOOKED OUT from the corners of her eyes at the Highlander who was going to be her escort. He had long, blond hair down past his shoulders, and dark brown eyes that seemed to mask anything he was feeling. That is, anything but lust. She knew this look, and it was one that disgusted her. She'd seen this Highlander in town before, even if he didn't know who she was. He always had whores from the tavern hanging on his arms. Of all the Highlanders to choose from, why did he have to be the one to escort her?

"Well, let's get our things and head on out," said the man they'd called Cam. "I hope there's enough room for both ye and the girl in the wagon."

"Nay. My things fill up the back," said Yvaine, getting an odd look from him. "The only place for us to sit will be up front with ye."

"With me? Nay. I willna be drivin' the wagon. I'll be on my horse."

"Nay. Ye'll be needed to drive the wagon, Cam," said Storm.

"Lucky ye. Ye get to sit with the nun," whispered one of the twins, causing both of the brothers to chuckle.

"I'm no'–" Yvaine meant to correct them, telling them she wasn't going there to take her vows. Then she decided not to mention it. Perhaps with a lustful Highlander along, it would be safer for her to let them all think she was going to take her vows, after all. At least then they wouldn't touch her. Or so she hoped.

"Ye're no' . . . what?" asked Cam, waiting for her to answer.

Yvaine stood up, glancing over at her brother, shaking her head slightly to warn him to remain silent. Thankfully, he didn't say a word. Keithen understood her warning.

"We havena been properly introduced," she said, looking back at Cam. "I am Yvaine and, of course, ye already ken my brathair, Keithen."

"I'm tired," said the little girl, clinging to her skirts.

"Ye can sleep on my lap once we get in the wagon," Yvaine told the lass.

"Cam," the man answered.

"Pardon me?" she asked, looking up at him. She knew what

he meant, but thought he sounded rude when he answered.

"My name is Cam. My friends are North, Nash, and Gavin," he told her, pointing to each of the men in turn.

"I'll secure some horses for the rest of us," said Gavin, heading away.

"I'll help him," said North. "We'll meet ye at the gate, Cam." He started to walk away, then noticed his brother, who looked like a twin to Yvaine. He still stood there gawking at her. "Let's go, Nash." North reached out and pulled the man along with him.

"I just thought the lass might need help, that's all," said Nash.

"That's what Cam is for," she heard North answer, and he and his brother started toward the door. "After all, Cam is always tellin' us how guid he is with the lassies. Let's see how guid he is with this nun-to-be." He chuckled as the two of them headed off after their friend, Gavin.

"Ye'll have to excuse them," said Cam. "I'm afraid they have no manners at all around a lady." He held out his arm to escort her to the wagon. She looked down at it but did nothing to take it.

"Well, dinna fash yerself, because I am no' a lady," she retorted.

"What?" He grinned crookedly, looking amused. Suddenly, she realized how bad this sounded.

"Nay! I dinna mean that I was a . . . a . . ."

"Whore?" he asked, raising one eyebrow. "Dinna worry, lass, I can tell ye are no'."

"I'll bet ye can," she said, taking the little girl's hand. "Come along, Avianca." She headed away, thinking of how many times she'd seen Cam with Violet and Red, the town's whores who worked at her brother's tavern. The last man in the world she wanted escorting her to the priory was a lustful cur like him. She swore, if he even tried to touch her, she would hit him over the head with a candle holder the way she did to Dun. Horrid thoughts of Dun laying at her feet in a puddle of blood filled her mind. She stopped in her tracks and swayed, feeling as if she were about to swoon.

"Are ye ill?" asked the little girl.

Feeling pressure on her shoulder, Yvaine's eyes sprang open. Clutching Avianca's hand, she whipped her head around to see Cam standing right there, boldly touching her. The feel of the man's hand on her only brought back terrible memories of Dun's hands on her as well.

"Nay! Get yer hand off of me," she spat through gritted teeth, pushing it from her. She jumped backward, almost tripping over the little girl. Fear filled her being, and she wanted to run. Her breathing labored and she felt heat rise to her cheeks quickly.

"My mistake," said Cam, holding his palms outward in surrender. "I didna mean to frighten ye, lass. I was only tryin' to keep ye from fallin' since ye looked like ye were about to faint."

"Well, I'm no'." Yvaine wondered if the man could hear her rapidly beating heart that pounded in her ears. "I – I am fine. Let's just please go to the priory." She turned to leave the great hall, not looking back at all.

"Ye're a little jumpy, lass. Is there a reason?" he asked from behind her.

"I'm just . . . still upset after what happened to my husband." She stopped and turned and feigned a smile. "I'm sure ye can understand. I'm in mournin'."

"Aye. Mournin'," he said perusing her up and down.

"Why are ye lookin' at me that way?" she demanded to know.

"I was wonderin' why ye werena wearin' black and also no' wearin' a head coverin' since ye are in mournin' as ye say. After all, it is proper."

"I wouldna think a man like ye even kent what the word proper meant," she threw the words back at him.

"Lass, I dinna even ken ye, but yet ye are so fast to judge me. Why?"

"I ken yer kind."

"My kind?" He looked confused. "Och, ye mean Highlanders?

Dinna worry, the rumors are no' always true. Besides, I'm a lover, before I'm a fighter."

"That's exactly what I meant," she said under her breath.

"What did ye say?" He cocked an ear toward her.

"I've seen ye comin' out of my brathair's tavern with no' only one, but two . . . wenches on yer arm." Her eyes shot down to the man's bastard daughter. She didn't want Avianca to hear her talking about whores, even if the girl's mother was one. After all, she was just a child, and didn't need to be exposed to the sins of the world.

"I can see this will be a long journey," Cam mumbled, walking past her, leading the way to the wagon.

# CHAPTER THREE

"ALL RIGHT, LET'S head on out," called out Cam to the others, holding out his hand to assist Yvaine up to the front bench seat of the wagon.

"I dinna need yer help, thank ye," she told the man, not wanting him to touch her. She'd heard of his amorous ways, and now there was a bastard child of his here to prove it. She couldn't trust him. She wasn't sure she could ever trust any men besides her brothers, after what she'd been through.

"Then if ye dinna want my assistance, I'll help the child instead." Cam reached out for Avianca, but the little girl cowered from him, clinging to Yvaine instead.

"It's all right, sweetheart," she told the girl in a gentle voice. "Go to yer faither."

"He's no' my da," said the little girl. "I dinna have a da."

"Look, I dinna want to believe it any more than ye do," Cam told the child. "We can figure this all out later but, right now, we need to get on the road. So, up ye go." He lifted up the little girl who was kicking and screaming. Then he plopped her down on the bench seat of the wagon.

"Ye need to learn how to treat children!" Yvaine scolded the Highlander, lifting her foot to climb into the cart.

"Ye need to learn how to hurry." Before she knew it, his hands closed around her waist and he lifted her up to the bench of the wagon, putting her next to the little girl. Partly, Yvaine wanted to reprimand him for touching her. Then again, something deep down inside her almost enjoyed the way his hands felt on her waist. The warmth of his fingers closing around her almost seemed protective instead of abusive, the way Dun's hands always felt on her.

Yvaine quickly shook the thought away. What was the matter with her? She didn't need thoughts like this filling up her already confused mind. Especially, not when it pertained to a Highlander. She reached out and pulled Avianca up against her, slipping her arm around the girl's shoulders.

"Just stay close to me and all will be all right," she consoled the girl in a soft voice.

Cam hoisted himself up and sat on the bench. His daughter was between them. Reaching down, he took the reins.

"Ye have a full load in this wagon. I hope it willna slow us down," he complained.

"Of course, it's a loaded wagon. After all, it is almost everythin' I own," she retorted.

He looked back over his shoulder at all her belongings, covered with a tarp.

"Are ye sure ye need it all? If we get attacked by the English, it'll be hard to get away from them quickly pullin' this heavy load. If it comes to savin' our necks or yer guids, I swear I'm goin' to leave it all behind."

"Attacked? Are we goin' to get killed?" cried Avianca, gripping tighter to Yvaine. "I'm scared. I dinna want to die like my mathair."

"Nay, of course no'. Everythin' will be fine," said Yvaine, running her hand over the girl's head to smooth her hair. Cam directed the horse forward. The Highlander named Gavin was in front of them, leading the way. North was on one side of the wagon, and Nash followed behind them. They were all dressed to the hilt with weapons. So was Cam. "Ye just lay yer head against me and close yer eyes and go to sleep," Yvaine told Avianca. "Before ye ken it, we'll be at our new home in the priory and locked safely inside its holy walls."

"Trapped is more like it," mumbled Cam, urging the horse to go faster, jerking the wagon and almost causing Yvaine to fall off.

"Haud yer wheesht!" she warned him. "What is the matter with ye? Ye are scarin' yer daughter. Plus, ye are drivin' the cart much too recklessly with a child on board."

Cam glanced over at her with a scowl on his face. "Do ye want to drive the cart, lass?" he asked with an edge to his voice. "Just say the word, and it's all yers."

"Nay. Of course, no'."

"Then mayhap ye are the one who should haud yer wheesht instead."

This irked her to no end that he spoke to her in this manner. The last thing she wanted was for the Highlander to think he was right. Or to order her around. She'd had enough abuse from her late husband, and wouldn't allow this to happen again in her life. It was time for her to start standing up to men, and there was no better time to do it.

"Actually, I've changed my mind," she told him. "I do want to drive the wagon."

"Ye do?" He seemed confused. Then he shrugged his shoulders. "All right, then."

"However, ye'll need to hold yer daughter."

He started handing the reins to her, but stopped in midmotion and shook his head. "Nay. I'll drive." He looked the other way.

"Humph. I didna think so." This just proved her point that he was just as afraid of the little girl as Avianca was of him. The man was terrible with children. He would never make a good father. Besides, she could see he didn't even want the girl. It was sad, in her opinion. Family meant everything to her, but not to him. All he seemed to care about was himself.

"What did that mean?" he asked.

"I have no idea what ye are talkin' about." Now, it was her turn to look the other way.

"I think ye ken exactly what I mean."

"Never mind," she answered.

"Nay. I want to ken. Why did ye say that?"

She didn't want to explain herself to him, nor to have to give him an answer if she didn't want to. "All this talkin' is keepin' Avianca from fallin' asleep. I suggest we refrain from conversation for now."

"Gladly," he grumbled, looking at the road rather than at her or the child. "God's eyes. This is goin' to be a long trip," she heard him say under his breath.

"Please refrain from cursin' around the wee lass. It's no' a guid way to raise yer daughter." Yvaine continued running her hand gently over the little girl's head. Avianca's eyes drifted closed and her breathing slowed.

"She's been raised in a whore house," he snapped. "There is no worse way to raise a child, believe me. Plus, I'm sure she's already heard every curse there is, as well as seen a few things no' meant for the eyes of the young."

"Mayhap ye're right," she answered. "After all, ye seem to ken more about whore houses than anyone."

"Ye have no idea," he said softly. When he glanced in her direction, she was surprised to see sadness and despair in his eyes. Still, her comment shut him up. When he turned his head, she noticed a slight tick in his jaw. It seemed he was clenching his teeth. Her work was done.

Yvaine smiled and released a deep breath. Closing her eyes, she reveled in the feeling of the warm breeze against her, and lifted her face to the sun. This was her road to freedom – a brand new life. She wasn't going to let anyone – not even this Highlander, ruin it for her. This was her second chance now, and she would embrace it, raising her baby by herself if she had to. No more would she have to fear for her unborn child's life, nor fear that she was going to be beaten again.

Yvaine felt good about everything, except that she'd killed her husband. That secret would go with her to her grave. Even though she'd have a new life now, deep in her heart, she knew that she'd never be happy until she found and married a man who would make a perfect father for her unborn child. It was crucial that she find someone who could protect her baby if she ended up not able to do it herself. If her secret was discovered, and she were condemned to die, the man would have to raise her child. The only problem was, she was starting to wonder if all men were alike. Dun was physically abusive, but other men could be just as bad by being mentally or verbally abusive instead.

Her eyes opened slightly and she peeked out at the handsome Highlander named Cam. Too bad he didn't even like children. It was a shame that he shunned his own child, because a Highland warrior was just what she needed, she decided. A Highlander would be able to protect her baby, should anything happen to her. However, not this one, she sadly realized. She closed her eyes again, trying to push away the vision of her dead husband that was embedded in her mind like a thorn in the thumb. Just the thought of what she had done would haunt her forever.

⊱⊰

IT HADN'T TAKEN much more than a half-hour before they made it to the Scottish border. Gavin held up his hand from in front, stopping the procession.

"Why are we stoppin'?" North called out.

"Is somethin' wrong?" asked Nash, riding up to join North.

Gavin turned his horse and headed back to them. "I suggest we stop here, and no' cross the border yet."

"Stop?" asked Cam, his only focus on making it quickly to their destination. "Why?"

"I dinna see Lord Rook or his men yet who were supposed to meet us at the border. We need to give them more time."

"We can keep goin'," said Cam. "I'm sure we'll meet them on the road soon."

"Unless ye've forgotten, this is the point where I turn around and head back to the castle to spend time with my new bride," Gavin reminded him.

"Och, I suppose ye're right." Cam hopped off the wagon, leaving Yvaine and Avianca, heading over to talk to his friends in private.

"Gavin," he said, glancing back over his shoulder to make sure Yvaine hadn't followed him.

"What is it?" asked Gavin, while Nash and North dismounted their horses, coming closer to hear the conversation.

"When ye get back to Hermitage Castle, see if ye can talk the chieftains into givin' me a different punishment."

"What for?" asked Gavin, looking down at him from atop his horse.

"I dinna want to spend the next fortnight or so with her," he said, nodding back at the cart.

"I dinna see what ye're complainin' about," remarked Nash. "I think the lass is very comely."

"That's exactly why," Cam explained. "I canna spend time near her, because I keep thinkin' about doin' other things with her, like kissin' her and makin' love. Of course, since she is soon to be a nun, I canna do any of those things. I swear, I will go mad before my sentence is over."

Nash and North laughed, and even Gavin smiled, liking the thought of him not able to woo a lass.

"Well, like Old Callum said, mayhap this will quench yer lust for the lassies, after all," Gavin told him.

"Aye, it could lead to a whole new side of ye," agreed Nash.

"Mayhap ye'll even end up bein' a monk when this is all over." North chuckled at the mere idea, but Cam didn't think it was funny.

Cam let out a long breath. "Nay, it willna change me in the least, I assure ye. Plus, now I have a daughter I dinna need or want. I am no' even sure how the hell that happened!"

"Let me give ye a clue," said Nash. "Her name was Isobel."

"I am no' daft. I ken that! But whores are supposed to have ways to keep from gettin' pregnant," protested Cam. "It never should have happened. Isobel was no' careful."

"Perhaps, ye're the one who should have been more careful," came a female voice from behind him, causing Cam to spin around on his heel. Yvaine was right there, having overheard him. He hoped to hell she hadn't heard the part about him wanting to kiss and couple with her, too. Thankfully, his daughter was still asleep back in the wagon.

"Yvaine," he said. "I was just tellin' my friends –"

"I heard what ye were tellin' them."

"How long were ye standin' there?" he asked, feeling like crawling under a rock from embarrassment. Why was he having illicit thoughts about a woman who was soon to become a nun?

"I heard enough to ken that ye are just like any other man, always blamin' the women for his mistakes."

"Now wait a minute."

"Ye were just as responsible for the conception of that poor child as was the whore ye laid with and got pregnant."

"That's no' so. The whore was responsible only. Right?" Cam looked over at his friends, but they were doing nothing to support him. Nash and North busied themselves tending to their horses. Gavin turned his steed and headed away.

"I'll keep watch at the border for English as well as Lord Rook," called out Gavin.

"We'll help ye," said Nash, quickly mounting his horse.

"The more eyes the better." North jumped atop his horse next, and the three of them rode off instead of giving Cam the support he needed right now.

When Cam turned back to look at Yvaine, she had her arms crossed over her chest and her chin jutted out in the air. "Well?" she asked.

"Well what?"

"Are ye goin' to admit ye are responsible for the child and accept her as yer daughter?"

"Listen. I am a Highland warrior, lassie. I dinna need anythin' or anyone tyin' me down. As soon as my sentence is completed, I am goin' back to the Highlands where I belong."

"Then ye'll be takin' Avianca with ye." It was more like she was telling him, not asking him a question.

"Nay!" Cam threw his hands in the air. "I canna take care of her, and that is all there is to it."

"If ye willna care for her, then who will?"

He raised a brow. "Mayhap ye can."

"Me?" she asked, looking shocked that he'd say that. "I have enough responsibilities of my own. This one is all on ye, no' me. Besides, I canna take care of my chandler business and another child on top of all that. It's totally out of the question."

"Another child?" he looked at her curiously. "What does that mean?"

DAMN. YVAINE HAD been careless with her words and she'd slipped up. Now he'd caught it. "Nothin'," she said, busying herself by brushing lint off her clothes.

"Do ye already have a child then?" He wouldn't let up with the questions, and she was going to have to think of something quickly. She didn't want him to know she was with child. She needed to cover her tracks.

"Nay. I dinna have a child," she said, which wasn't a lie. After all, her baby wasn't even born yet. Her hands subconsciously went to her belly, and his eyes followed. As soon as she saw it, she realized her mistake.

"Are ye . . . pregnant?" he asked, the corner of his mouth turning up in a wry grin.

"It is no' proper of ye to ask such a question to a lassie." Anxiety coursed through her, and she felt a bead of sweat forming on her brow. Her breathing shallowed, and she started to feel the way she always did when she was around Dun. She'd never told Dun she was pregnant, because of the fear he would blame her, or purposely do something to make her lose the baby. He'd made it quite clear to her right after they wed that he never wanted children.

"Tell me the truth," Cam said in a low voice, looking directly into her eyes this time.

Yvaine's heartbeat sped up, and her head spun. Her tongue felt two sizes too big to even be able to speak now.

"Is that why ye're goin' to a priory? Ye are pregnant and canna stay in Hermitage to run yer chandler business by yerself, because ye are goin' to have a bairn to raise, too? I'll bet the Chandler's Guild doesna allow a pregnant widow to take over the business. Admit it. I'm right, are no' I?"

She wanted to deny it, but when she looked back at the little girl in the wagon, her heart about broke. If she didn't acknowledge the bairn growing within her, then she wasn't any better than Cam, denying the fact he now had a four-year-old daughter. Her eyes closed and her body swayed as she suddenly became lightheaded. It felt, once again, as if life were crashing down upon her.

A dead husband.

A baby-to-be.

Her life was changing so quickly that it made her dizzy. Heat engulfed her body and her knees buckled beneath her. The next thing she knew, she was falling to the ground.

# Chapter Four

CAM SAW YVAINE falling, and shot forward, scooping her up into his arms before she could hit the ground. As he cradled her to his chest, her head rolled against him. Strands of her long hair drifted up around him in the breeze, smelling like rose-scented soap. The soft tips of her locks brushed gently against his cheek, feeling like the gossamer wings of a butterfly. It sent a delectable shiver through him.

This woman looked like a sleeping goddess in his arms. The sun lit up her smooth skin, and the rays settled upon her, almost making her glow like an angel. Rosy cheeks and full, pink lips only added to her undeniable beauty. Long, curved, dark lashes flickered, followed by her eyes slowly drifting open.

Big, round eyes, the color of chestnuts, stared up at him, holding fear and confusion. He also noticed something that surprised him, since the woman had been so mouthy and brash. He figured she was naught but a cold-hearted shrew, but now he wasn't so sure. In her eyes, he saw desperation. It was almost like longing . . . a need to be loved, if he wasn't mistaken. He'd been with many women in his lifetime. He could read them better than anyone, even if most of them had been whores he'd bedded who didn't want anything from him but his money.

Yvaine was different. She was more like the lassies of the clan who'd wanted more from him than just one night of bliss. Those women wanted a commitment that he had never been able to give. It just wasn't in his nature to do so.

In Yvaine's eyes, he saw a deep need . . . and despair. It made him want to protect her – especially since his strong suspicions told him she might be pregnant, even though she wouldn't admit it. His eyes shot down to her belly. If she was with child, it hadn't been long enough to even show yet. Mayhap she wasn't pregnant after all. He supposed it was just his imagination running wild. Besides, it wouldn't make sense. How was the girl going to raise a child when she was about to become a nun?

The scent of a chandler's shop – cinnamon, beeswax and honey – wafted up from her clothes, filling his senses. His gaze drifted back to her face again to find her eyes closed once more. When she wasn't awake and threatening or chastising him, she seemed so vulnerable and tremendously fragile. Her features were delicate and feminine, calling to him, tempting him like a siren of the sea. Her lips were full . . . just the perfect type for kissing. Curiosity and want filled his being. Now, he had to know how they tasted.

Without thinking about what he was doing, he brought his face closer to hers. His lips gently brushed against her mouth in a quick and simple kiss. He licked his lips, savoring her essence. She tasted sweet and enticing. He wanted nothing more than to go back for seconds, but knew it was wrong. After all, this woman was soon to take her vows! Far be it for him to keep longing for a woman who didn't want anything to do with men. Nay, she would never kiss or couple with a man again and, apparently, she didn't care.

Yvaine squirmed in his arms and moaned seductively, only managing to tempt his weak resolve. With her eyes still closed, her lips quivered. Then she raised her chin slightly, as if she were extending a welcome invitation to him that he couldn't ignore.

Cam was about to kiss her again when he heard a little voice from behind him, causing him to stop.

"What are ye doin'?" asked Avianca.

Startled, he turned with a jolt. That only managed to bring

Yvaine from her unconscious state, since he still held her in his arms.

"W-what's goin' on?" screamed Yvaine, struggling to sit up, gripping on to his plaid. "I demand that ye put me down. Now!"

"Sorry," he apologized, realizing the delicate goddess or angel was gone and in her place was the shrew again. "Ye fainted, and I caught ye before ye hit the ground," he tried to explain, but she wasn't listening. He gently placed her on her feet, hoping for a simple thank you. Instead, he was rewarded with naught but a harsh sting as Yvaine slapped him across the face.

"Damn! What the hell did ye do that for?" he grumbled, his hand going to his cheek.

"Please, dinna curse in front of the child." She pulled Avianca away from him, as if she were protecting the girl from some sort of monster. He didn't like the feeling at all. Especially since he was the girl's father.

"I saw ye kissin' her, just like ye used to do to my mathair," said the girl, making his heart drop in his chest.

Double damn. Had Avianca seen him when he was with Isobel? He hoped not. He never even knew the girl existed. Why the hell hadn't the whore told him they had a daughter together? His head spun from all these thoughts at once. Cam wouldn't be surprised if he were the next one to faint.

"Y-ye kissed me?" Yvaine asked, as if she were trying to remember. Her hand went to her mouth and she stared at the ground.

"I admit, I did kiss ye," he told her the truth. "When I did, ye moaned and lifted yer chin and puckered yer lips, wanting me to do it again."

"I did no'!" Her tongue shot out to lick her lips.

"Ah! So, I see ye tastin' my essence on yer lips after all, lass."

"I – I dinna ken what ye're talkin' about."

Before he could call her out on her lie, the sound of thundering hooves charging toward them caused him to turn around. Cam looked up to see his friends riding back to them with their swords drawn and raised. There was a sense of urgency about their actions, and he knew that something was wrong.

"Get the lassies to safety," shouted Nash.

"The stinkin' English are on our tails," yelled North.

"Where's Gavin?" Cam's hand automatically went to the hilt of his sword as he scanned the surroundings for their friend.

"He's distractin' the English to give us a chance to protect the lassies," announced Nash.

This is not what Cam wanted to hear. "Nay! He canna fend them off by himself. Damn it, go back and help him. I've got the girls covered." Cam reached out and scooped up Avianca under one arm, then took Yvaine by the hand. "Run," he told her. "I need ye to hide with the wee lass in the back of the wagon until this is all over."

"Will the English try to take my guids?" asked Yvaine as they reached the wagon and Cam put the girl down, pulling back a flap of the tarp.

"Damn it, lass, stop thinkin' about yer guids and start thinkin' about yer lives instead."

"I am. But everythin' I own is in this cart. Help to protect it, please."

Cam found the woman exhausting, but decided if she didn't think he'd help her that she'd never be quiet and hide from the English. He didn't want her or his daughter to be attacked.

"They willna get a thing if I can help it," he assured her. "I'll take them down, one by one, before they get anywhere near the wagon." He pulled out a few items to make room, throwing the things to the ground. "Get in," he commanded. "Quickly!"

"But I –"

"I dinna have time for ye to disagree. Now, in!"

YVAINE CLIMBED INTO the wagon, hiding in the hole under the tarp that Cam had cleared out for her.

"Take the girl, and keep her quiet," he instructed, pushing Avianca in next. "Whatever ye do, dinna let the English ken ye are here."

"I'm scared," cried Avianca.

Cam reached out, lifting the little girl's chin, looking directly into her eyes. "I need ye to help keep Yvaine quiet, Avianca. Can ye do that favor for me?" he asked the girl. "She has a habit of never shuttin' up."

"I can," said Avianca, nodding slightly even though she looked like she was about to cry.

"Guid." He pulled a dagger off his weapon belt and handed it, hilt first, to Yvaine.

"What is this for?" asked Yvaine.

"Just in case ye need it."

"I dinna like weapons. I dinna ken how to use them."

"Ye'll like it fine if it saves yer life. To use it, ye just aim and stab. There's nothin' to it. Now, stay quiet and dinna move from here until I come back to get ye. And . . . both of ye, keep yer eyes closed. Also, dinna let anythin' ye hear frighten ye. Ye need to stay quiet under all circumstances. Understand?"

"Aye," said Yvaine, pulling the little girl to her in a hug, gripping the hilt of the dagger tightly. She prayed to God that Cam and his friends wouldn't get killed by the English. She also prayed that she and Avianca would be safe and that she wouldn't be required to use the dagger, after all. The last thing she wanted was to kill a man . . . again.

Cam tied the tarp back down, but Yvaine could still see out through an open crack.

Shouting was heard, and then the sound of men yelling. Metal clashing against metal resounded in the air, making her realize that Cam and his friends were fighting off the English in a very dangerous battle.

"I'm scared," whispered Avianca, clinging to Yvaine. Yvaine was frightened, as well, but couldn't show it. She needed to remain strong for Avianca . . . and for her own unborn child.

"Shhh," she whispered. "Close yer eyes, lass." She held the girl's head against her chest, feeling the trembling of both their bodies. The sounds of fighting grew louder and louder around them. Through the small opening of the tarp, she could see Cam. He was on foot, fighting off the Englishmen, one after another. He killed one, his sword sinking into the Sassenach's chest. Yvaine closed her eyes, seeing the blood on the sword as Cam removed it. It only made Yvaine think of Dun's lifeless body lying in a puddle of blood at her feet. She couldn't push that image from her mind.

"Cam, behind ye," she heard one of his friends call out. Her eyes snapped open to see an Englishman at the foot of the wagon, about to stab Cam in the back. Cam spun around and sank his sword into the attacker's chest.

The air under the tarp became thick, and she found it hard to breathe. Anxiety coursed through her and her head spun. Still, she couldn't leave. She had to stay there and protect Avianca, as well as herself.

Then something shook the wagon, and she realized someone had hopped aboard. She looked up to see the tip of a knife slitting the tarp right above her head. Ducking down lower, she cradled Avianca in her arms, holding her hand over the little girl's mouth.

As much as she tried to keep the girl quiet, she still let out a soft whimper. The tarp ripped open right above their heads, and was pulled back to reveal their hiding place.

"Well, well, well, what have we got here?" An Englishman with blackened teeth stared down at her with lust in his eyes. "I'd say this is a treasure of the best kind."

He reached for her and she instinctively lifted the blade. It was sharp and cut the man on his hand. His blood dripped down on her face.

"Nay! Please, dinna hurt us," she begged, pulling Avianca closer.

"Oh, there are two of you," he spat, rubbing his injured hand.

"She's just a child. Please, leave her alone," begged Yvaine, thinking their lives were over.

"You cut me, bitch!" snarled the man, anger blazing in his

eyes.

Yvaine held up the blade again to protect them, but then her eyes fastened on the man's blood. It ran down his arm from the wound she'd given him, and drops landed on her chest.

It was too much for her to take. In her head, Yvaine was back in the chandler's shop once again, looking at the blood of her dead husband who had died by her hand. Her fingers opened and she dropped the knife, not able to even defend herself or that of the child anymore. Her body froze and she was unable to move.

As the man chuckled and reached down to touch her, she closed her eyes and cringed. Her arms wrapped around Avianca, protecting the little girl with her own life.

Then, just when she was sure the man would rape her, she heard him gasp. When she opened her eyes again, Cam was atop the cart, pushing the dead man to the ground. He gripped his bloody sword in his hand as he looked down into the wagon.

"Are ye all right, lass? Is my daughter all right, as well?"

Yvaine was so much in shock that she couldn't even answer.

"Here comes one of the Legendary Bastards of the Crown," shouted one of the Englishmen next.

"Run for your lives," called out another, followed by the sound of running feet and horses' hooves as the English headed away.

"Blethers, it's about time Rook showed up," grumbled Cam, looking out at what was happening before jumping down from the wagon. He came around to the back, pulling open the tarp. "It's safe now. Ye can come out," said Cam, wiping his blade off on his plaid and then pushing his sword back into his scabbard. He held out his hand to help them. "Come on, Avianca."

"Nay," cried the little girl, still clinging to Yvaine. "I dinna want to come out. Ever."

"It's all right, sweetheart," Yvaine finally managed to say, trying to calm the girl although her body still shook in fright. Finally, Avianca took Cam's hand and he helped her out of the wagon. Then he did the same, helping Yvaine to the ground as well.

At first, the air against Yvaine's face felt good. Then she looked at the surroundings, seeing all the dead bodies lying mangled and in puddles of blood. It made her sick to her stomach.

"Are ye all right, Yvaine?" Cam reached out for her but she pushed his hand away and covered her mouth. Spinning on her heel, she couldn't help but retch.

✦•◦◇◦•✦

# CHAPTER FIVE

"L ASS, I AM so sorry ye two had to see this." Cam reached out for Yvaine, but she pushed his hand away.

"Dinna touch me when ye have blood on ye." She looked so frightened. Her face became very pale.

"I want to go home." Avianca pouted and then she started crying. Yvaine pulled the little girl to her for comfort.

"Aye, we need to leave here at once," Yvaine agreed.

"I canna leave before we bury the dead." Cam looked around at the dead English, realizing it was a harsh scene for the two girls to have to witness. He wished it wasn't so, but he hadn't any choice in the matter. It was kill, or be killed. He did what he had to do in order to protect the lassies.

"There is a child present, and she shouldna be seein' such carnage." Yvaine turned her head and threw up again. Her hand went to her stomach.

"A simple thank ye for savin' yer lives would have sufficed. Get in the wagon and stay there until I'm ready to leave." Cam spun on his heel and headed back over to his friends who were now talking with Rook – one of the Legendary Bastards of the Crown. Rook was the son of King Edward III.

"I'm sorry we were late," said Rook, who was English. "I'm just glad we got here in time to help you."

"I kent this was goin' to be trouble," Cam snorted. "I dinna like this punishment I've been served. I should have been able to

41

stay in Scotland, like Gavin did for his sentence."

"We are in Scotland, ye fool," spat Gavin, since they were right on the border.

"Ye ken what I mean," Cam answered, glancing back at the girls who were climbing into the wagon. "I'm just glad the lassies werena harmed. Especially the wee one. I would have never forgiven myself if I hadna been able to protect them. They are very shaken and want to leave anon."

"Go, then," said Gavin with a shake of his head. "I'll stay and help bury the bodies before headin' back to Hermitage Castle."

"Aye, we'll help him," volunteered Nash.

"Nay, ye two were instructed to go with Cam," Gavin reminded them.

"I'll have my men stay and help Gavin," Rook offered. "I'll accompany you to the priory along with Nash and North, so we can get going."

"What if we meet up with more English . . . a lot more?" Nash asked him.

"Aye," agreed North. "Wouldna it be better to have more men along with us?"

"My men will follow us as soon as they are finished," stated Rook. "Don't worry. I know a shortcut to the priory that even the English don't use. We'll get there with no further problems, I assure you."

"How can ye be so sure?" asked Nash.

"You're forgetting, I lived in the catacombs of the priory since childhood, after Burnt Candlemas," Rook reminded them. "I know my way around trouble better than anyone."

"That's right," agreed Gavin. "Cam, take the lassies and go. I can hear the wee one still cryin'."

"Wee one?" asked Rook, looking over to the wagon. "I thought there was only one girl to escort to the priory."

"There's been a last-minute addition of a child," Gavin told him.

"A child?" Rook seemed confused.

"It seems Cam's amorous ways with whores got him into a little trouble." Nash chuckled when he said it, but Cam found it far from amusing.

"I still don't understand," said Rook.

"Avianca, it seems, is my four-year-old daughter," Cam explained. "Her mathair died and it was her last wish that the child be raised by me."

"Really." Rook raised a brow, looking amused. "A whore wants her child raised by a Highlander warrior?"

"We couldna believe it either," piped up North. "She probably figured that Cam knew more about women than anyone after all the visits he's made to brothels through the years."

"That's enough," grumbled Cam. "I am goin' to clean myself off as well as my sword in the river, and then let's get movin'. My ears canna handle any more of the child's cryin'."

"All right, I'll let my men know the plan," Rook told them, starting away, but stopping and turning back around. "Are you really going to raise the child yourself?" he asked Cam.

"Would it be so surprisin' to ye if I said I was?" Cam asked him.

"Well, I wouldn't expect it, that's for sure."

"And neither should ye," Cam answered. "I dinna ken anythin' about raisin' a child, and I dinna plan to do any such thing. Once we get to the priory, I'm goin' to tell the monks to find the wee lass a guid home with decent parents."

"I see," said Rook, sounding skeptical.

"I can tell ye dinna believe that either," snorted Cam.

"I am not doubting you," Rook told him. "It's just that sometimes things don't always go as planned."

"I certainly didna plan on havin' a child, if that's what ye mean." Cam's eyes darted back to the wagon once again.

"Have you considered getting married soon?" asked Rook.

"Never," snapped Cam, turning on his heel and heading back to the wagon with the bawling child and the bossy widow. Now he had to take them to a priory to make candles and spend time with monks. This was going to be a very long sentence indeed!

"STOP THE WAGON," Yvaine commanded after a short time on the road. Her stomach lurched from the continuous bouncing. She sat in back with Avianca who had finally cried herself to sleep.

"What is it?" Cam looked back over his shoulder. "Blethers, dinna tell me ye need to piss again. Or do ye want to retch instead? After all, ye seem to trade off between the two quite often."

"Haud yer wheesht and stop this wagon, I say."

"Fine," Cam grumbled, bringing the wagon to a stop, calling out to Rook and his friends to halt as well.

"What's goin' on?" asked Nash, riding quickly to the side of the wagon. "Why are we stoppin'?"

North followed him, riding up quickly as well. "It's no' a guid idea to stop until we reach the priory. There could be Sassenachs hidin' anywhere." His eyes roamed back and forth as he scanned the area for any Englishmen possibly hiding in the brush.

"I only want to get into the front of the wagon since I canna stand the bouncin' back here any longer," Yvaine told him. "My teeth are goin' to rattle right out of my head." Yvaine put one leg over the side of the wagon, meaning to get out. That's when she discovered the ground was farther down than she thought. Suddenly, she found herself stuck on the edge of the wagon with no way to get off.

"Blethers, this is no' what I wanted to do."

"Stay there before ye break yer fool neck." Cam shot out of the driver's seat and ran to the side of the wagon to help her. "Here," he said, reaching up and putting his hands under her arms, lifting her out before she could even object.

God, it was wrong to feel this way with a stranger, but Yvaine liked Cam's hands so close to her breasts. He no longer had blood on him, and that calmed her a little. His long, blond hair was wet and slicked back. She was sure he'd cleaned off in the river because of her comment earlier.

"Thank ye," she said as he set her feet on the ground. His head jerked back in surprise, as if it was the last thing he'd expected her to say.

"Did ye just thank me?" He blinked twice.

"Aye, I did," she admitted, starting to feel bad for giving him such a hard time. "I thanked ye no' only for helpin' me off the wagon, but for protectin' me and the child from the battle as well."

"It's my job. What did ye expect me to do?" He held out his hand to help her up onto the driver's seat.

That wasn't the response she wanted or expected. It took her aback. "Yes, I suppose I am naught more than part of yer punishment," she said, not taking his proffered hand.

"Yvaine, that's no' what I meant and ye ken it."

"Do I?"

"Take my hand, lass," he told her. "I only mean to assist ye. If we are goin' to be livin' together at the priory, we need to start trustin' each other, and gettin' along."

She thought about it for a moment, and the word trust scared her more than the rest of it. She didn't trust men! Not after the way her late husband had treated her. She couldn't be sure all men – besides her brothers – weren't going to treat her in the same way.

"Take it," he told her, shoving his hand closer to her in an abrupt movement.

Instinct made her jump back and whimper, holding her arm up to block her face.

"God's toes, what's the matter with ye?" he asked, lowering his hand slowly. "Ye act like I'm the enemy, when I'm just the opposite. I am yer protector."

She slowly lowered her arm, realizing how foolish she must seem to him. He wasn't that bastard, Dun. She knew now he wasn't trying to hurt her, but help her, like he'd said. Still, it was an instinctual reaction for her when any man came toward her with his arm flying.

"I – I'm sorry," she apologized. "I guess I'm just no' used to havin' a protector." She slowly reached out, waiting for him to take her hand. He looked down at it and then back up to her in thought before actually giving her his hand.

"That's an odd thing to say. I would have thought ye were used to havin' a protector," he told her, guiding her up to the bench seat. "That is, bein' married and all," he continued. "I'm sure yer husband watched over ye."

Thoughts drifted through her mind of all the times Dun had hurt her. It made her shiver. Her body stiffened as she took a seat. "I'd rather no' talk of my dead husband if ye dinna mind."

"I understand," he said. "Too painful yet, I'm sure." He pulled himself up and sat down next to her, taking the reins and starting forward.

"More painful than ye'd ever believe." Yvaine wrapped her arms around her and stared off into the distance, trying to think of anything other than men, blood, and death.

✦•◦◇◦•✦

# CHAPTER SIX

C AM WAS GLAD when they arrived at the priory because the woman sitting next to him was odd, and most likely out of her mind. The sooner he got this punishment over with, the better. He directed the horse through the main archway. The establishment was huge and made of red brick. It was much larger than Hermitage Castle. It was almost like a little village in itself.

He looked up high right before riding through the passageway, seeing pillars made of stone. Above them, long, tall windows welcomed them with religious pictures constructed in the ornate stained glass. It was a most impressive sight. Above that was a niche in the stone with a statue and the name of Mary Magdalene carved above it. Atop the main pinnacle of the priory was a large stone cross.

It was dark in the passageway as he followed Rook into the entrance of this holy place. The clip clop of the horses' hooves echoed loudly in the chamber. Nash and North followed right behind the wagon, silent for once. He figured they were probably in awe of the surroundings.

Then there was daylight and the tunnel ended, leaving them inside the courtyard. Just being inside the holy walls of the priory's courtyard made him fidget in his seat.

As soon as they stopped, several monks dressed in black robes hurried toward them. A handful of nuns stood in the shadows watching.

"This place looks great," said Nash, looking around at the archways and cloistered areas that had small gardens in between.

"Aye, it certainly is no' in ruins anymore," agreed North, hopping off his horse.

"I'm sure Storm told you that the priory has been restored, and is actually still in progress," said Rook, dismounting his horse as well. "It was many years ago when I lived here in the ruins, in the catacombs."

"I canna believe anyone would live in catacombs," said Yvaine, starting to get out of the wagon. Cam hopped out first and helped her.

"I canna believe anyone would live in a monastery," mumbled Cam under his breath.

"Sister," called out one of the monks, hurrying toward them. The rest of the monks remained silent.

"Brathair!" Yvaine hurried over to hug the man. The monk was short and stout, wearing a black, woolen tunic tied at the waist with a leather belt. Over it, he wore the traditional cowl – a long, sleeveless robe with a deep hood. Like all monks, his hair was in a tonsure, his head shaved only atop his head, making him bald with a ring of hair around it. "Gillies, this is Cam MacKeefe and his friends, North and Nash. They will be stayin' here with me for a while."

"How do ye do?" asked Cam, reaching out to shake the man's hand. The monk lowered his eyes and nodded, keeping his hands inside his cowl. "Hello," Cam called out and waved to a few more monks nearby. "What are yer names?"

They did not answer. Instead, they turned and walked away.

"No' very friendly, are they?" asked Cam.

"They don't answer you because the monks are not allowed to speak," Brother Gillies told him.

"Why no'?" asked Nash, looking over at the monks as they headed away.

"It is part of their training," said Gillies.

"How do ye call them for dinner?" asked North, scratching his head.

"We have a bell that rings for not only each meal but also before each of our prayer sessions throughout the day."

"I'm curious," said Cam. "If ye are Yvaine's brathair, why is it ye sound more like a Sassenach than a Scot when ye speak?"

"He's been a monk in England for a long time now," explained Yvaine. "Gillies has chosen to speak like those around him."

"Ah. Just no' like the monks around here," said Cam with a chuckle, realizing how quiet the courtyard was, even though there were a few dozen people present.

"Brathair, thank ye for lettin' me stay with ye, and for lettin' me bring the chandler business here with me," Yvaine told him.

"Well, Sister, it's the least I can do, after you lost your husband." He laid his hand on her arm.

"Thank ye," said Yvaine.

"Bless your late husband, Dun, dear child," Brother Gillies continued. "I didn't know the man well, but from what I remember, he was in perfect health. How did he come to die?"

"Aye, how *did* he die?" asked Cam, wondering the same thing since her story didn't sound feasible to him.

"I already told ye," Yvaine said to Cam. "He tripped and fell and hit his head. It all happened suddenly."

"Was he drunk?" asked North. "I dinna remember ever seein' him in the tavern while we were there."

"Me neither," said Nash.

"He mainly drank at home, but no' always," Yvaine told them. "Aye, he was very well in his cups that night, and also . . . clumsy," said Yvaine. Her face became pale and her gaze fell to the ground.

"And ye saw the whole thing but didna help him?" asked Cam.

Her head jerked upward now. "Aye, I saw it happen, but it was all so fast that there was nothin' at all that I could do to stop it. He brought on the situation himself."

"I hardly think anyone brings on a situation to die," said Cam, thinking the whole thing sounded odd, yet he couldn't prove the girl was lying. When she glared at him, he figured he'd better drop the subject. Honestly, he didn't care at all. All he cared about was doing what he had to in order to be accepted back into his clan.

"Where do ye want me to put my things?" asked Yvaine. "I hope ye have a room proper and big enough for makin' candles."

"There are many places in the monastery, with ample room," her brother assured her. "You will be all unpacked and ready to work after the main meal."

"Meal?" This took Cam's interest since he hadn't had time to break the fast this morning and was starving. "Great! I am really hungry. Let's eat."

The bell of the cruciform-style church at the far end of the priory started ringing, filling the air with musical notes.

"There's the food bell," said Cam to his friends. "Where do we go?" Cam looked around the large priory that was set up almost like a small town. The church was at one end, and buildings and a stable, as well as plenty of cloistered walkways made a square around the area. In the center was grass and shrubs as well as flowers.

"That's not the bell for eating," said Rook with a chuckle.

"It's no'?" asked Nash. "Then what is it for?"

"It's the bell that signals the midday prayer service," explained Brother Gillies. "We should all go to the church for mass now."

"Church?" squawked Nash, since Cam and his friends rarely attended a mass.

"Aye," answered Brother Gillies. "The meal will be in the refectory afterwards. You'll all be staying, won't you?"

"Unfortunately, my wife, Calliope is expecting me back at Naward Castle," said Rook, getting atop his horse.

"We'll come with ye." North reached for the reins of his horse. "I canna wait to see Naward Castle."

"Aye. Me, too," agreed Nash, putting his foot in the stirrup, ready to mount his horse as well.

Cam cleared his throat to stop them. "I believe Laird MacKeefe said ye two were to stay here at the priory with me. Ye are allowed to visit Naward Castle, but only at the end of each week."

"That's right. He did say that," agreed Yvaine.

"Well, then. Since that's settled, Rook, how about if ye show my friends and me the catacombs where ye lived?" asked Cam, trying to get out of going to mass.

"Mayhap another time." Rook turned his horse and headed away.

"My lay brothers will stable and tend to your horses," said Brother Gillies, giving a hand signal to call a few monks over. "They'll unpack your belongings, and put them in the hall next to the scriptorium where you can set up your candle making business, Yvaine."

Several monks rushed over.

"Lay brothers?" asked Cam curiously. "What do they do?"

"They tend to most of the chores, the orchard, and the crops," explained Brother Gillies. "That gives the rest of the monks more time for their studies, prayer, and illuminating and copying manuscripts."

"I see," said Cam, wishing he were a lay brother right now. He would accept any reason to get away.

When one of the monks peered into the wagon, they heard a scream and then the crying of a young girl.

"What was that?" asked Brother Gillies, rushing over to the wagon.

"Avianca," gasped Yvaine, running after him.

"Aye, Avianca," said Cam with a sigh, almost having forgotten about the girl since she'd finally fallen asleep and was quiet. But her crying reminded him he had a daughter now. It was something he'd rather forget for the moment.

"Are ye just goin' to stand here, or are ye goin' to calm yer daughter?" asked Nash.

"Me calm her? Hah!" spat Cam. "I dinna think anyone on either side of the border could get the wee lass to stop her cryin'."

All of a sudden, the crying stopped. Cam looked up to see Yvaine rocking the girl, holding her tightly to her chest.

"It seems like Yvaine has quite a way with the girl," said North.

"Mayhap ye can learn from her how to do it," suggested Nash.

"Whatever for?" asked Cam.

"She's yer daughter." North shook his head in disgust.

"Dinna remind me, and dinna try to make me feel guilty," Cam answered. "I dinna plan on raisin' her. I canna. It's no' possible. I am a warrior. I'll have to talk to Brother Gillies about findin' a suitable family for the lass soon. That is, right after we eat, I'll mention it."

The three of them walked over to join the others.

"Where did this child come from?" asked Brother Gillies in surprise.

"This is Avianca, and she is four years old," said Yvaine, reaching out to wipe a tear off the little girl's cheek.

"Yvaine, Keithen didn't say anything about you bringing along a child," protested Gillies. "She can't stay here. This is no place for her."

"She must stay," Yvaine said. "She is Cam's daughter."

"Yours?" asked the monk, looking him up and down. "Are you a widower then?"

"Nay, I've never been married," Cam told him, getting a nasty scowl from the man in return.

"This is no way to raise a child," said the monk. "You are taking her around with you, and now bringing her to a priory?"

"I agree, it is no' a guid way at all to raise a child," said Cam. "That's why I wanted to ask ye to find a good home for the lass."

"What?" The monk's eyes opened wide. "You want to give away your own child?"

"Her mathair died and, honestly, I'm no' even convinced she's really mine," Cam told the monk as the girl started crying again.

"I want to go home," wailed Avianca, taking one little balled-up fist and wiping at her teary eyes. "I miss my mama."

"Cam, ye need to comfort her." Before Cam knew what happened, Yvaine plopped the girl into his arms. "Avianca, this is yer faither and he will protect ye, dinna worry."

"Now wait a minute," protested Cam, not knowing what to do with the little girl he was holding.

"Hurry, or we'll be late for mass," said Brother Gillies. "We can all discuss this matter later." He turned and started toward the church at a brisk pace. Yvaine was right on his heels.

Cam looked over to North and Nash. "Someone take her," he said, feeling panicked, holding the little girl out to them.

North and Nash both backed away, holding up their palms and shaking their heads.

"I dinna ken a thing about children," said North, doing nothing to take her.

"Dinna look at me," said Nash. "We've got to hurry, or we'll be late for mass." They both turned and ran to the church, leaving Cam standing there holding the girl, feeling very confused and stranded.

"Papa, is it true? Will ye really protect me like Yvaine said?" asked Avianca. She looked up at him with wide, green eyes filled with tears. "I'm so frightened. I miss my mama."

"Avianca," he said, meaning to tell the girl that he wasn't even sure he was her father, and that he was going to find some good parents for her. But when he saw the hope in the innocent child's eyes, he didn't have the heart to tell her that. Not to her face, at least.

"Yes?" she asked, blinking several times. She had a frown on her face.

"Can ye run?" he asked her, putting her down on the ground.

"Aye. But why?"

"Because if we dinna run, we're goin' to be late for mass, and I dinna want that monk mad at us. If so, he may decide no' to feed us afterwards."

She giggled at that, turning and taking off at a run for the church.

"Avianca!" he called out, trying to be heard over the loud, noisy bell ringing in the tower. "Wait for me," he said, sighing and running toward the church instead of away from it, which baffled him more than anything that he'd even be doing such an absurd thing.

# CHAPTER SEVEN

T HE SOUND OF the monks chanting filled the church, sending shivers up Yvaine's spine. The church was magnificent, and huge! She felt so alive being here. Her eyes closed as she breathed deeply, feeling a good energy enter her body.

She had just started to relax when her eyes drifted open to see Jesus on the crucifix behind the altar, staring down at her. Suddenly, she didn't feel worthy of being in this holy place at all. She was a murderer now, and certainly God knew it! Her body stiffened, and her head dizzied. She needed to get out of here fast. She didn't belong here – not when God knew her terrible secret.

"Pardon me," she said, squeezing in front of Cam, trying to get out of the pew. His hand shot out and he gripped her around the wrist, almost making her cry out.

"Ye're no' leavin' if I have to be here," he whispered to her.

"Let go of me," she said through clenched teeth. "Ye're hurtin' me." She managed to twist out of his grip and hurried down the aisle, away from him.

"WHAT WAS THAT all about?" whispered North, looking over at Cam.

Cam shrugged. Then he leaned over and whispered to Nash. "Watch the child. I'm goin' after Yvaine."

"Nay!" said Nash in a loud whisper, looking terrified. Cam smiled.

"She willna bite," he said, looking down at Avianca, who was playing with a prayer book, pretending like she knew how to read. "However, I'm no' so sure about Yvaine."

Cam stepped out from the pew and hurried out of the church after Yvaine. He didn't see her anywhere, so he headed across the courtyard toward the stables. When he heard a whimper from inside one of the cloistered walkways, he stopped in his tracks and turned around. Quickly, he headed over in that direction.

"Yvaine?" he called out, stepping into the shadows of the covered walkway to find her sitting on one of the stone benches. She saw him and quickly wiped her eyes with the back of her hand. "What's the matter?" he asked.

She faked a smile, but he didn't believe it in the least.

"Nothin'," she answered.

"Then why did ye leave before mass was over?"

"I just . . . needed some air." She sniffled, looking in the other direction.

Cam walked over and sat down next to her. "I'm sorry," he said in a low voice.

"Sorry? Whatever for?"

"Ye said I was hurtin' ye when I took yer wrist. I never meant to harm ye, Yvaine."

"Oh, that." She sniffled again and flashed a quick smile. "Ye didna hurt me. No' really."

"Then why did ye say I did?"

"I – I just didna want to stay . . . I guess."

"Ye and me both," said Cam, making her giggle.

"Do ye think it'll really be that bad stayin' here at the priory?" she asked him.

"Ye tell me," he answered. This time, it was his turn to fake a smile. "It sounds like there's no' much that goes on here besides prayin'. They dinna even let the monks talk. Are ye sure this is the kind of life ye want?"

"Of course no'," she said. "Who would want that?"

"Nay? Then why are ye goin' to be a nun?" he asked, confused as to her true purpose here.

"A nun?"

"Aye. That's why ye're here, isna it? I ken it is what happens to a lot of lassies when they are widowed at a young age. They become nuns and give their lives to the church."

"I'M NO' THAT young," said Yvaine, eager to change the subject. She didn't want to mislead him, but if he thought she was in training to be a nun, mayhap it wouldn't hurt. Then, he wouldn't woo her like he did with all the lassies, especially the whores. Cam had a reputation for spending most of his time with a woman in his arms. She didn't want to be his next trollop.

"How old are ye?" he asked.

"I am three and twenty. How old are ye?" she wanted to know.

"I am two years yer senior."

"Ye are that old and yet ye've never been married?" Of course, a philanderer such as he would never want to settle down, so why should it surprise her?

"I've never felt the need to wed anyone," he told her.

"Until now," she said, sure that he knew exactly what she meant.

By the look on his face, she could tell he didn't like her comment.

"Look, Yvaine," he said in a stern voice. "I didna even ken I had a child until recently. Honestly, I still dinna really believe she's mine."

Yvaine let out a poof of air from her mouth and shook her head in disbelief of his reaction. "A woman on her death bed said the child was yers, and yet ye still deny it. I highly doubt she'd waste her dyin' breath on such a lie."

"Unless she wanted to make sure her bastard child was taken care of once she left this world," he added quickly.

Yvaine stood up and brushed off her gown. "Well, if that was her intent, then she certainly chose the wrong man," she answered with a sniff.

"What does that mean?" He bolted up off the bench, crossing his arms over his chest.

"It means ye've made no secret that ye dinna want the child. Ye even said it right in front of the poor, wee lass. How cold-hearted of a man are ye, Cam MacKeefe?"

"Me?" he asked. "What about ye? I think ye are the most cold-hearted of all, after what ye've done."'

Her head jerked around in surprise. "What do ye mean?" Fear filled her. God's tongue, she hoped he didn't know her secret.

"I mean that ye have been treatin' me unkindly since the moment we met."

"Oh, is that all?" Relief washed through her. He didn't know her dark secret, after all.

"Is that all?" he repeated, slowly uncrossing his arms, and squinting his eyes. "I am here only to serve my time and earn my way back into my clan. But I'll be damned if I'm goin' to have to live with the ice princess with a sharp tongue for the next fortnight."

"What was yer crime that put ye in this situation to begin with?" she asked, ignoring his accusation.

"It doesna matter."

"It's that bad. I see."

"Nay, it wasna anythin' bad," he said, waving a hand through the air in dismissal. "No' really."

"Then tell me. What did ye do to make yerself an outcast of yer clan?"

"I just broke a few of Old Callum MacKeefe's doitit rules of his tavern, that's all."

"He grabbed the wrong lassie and kissed her," said Nash, walking up with North, having overheard them. Little Avianca followed on their heels. The mass was over now, and everyone poured out of the church and headed over to the refectory to eat.

"Hmph. Women again," she said. "Why am I no' surprised?"

"Let's go get some food. I'm famished." Cam started to walk

away with his friends, so Yvaine cleared her throat to stop them.

"What's the matter?" Cam looked over his shoulder.

"Are ye forgettin' somethin'? Or should I say someone?"

"Well, I'd take yer hand, but I'm afraid ye'd rip off my head for touchin' ye," said Cam, making his friends laugh.

"No' me, ye fool." Yvaine looked down at Avianca, who was sitting on the ground, twirling a blade of grass in her fingers. "After all, she is yer responsibility now."

Cam opened his mouth, but never got to protest, since his friends agreed with her.

"That's right," said North. "She's yer child so ye need to look after her."

"Dinna even think of tellin' us to do it again." Nash pushed past Cam, followed by North as they made their way to the hall for something to eat.

"Well?" Yvaine crossed her arms over her chest and raised an eyebrow.

"Canna ye just –"

"Nay!" she spat. "It is time ye take responsibility for yer actions, Cam MacKeefe, starting right here, right now." Yvaine stepped around him and headed to the refectory as well. She didn't think he'd just leave the girl there alone. If she did, she never would have walked away. Peering over her shoulder, she smiled. Cam reached down and took the little girl's hand, talking to her as they followed the rest to the hall to eat.

Mayhap there was a chance for redemption for the fool, after all.

"WHAT IS THIS?" asked Cam, sitting on a bench in the refectory next to his friends. He put one bowl of food down in front of Avianca, and wrapped his hands around the other as he peered into it, thinking he'd made a mistake. Perhaps this was leftover paste from the scriptorium to glue the books together.

"It is cooked oats with a hint of cinnamon and honey." Yvaine put her bowl on the table and sat down next to him.

"I think it's supposed to be our meal." Nash held up a spoonful and made a face.

"Nay. This canna be real food. Can it?" North inspected the gruel, letting the thin slop fall from the spoon back into the bowl.

"It's what the monks eat." Yvaine dipped her spoon into the bowl, blowing on the hot oats and nibbling at them.

"Nay, really," said Cam, throwing down his spoon. "Where is the meal?"

"This is it." Yvaine nodded at the bowl.

"I like it," said Avianca, smiling and eating it without complaining.

"Well, I dinna like it," spat Cam, starting to stand up. "I'm goin' to talk to Brother Gillies and tell him –"

"My guests," said Brother Gillies, walking up behind him. "I want to make sure you have enough to eat, so I, and some of my brothers will wait until you have all had your fill before we take our food."

"Brathair, that is so noble of ye, but no' necessary," said Yvaine, continuing to eat.

"It is the least I can do for the men who protected you on your way to the priory." Brother Gillies smiled and nodded. "Cam, do you want me to bring more for you and your friends?"

Cam sat back down, not knowing what to say to the monk who was making a huge sacrifice for them.

"Cam, didna ye want to tell him somethin'?" asked Nash in a hoarse whisper.

"What is it?" asked Brother Gillies with concern in his voice. "I hope nothing is wrong. You are our guests and I want you to be happy."

"Go on. Tell him," North said, urging him on.

"Tell me what?" asked Gillies.

"Cam wanted to tell ye –" started Yvaine, but Cam cut her

off.

"I wanted to thank ye for yer hospitality," said Cam.

"That's no' what ye were goin' to say," mumbled North.

"Nay. He was goin' to say –" This time Nash was cut off by Cam.

"We wanted to tell ye the food is delicious." Cam glowered at the twins.

Brother Gillies looked down at the table and the bowls of the three men. "How do you know? It doesn't look like any of you have even tasted it yet."

"Go ahead," said Yvaine with a smile. "Show my brathair how much ye are enjoyin' the food, Cam."

Cam wanted to kill the girl right now. Or at least wipe the evil grin off her face. She was doing this purposely just to torture him. Well, he wouldn't let her see that it bothered him at all. If he did, it would probably make her too happy.

Picking up a spoonful of the oats, he opened his mouth and took a bite. Cringing, he was sure he would hate it, but it really didn't taste that bad, after all. With the cinnamon and honey, it was actually tasty.

"Mmmm, this is guid," he said, looking up at his friends. "Try it."

Nash made a face, wrinkling his nose and shaking his head.

"That's all right," said North, pushing his bowl over to Cam. "I'm no' really hungry. I think I'll go for a walk in the orchard."

"Orchard?" Nash's head snapped up. "That sounds delicious. I – I mean like a guid idea. I'll join ye." He hurried from the table, heading away with North.

"Well, that leaves more for us, right?" Cam pulled the two bowls over to him, giving Avianca one of them.

"Yummy! Thank ye," said the girl.

"Do ye want more?" Cam asked Yvaine, just to be polite.

"Nay, it's all yers," she said, finishing off her food and standing up. "Gillies, I would really like to have my wagon unloaded now. I need to start makin' candles soon."

"Aye, but not until later, Sister. After we eat, the brothers have to wash the dishes and then take time for inner reflection before starting chores."

"Dinna worry about it," Cam told them. "I will help her, and so will Nash and North. Just tell us where to put the things."

"Of course," said the monk, explaining where to set up shop.

"I can help, too," said Avianca, almost falling off the bench. Yvaine rushed forward to catch her.

"Cam, we dinna even ken where to find yer friends," said Yvaine, taking the little girl by the hand.

"I ken where to find them," said Cam. "They're in the orchard."

"Oh, mayhap they are helpin' the lay brathairs pick fruit," said Yvaine. "Perhaps we shouldna bother them."

Cam chuckled. "Oh, believe me, they are pickin' fruit, but no' helpin' anyone but themselves. And aye, they should be bothered. Now, let's go before they decide to check out the chicken coop or barns next."

"I've never seen a chicken coop," said the little girl.

"Believe me, ye're about to see somethin' else ye've never seen," said Cam with a chuckle thinking how upset his friends were going to be to have to help move Yvaine's things when they were busy eating apples.

# CHAPTER EIGHT

Y VAINE FOLLOWED CAM out to the orchard, holding Avianca's hand. The monastery was huge, surrounded by a tall stone wall for protection. Away from the church and living area was a field with crops and also an orchard filled with rows and rows of fruit trees. It was still within the confines of the priory walls. She could see apples, peaches, pears, and even plums on the trees. The monks were very self-sufficient. This almost seemed to be a small community away from the rest of the world where, hopefully, one could forget their problems and find peace and solitude instead.

Yvaine had yet to see the rest of the monastery, but her brother had promised to show her their living areas soon.

"There they are," said Cam, spotting his friends in the orchard.

Sure enough, Nash was standing under a tree using his plaid like an apron to collect the apples that North was throwing down from up above. North stood up in the branches, picking ripe apples that were too high to reach from the ground.

"Nash, North, yer help is needed with unloadin' Yvaine's things from the wagon," Cam called out, walking up to join his friends.

"Hello, Cam," said Nash, glancing over his shoulder. By raising his plaid up to hold the apples, he exposed himself, not really thinking about it until Cam said something.

"There are lassies present," said Cam, clearing his throat. "Or do ye mean to be on display? It's no' quite proper in a place such as this."

Nash's plaid was heavy with apples, but when he realized the girls could see beneath it, his expression changed. "Yvaine! Avianca!" He quickly dropped the ends of his plaid, therefore spilling the apples to the ground. They rolled away in all directions. Avianca giggled and ran after them, trying to collect them.

"Heads up," called out North from above. An apple smashed down upon Nash's head, followed by two more. Nash dodged the latter ones.

"Ow!" spat Nash, rubbing his head. "Stop it, North. I am no longer holdin' the apples."

"What's goin' on down there?" North looked down from the tree, stretching his neck to see who was there. "Oh, it's Cam. Hello."

"I can see up his plaid," said Avianca, giggling, pointing up into the tree.

"North, get yer arse down here," growled Cam. "And quit givin' the lassies an eyeful."

"At least I've got more than an eyeful to show," mumbled North, lowering himself from the tree. When he got to the ground, he brushed his hands together to clean them off.

"I'll give ye a snootful if ye two dinna stop this nonsense," Cam warned them. "Egads, ye fools, we're in a monastery, no' a brothel."

"It's food. We're gettin' real food to eat," said North, picking up an apple off the ground and rubbing it against his tunic to clean it. After he shined it, he held it out to Cam. "Want one? They sure beat that awful gruel."

"Nay, I dinna," Cam answered. "I already ate. And if ye two would have given the food half a chance, ye would have realized that it wasna bad at all."

"Now ye tell us," complained Nash, putting his hand on his

stomach. "I have a bellyache from eatin' so much fruit."

"I need ye two to help unload the lassie's belongin's." Cam wasn't so sure his friends were going to be cooperative at all. Thankfully, they didn't fight him.

"Come on, Nash," said North with a sigh. He bent down and picked up two more apples, taking them along with him.

IT TOOK LONGER to move Yvaine's things up to the empty room next to the scriptorium than Cam had guessed it would. The woman seemed to have brought just about everything from her shop in town with her to the monastery. Boxes of beeswax, jars of scents, and even tallow for making soap had filled up her wagon. Not to mention, she brought some of her furniture, along with trunks filled with personal items. He swore, the way it looked, Yvaine never planned on going back to Hermitage again.

"Careful with that," Yvaine instructed Cam as he put down the three boxes he was carrying all at once. "I already see several things have become broken from the trip. This is no' guid at all."

"Again, a simple thank ye would have sufficed," mumbled Cam under his breath.

"I'm tired." Nash stretched and yawned. "I wonder where we're goin' to sleep."

"I'm sure Brathair Gillies will tell us all the details as soon as he has the chance," Cam told him.

"Did I hear my name mentioned?" Brother Gillies stood in the open doorway with a smile on his face. "Oh, it looks like you don't need my help, after all." He entered the room.

"He timed that well," grumbled North, plopping down atop a chair.

"My lay brothers told me there were two Highlanders in the orchard, picking fruit earlier," said Gillies.

"Aye, that would be Nash and North," Cam informed him,

getting scowls from his friends for tattling on them.

"How kind of you," said the monk.

"Kind?" Nash looked over to North who shrugged from his chair. Just when it seemed they would be reprimanded, they were being thanked instead? This place was odd indeed.

"The lay brothers could use the extra help in harvesting the fruit. I'm sure you'll go back to help them finish now that you've moved all of my sister's belongings up here."

"Now wait a minute," said Nash, holding up his hand. Cam was sure he was going to object, so he intervened.

"They'd be more than happy to oblige," he answered for them. "After all, they've already tasted the rewards of their impendin' task. Isna that right, boys?"

"Well, that all depends. Are ye personally goin' to help pick fruit as well?" asked North, not happy at all about the way things were going.

"If that is what Brathair Gillies wishes, then I will," said Cam. "However . . ." He bent down and picked up Avianca whose eyes were already closing. The little girl was too tired to fight him. "I had hoped to get the tour of the priory along with Yvaine. My daughter is tired, and I'd like to see where she will be sleepin' so I can put her down to rest."

"Of course, we will do that right away. Come with me," said the monk, hurrying out the door. "You other two will find ladders, and baskets for the fruit in the stable," the monk called over his shoulder.

"Cam, that wasna fair," snorted Nash. "Ye answered for us. Plus, we ken ye dinna even care about the child."

"Aye. Ye just did that to get out of workin'," snapped North. "I swear this is turnin' out to be more our punishment than yers."

"Ye heard the monk. Now, haud yer wheesht and get to work," Cam instructed. "Yvaine, let's go see the rest of the priory." Cam headed out the door with the sleeping child in his arms as she lay her head against his chest.

It was true what his friends said. Normally, Cam didn't like being anywhere near children. He didn't know anything about caring for them, and neither did he want to. But when he looked down at the little angel sleeping in his arms, something changed. She didn't seem to have a care in the world when her eyes were closed. Avianca trusted him enough to sleep in his arms, that thought making his heart thaw just a little. She seemed so innocent – so vulnerable. If she really was his daughter, then all he wanted to do was to protect her. If. He could not know for sure. After all, the whore, Isobel, was not to be trusted. She had often lied to him just to get her way. Still, she was his favorite out of all the whores he'd ever bedded. Mayhap she wasn't lying, after all.

Damn, why did he have to be in this rotten position? He was in no place in his life to take care of a child by himself. Cam was a Highland warrior, free to do as he pleased. He fought men and protected the clan. But now, he would have to focus on protecting this child at all times . . . if she was truly his.

"Give her to me. I'll take her," offered Yvaine, holding out her arms for Avianca.

"Nay. I've got her," he said, not wanting to put her down just yet. They followed Brother Gillies down the stairs and across the courtyard.

"We both ken that ye only used the child to get out of work, just like yer friends said," Yvaine told him in a soft voice. "Cam, ye dinna even care about Avianca, so dinna pretend that ye do."

"Sister, how can you say such a thing?" Brother Gillies had good hearing, and her words to Cam did not go unnoticed. Her brother stopped and turned around. "The lass is Cam's daughter. Of course, he cares about her. How can you accuse him of anything less?"

"Really." Yvaine's chin jutted out as she looked from the corners of her eyes at Cam. "If that's so, then why willna he just admit aloud that he sired the lass? Plus, he means to ask ye to find Avianca a home with a guid family."

"What? Is that true?" Gillies looked to Cam in question.

"Well . . . I suppose it was my intention," said Cam, not wanting to lie to the man when he was inside holy walls. "But ye have to understand. There is no real proof that the girl is truly mine."

"We have the dyin' words of the wee lass' mathair that ye are the faither. I think that is more than enough proof," said Yvaine.

"If you really want me to find a home for the girl, I will," said Gillies. "I do know of several families in town that either have children and want more, or couples who are childless and would like one. I'm sure it won't be a problem to place her with a loving family."

"A lovin' family," Cam repeated, looking down at the girl once more. He thought of his own childhood that was so similar to what Avianca had most likely lived her entire life. No one deserved that! His wish for the girl was to have a normal childhood, living with peasants who farm the land and where she could play with other children. That is what any child deserved. It was also more than he could offer. "Aye. That would be fine," said Cam, not wanting to sound ungrateful. Yvaine obviously didn't agree with the decision. She all but snatched the little girl out of his arms, making Cam feel empty and alone.

"You've already seen the church," said the monk, "so we won't go there now. Next to it is our chapter house." He nodded to a long building attached to the side of the church.

"Chapter house? What is that for?" asked Cam.

"It is where we have our meetings, or where Bible readings are sometimes done." Brother Gillies entered the cloistered walkway that surrounded the area. The cloisters connected all the buildings and the church together. If it rained, one could walk under these areas to get from one place to another, all the while remaining dry. "Here are the cloisters."

"These archways are phenomenal," said Cam in awe, looking up to the high stone arches that made up the outside of the cloistered pathways. Some of them were still in the midst of repair. He could see a scaffold in one area and several lay brothers laying bricks to fix the partially demolished area. "It is amazin' how much has been repaired. After all, I heard Lanercost was naught but ruins, no' that long ago."

"Lanercost has constantly been under attack by the Scots through the years," said the monk. "As if it weren't bad enough that William Wallace and then Robert Bruce attacked the place, just over two decades ago was the worst."

"Ye mean when King David was here," said Cam, knowing the stories.

"Aye. Your Scottish king was by far the worst. He not only led the raid but stayed at Lanercost for three days causing havoc. He threw out the vessels of the temple, imprisoned the canons, and ransacked the church. He demolished holy relics, stole jewels, and plundered the treasury. He left this place pretty much destroyed."

"I'm sorry," said Cam, knowing how awful war could be. "But ye refer to David as my king, but yet ye are also Scottish."

"My mother was English," said the monk. "I think of myself more as English than Scottish."

They continued to walk. "Then ye are only half-Scot, too?" Cam asked Yvaine.

"Nay," she answered. "Keithen and I were from our faither's second marriage."

"So, Brathair Gillies is really yer half-brathair."

"Aye, but he is our family, and family is all that matters. Especially since my parents are no longer alive." She looked down to the little girl in her arms when she said it, making Cam remain quiet.

"Yvaine, let me carry her," said Cam.

"Nay," she answered stubbornly.

"Shhh," the monk told them with a finger to his lips. "The cloisters are where our brothers sometimes meditate, reflect, pray, or read. We need to be quiet."

Cam could see that Avianca was getting heavy for Yvaine. Without asking again, he reached out and took the child from her, receiving a dirty look from her in return.

"Lanercost Priory is a lot larger than I expected," said Cam softly.

"It once had a tannery, but that is no longer in use because of the destruction," said Gillies. "We do have a brewhouse and granary which we use, but they are both still not fully functional."

"Ye are self-sufficient with growin' yer own food as well, I see," said Cam, looking out to the orchard and crops growing in the fields.

"We are."

"How about livestock?" he asked. "I saw chickens and a few sheep but no' much more."

"At one time, we had cattle and pigs as well, but not at this time," Gillies explained.

"What do ye do for meat?" he asked. "At the MacKeefe Clan in the Highlands, we slaughter some of our cattle and other livestock to have food for the winter."

"They dinna eat meat," Yvaine told him, making Cam's stomach lurch just to hear it.

"No meat?" he asked. "Really?"

"We have ponds with fish that we do eat," said the monk. "However, our sheep are only for the wool, and the chickens for the eggs. We have a few milk cows, but we do not eat their flesh."

"Wonderful," Cam commented under his breath, wondering what Nash and North were going to say when they heard this. He felt sorry for them in a way since this was his punishment, yet they would suffer as well.

"Did I see vineyards, too?" asked Yvaine.

"Aye. The brotherhood makes our own wine," Gillies told them proudly.

"How many people live here?" asked Cam curiously.

"Right now, we have forty. That includes the monks, lay brothers, and half a dozen nuns. Of course, there are more here when we house travelers or those who are on pilgrimage."

"There seems to be a lot of work that is required here,"

commented Cam.

The monk smiled. "We all pitch in, and there is no idle moment day or night. You see, there are eight canonical hours as well, called matins, lauds, prime, terce, sext, none, vespers and compline."

"What does that mean?" asked Cam, the words sex and none ringing in his ears.

"He is speakin' of the times that are required for prayer," Yvaine explained.

"Eight hours a day of prayin'?" gasped Cam in disbelief.

"Although they are called hours, the prayer sessions really only add up to about five," Gillies told him.

"Only five hours? Och, well, that's a relief," said Cam sarcastically, wanting to be anywhere but here.

"However, private prayer and contemplation could add up to an additional five hours," added Gillies, making Cam's head spin and feel as if it were about to burst. This was truly a nightmare and he was smack dab in the middle of it with no way out.

"Will I be able to sell my candles to the church and possibly in town?" asked Yvaine.

"I will do my best to help you," her brother answered.

"Yvaine, I dinna ken how ye'll have time to even make candles when ye will be required to work and pray so much as a novitiate," said Cam.

Brother Gillies laughed at that. "My sister is not –"

"Where will the child sleep?" asked Yvaine, cutting off the man's sentence. "I'd like to put her down for a nap."

"Well, I suppose she'll be staying with Cam," said the monk, making Cam feel very anxious. "After all, I'm sure he'll want to watch over his daughter."

"Nay. That's no' possible," Cam protested.

"Why not?" asked the monk, leaving Cam speechless. He didn't have any good excuse, and couldn't think of how to get out of this with his head so full of thoughts of the horrible life of a monk. He'd now be living like a monk for his punishment.

Thankfully, Yvaine came to his rescue.

"She can stay with me." Yvaine rubbed her belly gently. Cam wondered if the gruel wasn't sitting right with her. Even though it had been tasty, it was settling like a rock in his stomach, too. Now, he wished he would have eaten fruit with his friends instead.

"My quarters are in the pele, on the ground floor." The monk took them to a square, stone tower that was several stories high. "Yvaine, you can take the room above mine and share it with the child."

"Thank ye," said Yvaine as they all started to climb the stairs to the tower.

"Where will I and my friends be lodgin' durin' our stay?" asked Cam.

"The dormitories are for the monks, the lay monks, and the nuns," he told him. "I do have an extra room or two but I must keep those open in case nobles should stop here during their travels. I'm afraid I'll have to ask you and your friends to sleep either in the infirmary, or mayhap even the stables."

"I see," said Cam, not even surprised by now that they wouldn't be offered better accommodations. "Or, we can just sleep in the catacombs, like Rook used to do," he replied facetiously.

"Cam! Stop bein' so disrespectful," said Yvaine as the monk opened the door and led them into a room. It was plain inside, with just a pallet on the floor, a crucifix on the wall, and one small table with two chairs.

"Put the girl down on the pallet," said Gillies. "Yvaine, you'll have to share the pallet with her, but it is a large one so it should still be sufficient. Unless you'd rather I bring up a bed that is up off the floor. Whatever is easier for you."

Cam thought that an odd thing to offer since he and his friends would be sleeping in much less than desirable quarters and probably in the hay.

"Nay. A pallet on the floor is fine." Her hand went to her

stomach again and she looked very tired.

Cam laid the little girl down and stood back up. "All right, I am ready to see the rest of the place now."

"I'd like to stay here and rest with Avianca, instead of goin' with ye," said Yvaine.

"Why? I canna imagine ye'd be tired already," said Cam. He and his friends had been the ones who not only fought a battle today, but also did all the work. Yvaine did nothing but watch.

"I – I just dinna want Avianca to be scared when she wakes up. I think it's best I stay with her for now."

"Have it yer way," said Cam with a shrug, heading out the door. Once he and Brother Gillies were back in the courtyard, the monk showed him the kitchen, the stables, and even the garderobe.

"This is our lavitorium where the monks wash. There are separate days and times for the nuns to use it." He opened a door and showed Cam a room with buckets of water, as well as small bath tubs where one could sit up to their waist in water if their knees were bent. On the far wall was a hearth with a large kettle that was used to heat the bath water. "Of course, if you and your friends want to use it, you'll have to ask and we'll need to schedule a special time to do so."

"Och, dinna bother. We bathe in the loch," said Cam.

"Isn't that cold? Especially in winter?" asked Gillies.

"We're used to the elements. Besides, no' much bathin' happens in winter."

"Well, in the priory, cleanliness is required. Please don't even think of bathing in our fish ponds." The monk seemed insulted by Cam's answer.

"Nay, I wouldna think of it. I guess we'll have to set up a time. To bathe, I mean." First, no meat, and now required bathing. Cam hoped to hell he and his friends weren't going to be required to do all the praying that the monk mentioned as well. If so, he was sure to die. Right now, all he wanted was to be in a tavern like the Horn and Hoof back in Glasgow with a tankard of

Mountain Magic in one hand and a wench in the other.

They left the room and headed over to the scriptorium next. "There are monks illuminating manuscripts inside right now. We don't want to disturb them, so you'll see the scriptorium later," said Gillies.

"Of course," said Cam, having no desire to see a dark room where they copied books anyway. "What is under the dormitories?" he asked. There were lots of passageways and staircases everywhere.

"That is the undercroft where the food is stored. The buttery is down there as well."

The buttery was where they kept drinks and vats of wine.

"Ye dinna happen to have any Mountain Magic on hand, do ye?" he asked, longing for a dram of whisky.

"Mountain Magic?"

"Whisky," he said, seeing that the man didn't understand. "It's the most potent whisky in all of Scotland and England, brewed by the grandfather of our chieftain, Storm MacKeefe."

"Oh, nay. We only have ale, mead, and wine," explained the monk. "When the apples are ripe, we also have cider."

"Why did I already ken that somehow?" Cam mumbled.

"Were you serious about wanting to sleep in the catacombs?" asked Gillies.

Cam laughed, but stopped when he realized the man wasn't jesting. "Why would I want to sleep with the dead, in a dark and dreary place like that?"

"Oh, nay. It's not like that at all," answered the monk. "I mean, if you were to use Lord Rook's old chamber which is down there, it wouldn't be. You and your friends are welcome to it."

"Chamber? Lord Rook actually built a room in the catacombs?"

"Aye, he did. And a magnificent place it is."

"Really," he said, not believing a word of this. "Then why dinna ye or the other monks use it, if it is so guid?"

"We can't. It is far too elaborate for us. We have taken the vow of poverty, and so the room has been vacant for years now."

"Elaborate?" This got Cam's interest and he had to see it now. He spied North and Nash coming out of the orchard, each carrying two bushels of apples.

"Where do ye want these?" North asked, looking tired, hot and sweaty.

"The fruit will go in the undercroft," said the monk. "You can leave it in the cloisters and the lay brothers will take it down a little later."

"Blethers, it is hot out here." Nash put down the bushels and wiped his brow with the end of his sash of purple and green – Clan MacKeefe's colors.

"It's cool down in Lord Rook's room," said Gillies.

"I suppose it would be, since it is underground," Cam answered. "Can my friends take a look at the room in the catacombs with me?"

"Of course. This way, please." The monk led the way.

"Our room is in the catacombs?" snapped Nash as soon as the monk walked away.

"Bid the devil, please tell me ye are jestin'," snorted North, wiping his brow with the back of his hand.

"It's either that, or we sleep in the stables or infirmary," said Cam.

"Anywhere is better than with the dead." North didn't like the idea at all.

"Come on. I'm curious to see this so-called elaborate room where Lord Rook lived for a guid part of his life." Cam led the way, and his friends followed. Even with the monk's description, Cam never expected what they were about to see.

$$\blacktriangleright\!\cdot\!\circ\!\Diamond\!\circ\!\cdot\!\blacktriangleleft$$

# CHAPTER NINE

"BID THE DEVIL, I dinna like it down here," said Nash, as Cam and his friends followed Brother Gillies down into the catacombs under Lanercost Priory.

"It is a wee bit eerie," said North, looking around the underground enclosure. The monk held a torch high that lit up the walls, showing skeletons lying in niches of the underground cavern.

They passed tomb after tomb with large carved crosses, and sarcophagi of nobles or knights with their bodies and faces carved right into the stone lids.

"So, this is where Lord Rook lived?" asked Cam, finding the whole thing unbelievable. He reached out and ran his hand over the carving of one of the tombs.

"Aye," said the monk. "But you have to remember that Rook and his brothers were split up during Burnt Candlemas in Scotland when they were just young lads. His brother, Rowen, was taken by pirates. His other brother, Reed, stayed in Scotland, and Rook was taken by a monk and brought here, in order to save his life from the hands of the English."

"But why did he stay here?" asked Nash jumping and looking at the floor. "That's a rat. I'm sure a rat just ran over my foot." Cam looked over to his friend, sure he saw him shiver.

"It's a long story and you'll have to ask him about it someday," said the monk. "Ah, here's the secret room." Gillies handed the torch to Cam. "I know there's a lever hidden here some-where." He slid both his hands behind a rock, searching for something. Before Cam knew what happened, a stone door slid open, revealing another door made of wood. The monk reached out and turned the latch to open the second door. Cam saw a very dark hole that led into a chamber.

"We're goin' in there?" asked Nash, peeking into the dark-ened room, reluctant to enter. "I bet there are more rats in there. Lots of them."

"Step aside," said Cam, holding the torch high, entering the room first. The firelight lit up the area, making Cam's mouth drop open.

"I'll light a candle or two," stated the monk. He found some candles on a table near the door and lit them.

Silence filled the room as Cam and his friends stared in awe at what they were witnessing. A large four-poster bed with carved spindles sat atop a small dais. Around it hung long, purple, dusty curtains that were partially closed.

Thick wooden beams on the ceiling led to small openings where air flowed through vents. Even though this room had been closed up, probably for years, the vents brought in fresh air, so the room wasn't at all musty. The floor beneath their feet was not stone, but made from wooden planks, making the place warmer.

There were woven tapestries on the walls, and beeswax-scented candles strewn about the area. Cam also noticed a table and chairs made of wood. The chairs had high backs and were carved with intricate designs. An empty water basin was atop another table, and there was actually a hearth across the room.

On the main table was a dusty chessboard with the pieces of the game all made from swirled marble.

"Ye werena jestin' about this place bein' ornate." Cam picked up a chess piece, inspecting it closer. "Why did Lord Rook leave all these things here, instead of takin' them to Naward Castle with him?"

"I'm not sure, but he mentioned something once that he

wanted to forget about his old life and start anew."

"This chess game alone must be worth a lot of money," said Nash, looking over Cam's shoulder.

"I agree," said Gillies. "However, Rook specifically said he didn't want to take the chess game with him. I believe it had something to do with his father, King Edward. However, it is very important to him, so please be careful with it."

"Why didna ye sell his things to pay for some of the repairs at the priory?" asked Cam, picking up a golden goblet and inspecting it.

"Nay, I couldn't do that. These things don't belong to us. I am sure Lord Rook won't mind if you men stay here, but you must promise not to take anything from this room."

"Are ye callin' us thieves?" asked North, sounding highly insulted.

"I promise, we willna," said Cam, not wanting trouble, or an argument of any kind. "I'm sure Brathair Gillies did no' mean to insinuate that we were dishonest, North."

"Nay, I didn't," said the monk.

Through the vents in the ceiling, the sound of ringing church bells could be heard.

"What's that?" asked Nash, looking upward.

"It's time for none," answered the monk, taking the torch back from Cam.

"None? None of what?" asked North.

"I think he means it's another prayer session," Cam told his friends.

"Aye." Brother Gillies nodded and headed toward the door. "This one is mainly the reading of psalms, followed by more chanting." He stopped at the door and turned toward them. "Well, we'd better hurry so we're not late."

"I'll stay here." Cam sat down on the bed.

"Me, too. Want to play chess, North?" Nash sat down and started arranging the pieces.

"Nay, I need a nap," said North, stretching one arm behind

his head.

"Men, I'm sorry, but I was told by Laird MacKeefe that as part of your punishment, you were to live as the monks do. Therefore, you'll have to come with me."

"Nay," said North, shaking his head. "This is no' my punishment, nor is it my brathair's."

"That's right," agreed Nash. "We're here only as . . . support for Cam. We are no' the ones bein' punished. No' yet, anyway."

"I see," said the monk. "Well, then, Cam, you and I should get going. It is a far walk out of the catacombs and to the church and we don't want to arrive late."

"But I –"

"Go on, Cam," said North, heading for the bed. "We'll wait for ye here."

"Damn it," swore Cam, running a hand through his hair. "I canna pray for eight hours a day."

"It's really only five, remember," the monk reminded him. "Plus, I won't hold you to the personal reflection and prayer time that the other monks endure."

"See ye when ye get done chantin'," said Nash, chuckling, still arranging the chess pieces on the board.

"Oh, you two won't be able to stay here. Not now," said the monk.

"Huh?" North was about to sit down on the bed, but looked up in surprise.

"What do ye mean?" asked Nash. "Ye just said we dinna have to go to church like Cam."

"Nay, but there are many chores to be done. Everyone in the priory helps out."

"But we're guests," protested North.

"Not really," said the monk. "But don't worry, I won't ask you to do anything too hard or too messy, like cleaning out the garderobe."

"The garderobe?" Nash sprang to his feet. "Well, what is it that we have to do?"

"I'd like you two to head out to the vineyard and help the lay brothers pick grapes. Afterwards, they'll show you how to stomp the grapes in preparation of turning it into wine."

Cam about burst out laughing when he saw the looks on his friends' faces. "I'll bet ye're both sorry ye complained about goin' to a prayer service now."

⟫⟫✕⟪⟪

YVAINE WAS AWOKEN by a small knock on the door. Opening one eye and then the other, it took a minute for her to remember where she was. She looked over to see Avianca lying on the pallet next to her, stirring. That's when she realized she was no longer in Hermitage, but now safe in the priory instead.

Another knock, and then the door opened and Cam stuck his head inside.

"Yvaine?" he asked. "Can I come in?"

"Oh. Of course," she said, jumping up, running a hand over her mussed hair to smooth it.

Cam walked into the room, leaving the door open behind him. He stopped, and stared at her, which allowed Yvaine a chance to drink in his manly beauty. The sun shone in the door behind him, lighting up his golden hair. It was almost as if he had a halo around him. Dressed in his plaid, the colors of purple and green seemed so vibrant in the midday sun. He looked strong, sturdy and handsome. For some reason, she found herself attracted to this rugged Highlander who was really naught but a stranger to her. She didn't understand her feelings at all.

"Where were ye?" he asked, taking one step forward, and then stopping as if he weren't sure if he should stay or go.

"What do ye mean?" she asked, feeling heat rise to her face. "I – I was here. Nappin' with Avianca." She straightened her clothes, her eyes going right to his this time. While his hair was light, his eyes were dark brown, drawing her in because they looked so mysterious . . . and intriguing.

"I ken that. But why werena ye at some?"

"Some what? I have no idea what ye are talkin' about, Cam. Ye are makin' no sense at all."

"The prayer service," he said, sounding frustrated. His hands moved through the air in a jerky gesture.

"The prayer service?" she asked, finally understanding what he meant. "Ooooh, ye must mean none."

"Dinna tell me there was none, because I was there, so I ken all about it. And believe me, there was nowhere else I would have rather been. Except mayhap stompin' grapes," he added as an afterthought which made no sense to Yvaine either.

She giggled, and made her way over to him. "I ken ye were there, in church, and I am sure there was a prayer session. That isna what I mean. I am just tellin' ye the proper name of it is none. I believe all the canonical hours are derived from Latin and each stand for an hour of the day."

"None, some, I dinna care. Whatever, ye want to call it, I was there and ye werena!" His hands were in the air again. "I was forced to go listen to psalms and chant with monks while North and Nash were off stompin' grapes."

"Stompin' grapes?" She laughed again. "So that's what ye meant. Well, I'm sure they werena very happy about that!"

"That's beside the point. What I'm sayin' is that I had to go pray and I'm no' even the one who is in trainin' to be a nun."

"Of course, no', silly. Ye are a man and couldna be a nun if ye wanted to." She knew exactly what Cam meant and was just having fun with him. "I need to wake up Avianca, or she willna sleep tonight. I'm sure she'll need to use the chamber pot, so excuse us, please. We will meet ye in the courtyard." With one hand on the door, she nodded for him to leave.

"I hate this punishment already," he complained. "Plus, I am sure I'm no' goin' to be likin' it any better anytime soon."

"Well, mayhap ye should have thought of that before ye went grabbin' the wenches and kissin' them in the tavern," she boldly remarked, pointing out that he was the one at fault here.

His head snapped up and his intense stare just about bored a hole right through her. Her words must have really affected him. Suddenly, she was sorry that she had said them aloud.

"I'll grab any wench I choose, and kiss her anywhere I want, and ye'll have nothin' to say about it. Do ye understand?"

He sounded aggravated, and looked dangerous. Her insides started to quiver because thoughts ran through her head that he might try to hit her or hurt her, like her late husband had done to her so many times before. She tried to be strong and stand her ground. Mayhap if she stood up to him, she wouldn't seem like such easy prey.

"Well, I dinna think ye'll be grabbin' or kissin' any wenches for a long time now, so get used to it," she snapped, feeling her heart pounding in her chest. She knew she should stop taunting him, but something deep inside urged her to continue. "After all, ye are in a priory now," she pointed out. "Ye'll be too busy prayin' and chantin' to even think about lassies at all anymore." She took a step backward, making room between them.

"Dinna fool yerself," he said in a low voice, making her feel scared. Then he took a step closer to her, all the while his eyes holding her captive, making her unable to move. "I still am thinkin' about lassies, and there is nothin' ye can do about it."

He stared at her with a hungry look in his eyes, but it was different than the anger she'd often seen in the eyes of her late husband. This look was dangerous, but in a sultry sort of way. Before she knew what happened, he'd pulled her into his arms and was kissing her so passionately that, for a moment, all her worries and cares fled her head, and she surrendered to the feeling of enjoyment. It was something she hadn't ever felt while in the presence of Dun.

Cam's lips were soft and sensuous, and he tasted like wine if she wasn't mistaken. Her fingers curled around and she gripped on to his tunic, not wanting to break the embrace. Then her hands brushed against the crisp, curly hair on his chest, and his manly essence filled every one of her senses. The kiss lasted longer than she would have expected, and it wasn't until their lips actually parted that she realized what had just transpired between them. He was a lusty Highlander – a virtual stranger. She was a new widow . . . and a murderer as well. She had no right to feel happiness or excitement. He had no right to touch her or kiss her in such a familiar manner. Neither of them should be doing this at all, and certainly not here, in front of a sleeping child. This kind of behavior was not tolerated inside the holy walls of the priory.

Shaken, she pushed away from him, already regretting what she'd let him do. Her hand went to her mouth, and her breathing became labored. "W-why did ye do that?" her voice trembled as she asked him in a breathy whisper.

"I dinna ken." He stepped backward, looking as confused as she felt at this moment. Then he ran a worried hand through his long hair. When he looked back at her, their eyes interlocked once again. "I suppose it was just that . . . I couldna help myself, lass."

"Well, ye certainly seemed to have helped yerself to a kiss without even askin' me for permission first. That tells me that ye are naught but a lustful cur!" All of a sudden, she started to feel like just another one of his whores. She glanced back at the bed to see the sleeping child. Here was proof of what would transpire from his amorous actions. Yvaine didn't want to be just another of his mindless follies.

"Nay, ye are wrong," he told her, shaking his head, causing his long hair to move over his shoulders.

"Dinna try to deny the kiss, because as ye would say – I was there so I ken it happened."

"I wasna speakin' of the kiss, lass. I'd be a fool to try to deny that action between us. What I meant is that I am no' a lustful cur. I mean . . . mayhap I usually am, but no' this time."

"What is it ye are tryin' to say, because ye are makin' no sense at all?"

"I didna kiss ye because I wanted to bed ye."

"What?" She raised one brow, not expecting him to say that. Now her mind was really going in different directions. Part of her was relieved, yet another part of her wondered why he didn't want her and if she was desirable to him at all.

"All right, mayhap that isna exactly true," he said, sounding frustrated as his hands waved through the air again. "What I am tryin' to say is that I kissed ye because ye are so beautiful."

"Really?" That made her feel a little better, but she couldn't let him know she liked the compliment. "I am sure ye say that to all the lassies ye want to undress."

"Stop it, Yvaine. I am tryin' to tell ye my feelin's and ye are no' makin' it easy."

"Go on, then." She raised her chin in the air, wondering how he was going to get out of this mess. Once a womanizer, always one, she thought. And Cam MacKeefe was the biggest one in all of Scotland.

"I am attracted to ye, Yvaine, even though I canna understand why."

"Well, that's no' goin' to win ye any favors," she said, scowling at him for making her feel suddenly undesirable once again.

"I only mean that in the way that ye havena been very kind to me at all."

"That's no' true."

He held a halting hand in the air. "Let me finish, please. I want to tell ye that I havena been able to stop thinkin' about kissin' ye since the moment we met."

That shocked her to hear him say it. He almost sounded as if he meant it, and that surprised her. Especially since she didn't think he really liked her at all. Then again, if he was attracted to her that quickly, it had to be naught but lust.

"I – I'm sorry," he said. "I ken it was wrong of me to do it, and I swear it will no' happen again. I didna mean to scare ye, lass."

His kiss hadn't scared her. Not really. But what did scare her was how much she liked it when his lips touched hers and he held her close to him in his strong arms. It felt right, and comforting for some reason that she could not explain. She'd never felt comfortable around any men besides her brothers. This man was a stranger and a Highlander, which meant she should fear him more than any other. So why didn't she?

Yvaine had never been kissed by any man with so much passion before. At three and twenty years of age, she had kissed several men before actually marrying Dun. However, Cam's kiss was different. It was a claiming kiss for sure but, at the same time, it didn't feel forced or unwelcome. It felt like he actually cared for her, and she liked it. Her lips continued to tingle, and her heart fluttered like a butterfly flitting through the sky. This was a feeling she'd never experienced with any man, and especially not with her late husband.

"Da?" came Avianca's voice as she sat up and rubbed one eye.

Cam's head turned quickly, and his body seemed to stiffen. "Dinna call me that," he mumbled, seeming very upset now.

"Well, that's what ye are to her," said Yvaine. "She is yer daughter, Cam, and ye are her da."

"Nay. We dinna ken that for sure," he ground out, being in total denial. By his actions, she guessed that even if he did have bastards walking the earth, this was the first time he really knew about it.

"Well, what do ye want her to call ye?" asked Yvaine.

"She can call me Cam. Just like anyone else does."

The little girl walked over and looked up at Cam. "Since my mama is dead, are ye goin' to take me home with ye to live?" she asked him with wide, innocent eyes.

Cam's gaze darted over to Yvaine and then back to the girl. His lips quivered, but he didn't answer. Yvaine could see the sun reflecting in his dark brown orbs, and she noticed something she hadn't seen earlier. In his eyes, she witnessed fear if she wasn't mistaken. Fear masked by a tinge of desperation. She knew that look well because she'd seen it in her own eyes many times before. Every time she'd looked into the reflection of a candle holder as she'd polished it back in her chandler's shop in town, she saw the same thing she was witnessing now. The man was afraid of having a child – or perhaps he was just regretting his past actions now. Either way, he couldn't change the past.

Cam's jaw clenched, and he turned his head to look out the door, rather than to look at his daughter. "I have to go find my friends now," he mumbled. "I'll meet up with ye later, Yvaine." He didn't even mention the girl, nor did he acknowledge her by answering her question. Yvaine found herself wondering if all Highlanders were this rude.

"Why canna I call him Da?" asked Avianca, watching Cam walk out the door and down the stairs.

Yvaine pulled the little girl to her in a half-hug, not knowing exactly how to answer.

"I suppose it's because everyone has demons that haunt them, Avianca. Even though, sometimes, we might not ken exactly what they are."

"So, my da . . . I mean Cam, is bein' haunted by the devil?" Avianca seemed very concerned.

"I wish I kent but, alas, I am no' sure." Yvaine didn't want to scare the girl but, at the same time, she didn't want to lie to her either. She didn't know what shadows were lurking inside Cam. All she knew was that the devil was on her tail and probably would be for the rest of her life.

As Yvaine watched Cam hurry down the stairs and through the courtyard, she got the feeling he was running away from something . . . or someone in particular. She had thought it had something to do with his daughter, or mayhap he was running from himself. Then again, perhaps it was neither. After that kiss they'd just shared, she started wondering if mayhap she was the one who Cam MacKeefe was really running from, after all!

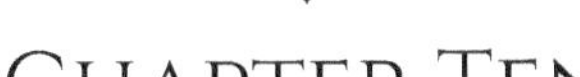

# CHAPTER TEN

C AM WENT BACK to the hidden room in the catacombs, needing to get away from Yvaine, as well as Avianca. Lighting a candle, he entered the room, liking the dead silence in the underground place. With the cacophony of voices in his head right now, all he wanted was a moment of peace. He wasn't a man easily shaken by anything, but he felt out of sorts because of what just happened.

"What is the matter with ye?" he asked himself aloud, heading over to the bed and flopping down upon it. He lay on his back staring up at the ceiling. Shadows danced above him from the flicker of the flame, and he swore he saw the silhouette of Yvaine above him.

Letting out a sigh, he buried his face in his hands, closing his eyes and wishing this punishment was over. Did he really just kiss a woman who'd not only just lost her husband, but who was planning on giving the rest of her life to the Order? What the hell was he thinking? Mayhap he really did have a problem with the lassies, after all, since he just couldn't stop himself from doing it.

All he could seem to think about was Yvaine. He blamed it on the fact that it must be because she was one of the only women inside these walls who wasn't already a nun, and it was making him feel desperate. Or was it?

Who was he fooling? It had nothing to do with that at all. He'd already been attracted to her from the moment he met her back at Hermitage Castle. There were plenty of women around him then, so desperation wasn't what made him feel this way, after all. Something about her pulled him in. Was it the fact that he felt sorry for her? After all, she was a young widow who was about to give up her life to the Order. Mayhap, his attraction to the lass had something to do with the way she looked after Avianca who wasn't even her daughter.

The wee lass was his daughter.

Or was she?

Confusion filled his brain.

Cam's life was changing so quickly that it made him feel unsettled. It also threatened any belief he'd ever had in his life. As if finding out he had a four-year-old daughter wasn't shocking enough, now he was insanely attracted to a woman who didn't even like him, not that he could ever have her anyway.

"I just want to go back to the Highlands," he mumbled, drifting off to sleep and wishing to escape his new prison. Perhaps his prison wasn't the priory, after all. Mayhap his thoughts, wants and beliefs were the only things holding him captive right now.

"WHERE IS MY faither?" asked Avianca as Yvaine walked with the little girl from the church after compline – the last prayer service of the day before bedtime.

"I dinna ken, but ye'd better call him Cam like he asked," said Yvaine, noticing the monks lighting a few torches in the court-yard since the sun had already set. Yvaine looked around, walking up to one of the monks who might have seen Cam.

"Excuse me, but do ye ken where I can find the Highlander named Cam, or perhaps his friends?" she asked the monk, but he remained silent. "How about ye?" she asked another, but he didn't answer either.

"Why willna they speak to us?" asked the little girl.

"I'm afraid it's because they've taken a vow of silence, and arena allowed to speak." She let out a sigh. This was already proving to be harder than she thought it would be. She looked down to the black robe of a nun that she wore. She hadn't wanted to don it, but her brother gave it to her to cover her gown so it wouldn't become soiled while she unpacked the chandler tools.

Being pregnant made Yvaine tired. She was nearly four months along now and although she wasn't really showing, she could feel herself starting to thicken around her middle. It wouldn't be long before her gowns no longer fit and she had to wear these ghastly robes every day. Mayhap she could make herself some new clothes. At least she thankfully had the skill of knowing how to sew.

"Why dinna they speak?" asked the curious little girl. "Dinna they have anythin' to say?"

"I'm afraid I dinna ken the answer to that."

Yvaine heard voices in the dark and looked up to see the silhouettes of Cam's Highland friends making their way across the courtyard from the vineyards.

"Nash! North!" she called out, waving them down. When they got closer, one look at them almost made her laugh aloud. "What happened to ye two?" she asked, stifling a giggle. Both the men were barefooted and carrying their shoes. Their legs were dyed purple all the way up to their knees, and she guessed probably up higher under their plaids as well.

"We were dancin' on bluidy grapes for hours," griped Nash.

"I never want to have to do that wretched job again," added North. "I am tired and hungry and need to sleep."

"Oh, my," said Yvaine, holding her hand up to her mouth, hoping they didn't see the smile she tried to hide in the dark. "Was Cam stompin' grapes with ye?" she asked.

"Nay, but he should have been," complained Nash.

"This is supposed to be his bluidy punishment, but my brathair and I are the ones doin' all the chores," North added.

"Well, where is Cam?"

"If he's no' with ye, my guess is he's lyin' on a soft bed, dreamin' of girls," snapped Nash.

"Oh, so did Brathair Gillies give ye three a nice place to stay?" she asked.

"Aye. We're stayin' in Lord Rook's old room in the catacombs," North answered with a yawn.

"The catacombs?" she asked in disbelief. "No one should have to stay there. That is horrid!"

"Ye wouldna say that if ye saw the elaborate secret room that we are stayin' in," Nash explained.

"If Cam thinks he's takin' the bed, he's got another guess comin'," griped North.

"Oh, there you all are," said Gillies, spotting them and walking over to join them. He had a nun with him.

"Yvaine, this is Sister Edna who I've assigned to help you with the child until I can find the girl a good home with a caring couple who will have her."

"I dinna want to live with someone I dinna ken." Avianca held tight to Yvaine's skirt. "I want to live with Yvaine and Cam."

"Oh, I didn't realize you were married," said Sister Edna. "Is one of these men your husband?" She looked over at Nash and North.

"Nay, we're just Highland warriors," said North, holding up his hands and taking a step backward, seeming spooked by the thought of marriage. He stepped on Nash's bare foot and Nash let out a curse.

"Please, no cursing!" Gillies reprimanded them.

"Sorry," said Nash, rubbing his bare foot.

"I am the widow of a chandler," Yvaine told the nun. "These men were kind enough to escort me to the priory."

"I see," Sister Edna answered. "So, the girl is an orphan?"

"Aye. Nay," said Yvaine, changing her mind. "I mean, her mathair died recently, but her faither is here somewhere in the priory."

"Oh!" The nun looked over to Gillies in shock.

"Her father is not a monk, Sister," explained Gillies. "It is a Highlander named Cam."

"Ooooh," she said, sounding and looking so relieved to hear that. "Her father wants to give her up to another family? I don't understand."

"Neither do I," Yvaine answered softly, running a loving hand over Avianca's head.

"Excuse me, Brathair Gillies, but can we have somethin' to eat?" asked Nash.

"Aye. We have been stompin' grapes all day and we're powerful hungry," said North.

"Of course," said Gillies. "The main meal is over, but you two are welcome to eat with the kitchen staff. Sister Edna, please go with Yvaine and help her with the child, while I show the men to the kitchen."

"My pleasure," said the nun, reaching out for Avianca.

"Nay. Leave me alone," screamed the little girl, hugging Yvaine's knees and not letting go.

"Thank ye, Sister, but mayhap I should tend to puttin' her to bed for tonight," Yvaine told her. "However, mayhap ye could be of assistance tomorrow when the girl isna so tired and frightened."

"Whatever you'd like," said the nun, looking at Avianca with pity in her eyes.

Yvaine wanted to go and find Cam, but now she couldn't. She supposed anything she had to say to him could wait until the morrow, after all.

$$\cdot\bullet\cdot\diamond\cdot\circ\cdot\bullet\cdot$$

# CHAPTER ELEVEN

C AM AWOKE TO the sound of church bells ringing, the muffled sound drifting through the air vents in the ceiling above his head. He rolled over, realizing he had fallen asleep earlier. He was still in the bed of the secret room in the catacombs of the priory. The mattress was very comfortable. He'd been so tired and upset that he must have slept through the night.

The candle had burned out and the room was as dark as a tomb. Well, it was a tomb he supposed, since he was sleeping with the dead down in the catacombs which wasn't a reassuring thought at all.

He heard something that sounded like a low growl coming from the floor. His hand automatically reached for his weapon belt on the bedside table. Finding the hilt of his sword, he gripped it firmly. The noise was almost human, but with a tinge of animal mixed in. He wasn't one to believe in ghosts or the walking dead, but if it was ever going to happen it would probably be in a place like this.

Silently sliding to the edge of the bed, Cam started wondering if it was perhaps a rat. He'd seen quite a few of them while walking through the catacombs yesterday. Well, rat or ghost, he wanted neither of them in the room with him and would put an end to this once and for all.

Standing up, he slowly made his way down the three stairs of the dais as he gripped his sword steady in two hands. Right as he stepped away from the bed, his leg hit something and he tripped. Cam tried to steady himself, but it was too late. He reached out for the table, knocking it over, hearing the sound of the marble chess pieces hitting the floor.

"Aaaaah!" came a loud scream, that wasn't from him. Then something heavy landed atop his chest, pinning him to the ground.

"What is it? Is it a rat? Kill it, North. Kill it!" came a shout that sounded a lot like Nash. Once Cam heard it, he knew exactly what or who was atop him now.

"It's me, ye fool," spat Cam, releasing his sword and pushing North off of him and onto the floor. Cam jumped to his feet.

"Is that ye, Cam?" came Nash's voice in the dark.

"Of course, it is! Who else would it be?" Cam made his way over to the table and managed to find and light a candle. When the flame lit up the room, he turned to see both Nash and North sprawled out on the floor, looking up and blinking like deer in the torchlight. If he wasn't mistaken, they both had purple legs. "What the hell?" he mumbled, wiping his eyes, thinking he was seeing things. "Are yer legs purple?"

"Aye," answered Nash for both he and his brother.

"Why?" asked Cam.

"If ye hadna been hidin' out here sleepin' all day, ye would have remembered we were workin' in the vineyards pickin' and stompin' bluidy grapes yesterday," spat North.

"Och, that's right," Cam answered with a smile, glad he hadn't had to do it. He supposed going to prayers was the lesser of the two evils, after all.

"It's no' funny, Cam," Nash ground out, sounding angrier than Cam had ever heard him in the past. "We're doin' all the work when this was supposed to be yer punishment, no' ours."

"Sorry about that," he said with a yawn. "I had no idea that bed would be so comfortable. I canna believe I slept so long. What did I miss?"

"A lot of doitit chores is what ye missed," snapped North,

getting to his feet. Nash did the same.

"I'm hungry. Did ye two get anythin' to eat by any chance?" asked Cam, rubbing his hand over his tunic.

"We did. We had food, and lots of it, too," said Nash, stressing the point. "What's it to ye?"

"Lots of food?" Cam felt his stomach grumble. "What kind of food?" Visions of beef, pheasant, and sweetmeats filled his head.

"Wouldna ye like to ken?" came North's snide reply.

The church bells continued to ring, causing Cam to look back up to the ceiling. "I guess that means it's mornin'. There is most likely some sort of prayer session we're supposed to be attendin' right now."

"We?" asked North, glaring at Cam.

"No' us, just ye," Nash corrected him. "Remember, we are no' required to go to the prayer sessions, but ye are as part of yer sentence."

"Ye'd better get goin'," said North. "After all, ye missed both vespers and compline last night."

"No' to mention, matins and lauds that took place durin' the night as well," added Nash.

"What?" Cam was surprised that his friends knew the names of all the canonical hours when he neither knew nor cared about them at all. "Did I really miss all that and a meal, too?" He scratched his head and then stretched.

"Go on, then," said North, nodding to the door. "Ye'd better hurry."

"That's right," agreed Nash. "I dinna suppose ye'll be needin' this big cozy bed anymore since ye're up for the day." As soon as he said it, he looked at his brother and then they both turned and ran to the bed, diving atop it at once.

"I get the bed," yelled Nash.

"Over my dead body," shouted North.

"Dinna anyone get hurt," Cam called out with a chuckle, taking the candle and heading out into the dark catacombs. Thoughts of food filled his head.

When Cam stepped foot out into the courtyard, he saw the beautiful sunrise that greeted him there. Pink and orange hues lit up the sky as the sun poked its head over the horizon in the start of a new day. The fresh breeze filled his lungs, feeling vibrant since there was limited airflow underground. He saw the monks and nuns heading to the church, but his stomach kept growling and all he could think about was food.

He was about to sneak off to the kitchen to find something to eat when he saw a nun heading down from the tower where Yvaine was staying. He did a double take when the early morning rays hit the woman's face and he realized that it wasn't just a nun – it was Yvaine.

"Blethers," he mumbled as all his troubles came crashing back at once. Yvaine was now dressed in the robes of a nun and that only reminded him of how wrong it had been to kiss her. Even though he wanted to turn and head to the kitchen right now, he knew he owed the woman an apology. Again.

He hurried over to catch up with her, secretly glad that Avianca wasn't with her. One problem at a time was more than he could cope with.

"Good mornin'," he called out, coming up behind her. His greeting caused her to stop and turn around.

"Ah, it's ye. I should have kent it was ye since no one else around here ever seems to speak." She sounded as aggravated as he felt being here in this pious place.

"It's unnervin', isna it?" He came up beside her. "I am no' used to so much silence."

"Brathair Gillies has been askin' for ye since yesterday. Tell me, Cam MacKeefe, where have ye been?"

"In the catacombs," he said, getting an eyeroll from her. She turned and continued walking.

"Please, dinna try to humor me so early in the mornin'. I am no' in a playful mood at all," she told him.

"Nay, it's true where I've been." He hurried to catch up to her and they continued walking to the church as he talked.

"Didna my friends tell ye that yer brathair is lettin' us stay in Lord Rook's secret chamber in the catacombs?"

"They did," she said, not even looking at him as she continued to walk.

"Well, that should tell ye somethin'."

"It does. It tells me that they are as big of liars as ye are."

"I'm no' lyin'," he protested, but she wasn't believing him at all. "Yvaine, wait. Please," he begged, causing her to stop again and turn around.

"What is it? Prime is startin' and Brathair Gillies will expect us both to be there, so we shouldna be late. He is already threatenin' to tell yer chieftain, Storm MacKeefe, that ye are no' keepin' yer end of the bargain."

"I am tryin', but it isna easy," he explained. "I would have been there, but I fell asleep last night. If no', I swear I would have gone to martins and laids and all the rest of them."

"It's matins and lauds, and nay ye wouldna because ye only care about yerself."

"What is that supposed to mean?" he asked, not liking this quarrel so early in the morning.

She turned around and put her hands on her hips. "It means that ye are a selfish brute, Cam MacKeefe, who canna take responsibility for his actions."

"Och, I see what this is all about now. Listen, I told ye I'm sorry I kissed ye. I promise, it willna happen again."

Her face softened and she slowly dropped her hands to her sides. "Nay, it's no' about that," she said, no longer sounding so angry. "I am talkin' about yer daughter."

"Avianca?" he asked, his mind still on the kiss.

"Of course, I mean Avianca, so why do ye even ask? Are there other bastards of yers that I am no' aware of?"

"No' that I've heard," said Cam with a shrug. "Where is the wee lass anyway?"

"Avianca is sleepin' and I decided I wouldna wake her."

"Ye left her alone?" His eyes shot up to the tower. He wasn't one to normally worry, but still, he didn't think it was a good idea to leave a four-year-old girl alone in a strange place. Especially not at the top of the stairs!

"Sister Edna is with her and will be helpin' me out until Brathair Gillies can find a family to take in the girl permanently."

"Oh." His eyes swept up the stairs again. "So, that is what ye're so angry about."

"Aye, it is."

"You dinna agree she should have a guid family?"

"Yes, I do. I want that more than anythin' for the girl, but no' with strangers. Ye are her faither and ye are the one who should be watchin' her, and takin' her home with ye to the Highlands."

"Me?" His hand thumped against his chest. "I dinna even ken the girl," he said in his defense. "I only just met her."

"Then take the time to get to ken her. She wants to live with ye, no' someone else. She cried about it all night long."

"She did?" Now Cam felt really bad. Perhaps he was being selfish like Yvaine said. As much as he didn't want to be tied down with a child, he also didn't want to abandon Avianca either. This all brought back too many memories that haunted him since he was a child. "Well, mayhap I could get to ken her," he said softly.

"Do ye really mean it?" Yvaine sounded hopeful, but he could tell she didn't believe he would actually do it either.

"Yvaine, I'm no' sure I'm the best one to take her in. I dinna ken a thing about children. I'm no' sure I'd make a guid faither."

"Well, then I suppose she'll go to another family, after all."

The words cut him like a knife. When this first started, he didn't care, and wanted to be rid of the child. But when they were attacked and the thought entered his head that the girl could have been killed, everything changed. He had actually started to care for the child. Now, he was wondering if mayhap he'd made a mistake in wanting her sent away. Still, he couldn't be sure. He also could never be a father. "Why dinna ye take her?" he suggested, watching Yvaine's eyes open wide at the suggestion.

"Me? Why should I? I'm a widow, if ye havena forgotten. How do ye expect me to raise a child on my own and support her without a husband?"

"Ye'll be livin' here in the priory. Ye'll have everythin' ye need, since the monks are so self-sufficient. Besides, ye will have no' only the monks but also the nuns to help ye raise the girl."

"Is that so?"

"Aye. It sounds like the perfect solution to me. I mean, since ye'll be livin' here and all."

"Nay, I willna. I will only be here for a year or two at most, so that is no solution at all."

"Only a year or two?" he asked. "Will ye be goin' to a nunnery after that? Is that what happens after ye take yer vows? How long will ye have to be a novice?"

Yvaine didn't answer any of his questions. Instead, her face seemed to pale, and her hand went to her stomach as if she felt ill. He wasn't at all sure she wasn't going to swoon.

"Ah, there you are," said Brother Gillies, hurrying across the courtyard to join them. "Cam, you seemed to have disappeared last night."

"I'm sorry about that," apologized Cam. "However, I'm here now, and ready to continue workin' off my sentence."

"Good," said the monk with a quick nod. "Yvaine, were you able to get your things from the chandler's shop set up yet?" asked Brother Gillies. "I know how anxious you are to start making candles again. Our beekeeper says we have more wax this year than ever, so you can use it. Plus, I have ideas of potential customers I will talk to – that is, after the church has purchased their candles from you first."

"Nay, my shop isna ready yet. I'm afraid I was busy watchin' the child yesterday, and time got away from me. Nothin' is done."

"I'd be happy to send a few lay brothers over to help you," offered the monk.

"Nay. There's no need. I'll help her," Cam spoke up, eager to make amends with Yvaine.

"Ye?" asked Yvaine. "Oh, I dinna think –"

"Great," said Gillies. "Then it is all settled. Cam, I'll allow you to miss a prayer service or two each day since you'll be helping Yvaine get settled."

"Thank ye," he answered. "But what about Yvaine?"

"What about her?" asked the monk.

"Willna she be required to go to each of the cana – canol – the prayer sessions?"

"Why would she?" asked Gillies.

"Shhh," said Yvaine as they reached the church. "Cam, we must be quiet."

"Right," he said, entering the church after her, getting the distinct feeling he had been left out of some conversation, because he didn't understand at all what was going on where Yvaine was concerned.

"HERE WE ARE," said Yvaine, entering her temporary workshop later that day. They'd not only gone to prime at sunrise, but spent time with Avianca at the first meal, and afterwards took a walk down to the fish pond so the little girl could look for frogs. It had been Cam's idea, which surprised Yvaine completely that he even suggested it. She had thought his only concern would be for himself and his personal needs. Men like him usually thought they were more important than anyone else. Mayhap she was wrong. There might be hope for the man, after all, since he was showing promise.

"I'm sorry we didna get an earlier start, but Avianca wanted me to go to church with her since she wasna with us this mornin'. I didna want to disappoint her," said Cam. "Besides, I figured if I showed my face, I'd win some favors with yer brathair by attendin' terrace."

"Terce," she corrected him with a giggle, speaking of the 9 a.m. prayers.

"I'll never get the names right," he said, running a hand through his beautiful, long blond hair. "Well, what do ye need me to do?" he asked, looking back out the door as Sister Edna took Avianca across the courtyard. "I suppose it'll be easier to work since they've left." The nun was even bossier than Avianca, and Cam was happy to be rid of her.

"That was nice of ye to spend some time with her," she told him, opening up a box. "I think she really enjoyed it."

"Ye do?" He shook his head. "Nay, I dinna agree. She kept givin' me the evil eye, I swear. I'm sure she despises me as well as all Highlanders."

"How can ye say that? She worships ye, even though ye canna see it."

"Worships me?" he asked, making a face, looking out the door again.

"Aye, she does. Mayhap she didna at first, but her opinion of ye has changed since ye saved her life from the English."

"What?" His head snapped around and his mouth fell open. His gaze darted out the door again and then back to her. Slowly, a grin spread across his face. "Ooooh, ye're talkin' about Avianca."

"Yes, I am. Why? Who did ye think I meant?"

"I thought ye were talkin' about Sister Edith."

"Edna, no' Edith," she corrected him, getting a deep sigh from him in response.

"Edna. Sorry. I never was guid with names," he said, sinking atop a chair, looking so forlorn.

"It's no' important." Since it seemed to bother him so much, she tried to make light of the situation. "Ye're doin' fine," she remarked, hoping to convince him, even though she'd never seen anyone before who could forget so many names or use the wrong words so often. Yvaine wondered if he was so self-absorbed that he didn't listen when anyone talked to him. Still, since he seemed so bothered by his mistake, she supposed he truly was trying.

"Is Cam short for Cameron?" she asked, trying to strike up a conversation between them.

"Nay." He got off the chair and started to open a box, but didn't expound on his answer.

"So, yer mathair just named ye Cam, then. I see."

Silence.

"What does Cam mean?" she asked. "Every name has a meanin'. For example, my name, Yvaine, means stardust." Yvaine smiled as she unwrapped a few candle holders while she spoke, wondering why he had become so quiet all of a sudden.

"Crooked," he said softly.

"Pardon me?" She looked up and smiled. "What is crooked? One of the candles, or a candle holder?"

"Nay. That is the meanin' of my name."

"Cam means crooked?" She found that odd. "Well, I'm sure yer mathair just liked the name, no matter what it meant."

"When I was a child, she told me that she named me Cam because I had a crooked mouth when I was born."

"Really? I didna notice. Let me see." She walked over to him and lifted his chin in her hand, studying his mouth. Perusing him this close only made her want to kiss him, but she would never be so bold. "It doesna look at all crooked to me."

"It's no'," he answered, sounding sad.

"Then why would she tell ye that? I dinna understand." She released him, looking him in the eyes. Unspoken pain emanated from his gaze. "Cam, tell me. Please."

"It doesna matter." He took his attention back to the box. She stepped closer and put her hand on his shoulder.

"I can tell somethin' is botherin' ye. Please, I want to ken what it is."

"All right," he said with a sigh. "I suppose if I dinna tell ye, that ye will eventually hear it from my friends."

"Ye sound like ye have some sort of deep, dark secret," she said playfully, but her smile disappeared with his next words.

"Dinna we all harbor secrets that we dinna want others to

ken?"

"W-what do ye mean?" She nervously pulled her hand away and looked at the ground. "Are ye sayin' that ye think I have a deep, dark secret I'm hidin'?" God's eyes, had he somehow found out?

"Nay, dinna be silly. No' ye, lass," he said, causing her to release the breath she'd been holding. "Ye are an innocent widow and soon to become a nun. What secrets could ye possibly possess?"

If only he knew what he was asking. She never wanted him to find out. It upset her so much that her legs shook. "I need to sit," she told him.

To her surprise, his hand was on her arm as he guided her over to a chair.

"Are ye ill, lass?" he asked, sounding as if he truly cared.

"Nay," she responded, flashing him a quick smile, trying to hide her emotions. "I think I just ate too much pottage and bread earlier. It is makin' me sleepy."

"Too much?" he asked with a chuckle. "These monks dinna eat enough to satisfy a mouse."

"Ye were sayin'? About yer name?" she asked, wanting to turn the conversation back to him.

"Och, that's right. I am ashamed to admit it, but eventually my mathair told me the truth that she named me after a crooked man who got her pregnant."

"I'm sorry. Then ye are a bastard, just like Avianca?"

"More so than ye think." He sat down on a chair next to her, looking very shaken.

"Cam? Tell me what has ye so upset."

"If I tell ye, do ye promise no' to judge me?" he asked. "I couldna bear ye lookin' at me differently because of somethin' that happened in my past."

Her heart sped up, making her want to spill her secret now that he'd said that. Still, she wasn't sure if she should, so she remained quiet.

"I dinna think anyone should be judged or have somethin' held against them for things they might have done in the past."

"Well, it's nothin' that I did. No' really," he said, opening up to her just a little, and then looking like he was about to put up walls again.

She spoke gently, trying to coax him to say more. "Ye can tell me anythin' about ye, Cam, and I promise I willna judge ye. What is it that is troublin' ye so?"

"First of all, let me tell ye that I am no' as cold-hearted as ye think. I only said I couldna be Avianca's faither because of my past."

"I dinna understand."

A worried look creased his brow, and finally he continued. "My mathair wasna married. Ever," he told her.

"Och, I see. So, a man forced himself on her then? That is terrible."

"Nay!" He stood up and paced the floor. "Ye dinna understand. No one forced themselves on my mathair. Believe me, it was all more than a willin' act."

"Then she had a lover. A man who laid with her and wouldna marry her afterwards. Isna that what ye mean?"

"No' exactly," he said, stopping and looking back at the door as if he didn't want anyone to hear them.

"Go on," she urged him.

"I was – I was born to a whore," he spit out. "So, ye see, I'm just like Avianca."

"What?" Shocked to hear this, Yvaine sprang to her feet. "I canna believe it."

"It's true," he told her, looking like he'd just lost his best friend in the world. "I am naught but the bastard son of a whore. I grew up in whore houses across Scotland as my mathair took me with her every time she moved from one place to the next."

"Oh, Cam. I am so sorry."

"I ken I have a bad reputation for visitin' brothels, but it is only because that is where I feel the most comfortable. Ye see, whore houses are the only place I ever kent as home."

Yvaine didn't know what to say to this. It truly was a horrible secret. Still, she promised him she would not judge him, and neither would she. After all, her dark secret was so much worse. "So, this has somethin' to do with the reason why ye didna want to take Avianca."

"It does," he admitted. "My childhood didna exist, since I was forced to grow up so fast. I kent things from an early age that most lads didna find out until later in life."

"Oh, that must have been horrible for ye."

"Please, I dinna want yer pity," he hissed. "My mathair loved me, but she realized it wasna right to keep me with her, so she did what she had to do. It was no life for a child. No' with the things she had to do to make a livin' to raise me. She kent I would be better off with a family. A guid family. A real one."

"She gave ye up then?" asked Yvaine, her heart about breaking for this man.

"Aye. When I was only six, she told me she was wrong and bein' selfish by keepin' me there with her. I hadna had any proper education, and everythin' I knew, I learned from experience."

"Ye're no' sayin' ye . . . I mean, no' that young. Did ye actually . . ." she asked, hoping he wasn't speaking of sex.

"Nay! Of course no'," he said. "It wasna like that at all. My mathair gave me a ring that was once my faither's. She told me she wanted me to have somethin' to remember her by. But when I was to go to my new family, I ran away. I stayed hidden in the woods at first. I didna want to leave my mathair and my home, no matter how bad it was. Still, I kent if I went back home, she'd only send me away again."

"How horrible for ye."

"At first, it was. But it wasna long before the MacKeefes found me. They are a guid clan and took me in when they discovered I was an orphan."

"But ye werena an orphan, Cam. Ye still had parents," she pointed out.

"I did. However, I didna tell them that. I was so angry with my mathair for no' wantin' me, and with the faither that I never kent, that I didna want to ever think about them again. I wanted no memory of them, and even gave the ring away to another little boy who I found fishin' in the loch one day."

"Is yer mathair still alive?" she asked curiously.

"Nay." He looked down and shook his head. "When I became an adult, I decided I was wrong in runnin' away. I desired to make amends with my mathair. I wanted it, but it was too late."

"She died then."

"I didna ken where to look for her at the time. I went out searchin' one brothel after another, hopin' to someday find her."

"Is that why ye are always in brothels?" asked Yvaine, finally starting to understand something about this mysterious man.

"Aye, and nay. Ye see, it's true what everyone says that I like the lassies too much. I do have a strong lustful side, and I guess it is in my blood."

"I wouldna say that." Yvaine didn't think this was a family trait passed down.

"I visited brothels across the land and, of course, spent more and more time with the – well, with the lassies while I was there."

"Did ye ever find yer mathair?"

He nodded slowly. "I did. It was about five years ago, after I had long since given up hope. I accidentally ran across her."

"Where was she?"

"I found her in an infirmary in a priory, much like this one, and she died in my arms," he explained. "She had been very ill for years, but I didna ken that. It seems once I ran away, she had a change of heart and wanted me back. She searched for me, and thought she found me. A young lad was mauled by a bear, and he was wearin' the ring. She thought it was me who died since the child was too mangled to see his face anymore. She blamed herself for my death. Her heart and spirit had been broken and could never be mended after that. That's why she left her profession and confessed all her sins to a priest, hopin' to be forgiven."

"She did? I dinna understand. Why did the monks let her stay with them if she was once a prostitute?"

"She gave them the ring she'd taken off the mangled child's body. The ring that came from my faither. It was worth much, and the monks were able to sell it and use the money for their own needs."

"I'm still confused. Why would an English nobleman give such an expensive ring to someone like her in the first place?"

"He didn't. My mathair stole it from him after they . . . after I was conceived. I am no' proud of the things my mathair did. Still, with her dyin' breath, she told me the man had promised to marry her. That is why she did nothin' to protect herself from gettin' pregnant. The next mornin', my faither changed his mind. My mathair thought she might be pregnant, and stole his ring to sell it to help raise me, once I was born. The problem was, she was in love with the man. She could never bring herself to sell the ring, after all."

"I understand now. She was able to stay at the priory because she bought her way in."

"No' exactly. Ye see, once she thought I was dead, and she'd confessed her sins, she devoted her life to the Order."

"She became a nun?" gasped Yvaine.

"Nay. She couldna be one since she had a dark past. Instead, she worked as a cook in the monks' kitchens."

"Cam, who was yer faither? If he had a signet ring, he must have been a noble."

"I dinna ken the answer to that. My mathair never told me his name. I still remember the ring to this day. It had a big square, blue stone in it. It was a gold band, with circles around a wild boar in the middle."

"I'm sure ye could have found out which Englishman bears that crest. It wouldna be hard to do."

"I suppose I could have, but I didna want to. That is all in the past now, and I no longer care. Right now, all that matters to me is that I dinna repeat the mistakes of my mathair. I willna let Avianca grow up the way I did."

"She's already lived the first four years of her life in a brothel," Yvaine pointed out.

"Aye, and that is damage I can never undo. I have been wonderin' if perhaps I should bring her to live the rest of her life with me and the MacKeefe Clan."

"Do ye really mean it?" asked Yvaine excitedly, so happy that Cam had not only told her of his past, but that he'd decided to be a father to the girl, after all.

"I was confused at first, but I ken now that it is the right thing to do. After I am accepted back into the clan, I will take her with me."

"Oh, Cam, that's wonderful," cried Yvaine, reaching up and kissing him passionately on the mouth the way he had done to her. His hands slowly encircled her waist, pulling her closer as he returned the kiss. She wanted another kiss, but he gently pushed her away, and held her at arm's length.

"Nay," he said. "I canna kiss ye. It isna right."

"Why no'?" she asked.

"Because, ye are goin' to be a nun." He shook his head, looking like he was struggling hard with this decision.

"What if I told ye that ye can kiss me? Would it be all right then?"

"What are ye sayin'?" he asked, looking as if he thought her disgusting to even allow it.

"Before ye judge me, let me explain. I am no' goin' to be a nun, and neither was I ever."

"What are ye sayin'?" He looked so lost and confused.

"Ye are the one who thought I was goin' to join the Order, but I never told ye it was true, did I?"

"I – I suppose no'," he said, slowly sitting back down on the chair. "Why did ye no' tell me all this sooner?"

"I was scared," she admitted. "I didna ken a thing about ye, other than ye liked the lassies. I am sorry that I allowed ye to believe a lie, but I had just lost my husband and I – I guess I –"

"Shhh," he said, pulling her over to him, and sitting her atop his lap. He gently rubbed his fingers over her arm to comfort her. "I understand, lass. If I were ye, I'd be leery of an awful man like me as well."

"Nay! Dinna say such things. Ye are no' awful, Cam," she told him, throwing her arms around his neck and kissing him once again. "I am the awful one, no' ye."

"Now ye are wrong. Dinna ever say that about yerself. Ye are a lovely person, Yvaine."

"I hope ye still believe that no matter what happens."

"What do ye mean?"

"I dinna mean a thing. Make love to me, Cam," she said, tears dripping down her cheeks.

"What?" He looked up with surprise showing in his deep brown eyes. "Ye dinna ken what ye are sayin'."

"I do ken what I'm sayin'. I never felt love with my husband the entire time we were married."

"What do ye mean, lass?"

"Look," she said, opening up her bodice enough for him to see the bruises on her chest.

"My God! He hurt ye," he said in a low whisper. His shaking hand reached out and he touched her bruise so gingerly that she barely felt it at all. "This is why ye reacted the way ye did when I grabbed yer wrist. Ye seemed so scared of me and now I understand. Lass, no man should ever hurt a woman in this way." He looked up to her and she started crying. She sobbed so hard that he picked her up in his arms and carried her to the far end of the room where blankets from the packing were thrown on a pile on the ground. Then he kissed her once more and gently laid her atop the soft pile, kneeling down at her side.

"I dinna ken if I can show ye love, because I have never learned how to love a woman."

"Dinna say that. Ye ken more about the lassies than anyone, Cam.

"Aye, I know how to make them happy and feel guid. But if we couple, it will only be in lust, no' in love that I do it. That is all I can offer, because it is all that I ken."

"I dinna care if it is done only in lust. I need ye, Cam. I need to feel guid. Is that so wrong of me to want it?"

"Nay. No' at all." He gently pushed aside her bodice, lowering his head to place his lips on her bruise. Kissing her ever so gently, her head fell back and she pulled him closer. All she wanted was to know how it felt to make love willingly, and not be forced upon roughly the way Dun always did with her.

"I want to do this, Cam. Ye have my willin' permission," she whispered as he started to kiss every bruise he found.

"Are ye no' worried that ye will burn in hell for couplin' with me, right here in a priory?"

She looked him in the eyes when she answered. "Ye said everyone has secrets, and so now ye ken some of mine as well. Nay, Cam, I am no' worried, because I already ken I am goin' straight to hell when I die. It doesna matter."

"Why would ye say such a thing?" he asked.

"Cam, please, dinna make me beg for this."

"No lassie has ever had to beg for me, and I dinna think it suits ye, so I will stall no longer." He stood up and removed his clothes. Her eyes fastened to his naked body. He was hard and ready. This excited her tremendously, as well as scared her, but she no longer cared. She couldn't wait to know how it felt to enjoy coupling with a man. If she enjoyed it, it would be the first time ever.

He kneeled down next to her, and slowly reached out to continue untying her bodice. Yvaine closed her eyes and winced. Then she whimpered. Somehow, she couldn't get the visions out of her head of the rough way Dun used to take her. He was always hurting her and never cared.

"Dinna be afraid, love," he whispered, causing her eyes to flicker open. "I promise ye, I would never hurt ye. I am Cam, and no one else. Ye need to remember that. Can ye do that for me?"

"Aye," she said, sniffling, feeling her emotions pent up so tightly that she thought she would burst.

"Just close yer eyes and relax," he instructed. "I want ye to think of happy times, happy thoughts. Think of a place where ye feel safe. Where no one can harm ye."

His words worked to calm her. She thought of a sunny glen she used to visit as a child. She and her friend would pretend they were queens and that the surrounding plants and trees were their subjects. They would imagine they were in a castle and that their knights were coming to marry them and take them away. The sound of the imaginary brook echoed in her ears, making her feel safe . . . and happy.

"That's right," Cam whispered, untying her bodice, kissing her chest as he pulled down her clothes, removing them one by one until she was totally naked.

"Just relax, and let yerself go." His fingers closed over one breast and, for a moment, she stiffened. "I willna hurt ye. I promise," he told her, making her feel safe and calm once again.

With her eyes still closed, she felt his mouth on her breast as he continued to kiss her. Then his lips closed over one nipple and his tongue shot out, making a tingle of excitement shoot through her. Her eyes snapped open.

"Cam!" she exclaimed.

"What is it? Did I hurt ye, lass?" he asked in concern.

"Nay. Just the opposite. I felt – I felt a tingle of excitement that I've never experienced before."

"That is just the start of things, sweetheart. I will help ye to experience a lot of guid feelin's that ye seem to have been missin' out on lately."

"Do more," she urged him. "Kiss me again."

He chuckled and leaned over and kissed her on the mouth. "Slow down," he told her. "There is no rush. These things take time."

"But I want to feel more. Please, hurry." She was so excited that she could barely stand it.

"All right," he agreed, running his hands down her body,

kissing her arms, her chest, her breasts, and even running his tongue around her navel.

She giggled and squirmed beneath him, liking the way this felt. "Is it supposed to feel this wonderful?" she asked him, since this was all a new experience for her.

"Am I only the second man ye've ever been with?" he asked, being careful not to say the name of her late husband and ruin the moment.

"I am ashamed to tell ye that is true, especially at my age. No other opportunity ever arose in my life before."

"There is nothin' wrong with it. Yvaine, I promise ye, there is an opportunity arisin' very quickly."

She knew exactly what he meant when he parted her legs with his knee and pressed his erection up against her belly. He felt so big and strong. She wanted him badly. Something dormant inside her was coming to life with every one of his kisses and each stroke of his fingers over her skin.

"I – I feel somethin' happenin'," she whispered. Her breathing labored and her back arched. Of her own accord, she lifted her knees around him.

His hand dipped down and he tested her wetness between her thighs by gently slipping a finger inside.

"I want to feel ye – all of ye in me," she told him, not sure she could wait. Her excitement grew quickly and she was near to shattering in his arms.

"Ye are ready," he announced with a big smile. Her hands ran down his sturdy chest and she realized that his nipples were taut as well.

"Are ye sure it willna hurt?" she asked, feeling doubt creeping back in.

"If ye stay relaxed, I promise it will feel like heaven."

"Heaven," she repeated, closing her eyes. He slowly and gently slipped his hardened length inside her, making her feel happy and alive as he filled her completely.

"Oh, ooooh," she murmured as Cam slipped his manhood in and out, constantly checking to make sure she was comfortable.

"Is this all right, love?" he asked. "How does it feel?"

"Yes . . . yes!" she cried out as she felt her excitement rise and saw colors explode behind her closed lids. "Somethin' is happenin', Cam. I feel it," she cried out with joy.

"Let go, Yvaine. Dinna hold back. Ye deserve to feel guid, now enjoy it."

She did enjoy it. More than she ever thought she could. And when she'd reached her peak, and he knew it, he found his completion, too.

Feeling sated, happy and safe, she lay in Cam's arms feeling as if she had been reborn.

"Ye were right," she told him, breathing heavily. "I never kent it could feel that guid, but now I do."

"I'm glad," he said, kissing her gently on the tip of the nose. "And I am happy ye were able to put yer past experiences behind ye."

The door burst open, and Cam quickly threw a blanket over Yvaine to hide her nakedness.

"Cam, are ye in here?" North walked into the room, letting his eyes get used to the dimness after being out in the bright sun. He was followed by Nash. They had fishing poles in their hands.

"Brathair Gillies wants us to catch some fish for supper. We wanted to ask if ye'll come with us." Nash looked over to the dark corner and his mouth fell open. Next, he dropped his pole.

"Why did ye do that?" asked North.

"Hello, boys," said Cam, smiling and waving at his friends.

North's head snapped around to see Cam and he dropped his pole next.

"I guess he willna want to go fishin'," mumbled Nash.

"I suppose no'," added North. Neither of them looked away.

"I'm a little busy, so I'll take a pass on the fishin'. Now, if ye'll kindly leave and close the door behind ye, I'd greatly appreciate it."

"God's teeth!" said Nash, as he and North picked up their poles and hurried out the door. "I canna believe that Cam just bedded a nun."

# CHAPTER TWELVE

"WHAT IN THE name of the devil did ye do?" Nash asked Cam the next day in the secret room of the catacombs. He and North had been busy fishing until late yesterday, and then the monks kept them busy cleaning the fish afterwards. By the time they'd come back to the room, Cam was already fast asleep atop the bed again as usual.

"I have no idea what ye're talkin' about." Cam sat up and stretched. They'd all overslept today. Through the vents, they heard the church bells ringing. That was the signal, telling the monks it was time for some prayers or chants, or reading of psalms. Cam decided it was all the monks ever seemed to do. By the amount of sunlight streaming in through the overhead vents, he could tell it was past sunrise, but not yet noon.

"Ye ken exactly what we mean." Nash sat up from sleeping on the floor, rubbing his back. "Ye bedded a nun, ye fool! How could ye?"

Cam chuckled, got out of bed, and started to dress. "Ye two dinna ken what ye're talkin' about."

"Dinna try to deny it," said North, dressing as well. "We both saw ye lyin' naked on the floor with a nun!"

"Yvaine is no' a nun." Cam sat back down on the edge of the bed to don his boots.

"Mayhap no' yet, but soon she will be," said Nash. "So, ye see, it is nearly the same thing."

"Aye, it is," agreed North. "No' to mention it is wrong. What do ye think Storm and Ian are goin' to say when they find out what ye did?"

"They willna find out, because neither of ye are goin' to tell them," Cam answered.

"Dinna worry about Storm and Ian. I'd worry about what Old Callum is goin' to do to ye." Nash stretched, got up, and started to dress as well. "The whole reason ye are here, in case ye've forgotten, is because ye were kissin' the wrong lassie. Ye obviously have learned nothin'."

"I am no' in the wrong," Cam protested, running a comb over his head and tying his hair back with a leather band. "We were all mistaken. Ye see, Yvaine told me she is no' becomin' a nun at all."

"No' anymore," mumbled Nash in disgust. "No' after ye ruined her the way ye did."

"She is a widow, ye fool," snapped Cam, standing up and strapping on his weapon belt. While they could wear their weapons inside the walls of the monastery, they were not allowed to bring weapons into the church. "I didna spoil her in any way. She never intended on becomin' a nun. Plus, she wasna a virgin to begin with. The lassie all but begged me to make love to her."

"I dinna believe that at all," snorted North.

"Neither do I." Nash scowled at him. "Cam, sometimes ye just go too far."

"I dinna care what ye two believe or think. It is the truth, I tell ye," Cam answered.

"Ye are no' usin' yer head! What if ye got her pregnant?" asked Nash. "Cam, she is no' one of yer usual whores and most likely doesna ken how to prevent things like that from happenin'. What are ye goin' to do now that ye've planted yer seed in her?"

"Aye," asked North. "Are ye goin' to marry her if she is carryin' yer bairn?"

"Stop it. Both of ye," growled Cam. "Ye are worryin' way too much. I'm sure she is no' bairned, so there is nothin' to concern yerself with."

"But what if she is?" asked North. "Would ye just leave her here after yer sentence is over? Or would ye do the proper thing and marry her, bringin' her back with ye to the clan?"

Cam didn't like hearing all this talk about the future nor about doing what was proper. He didn't live by anyone's rules but his own. He would not condone this doitit clishmaclaver from his friends any longer. "I dinna want to hear another word about it. Do ye two understand?" Cam held up his hand in an attempt to stop their barrage of questions. "It was just one time, and I'm sure it'll probably never happen again. Therefore, I dinna see the purpose of continuously mentionin' it."

"*Probably* never happen again? That doesna sound like ye're sure at all," remarked Nash.

Cam shrugged. "We'll see what happens, I guess. In the meantime, I'd appreciate it if neither of ye mentioned it to anyone. Especially no' to Yvaine's brathair."

"Aye, we wouldna want word gettin' back to the MacKeefe Clan or ye might have to start all over with yer sentence," stated Nash. "If Callum even gets a whiff of this, he is sure to make the next punishment ten times worse."

"I didna think of that," said Cam, starting to get a little worried. All he wanted was to be done with all this nonsense, and welcomed back into the clan. To have to prolong the agony much longer would kill him. "Do ye two promise ye willna tell anyone?"

"Why would we?" asked North. "If ye get a new punishment, they'd only send us along with ye. I just want my turn so I can get my sentence over with and stop livin' yers as well."

"Me, too," agreed Nash.

"Hello? Is anyone here?" came a muffled female voice from outside the room that could only be Yvaine.

"She's here," said Cam, feeling his heart beating a little faster. He'd been dreaming of making love to Yvaine all night long. Just thinking of seeing her again was already making him excited.

"Open the door. Quickly," he told North as he picked up a shiny platter and checked his reflection in it. He quickly pushed back a stray hair.

"Ugh," mumbled North, making a face at what Cam was doing. He walked over and flipped the lever. The stone door slid open to reveal Yvaine, Brother Gillies, and Avianca standing there waiting for them.

"It's like magic," said Avianca in awe. Although her eyes were wide in amazement, Cam was sure part of the reason was because she was scared of the dark and dreary catacombs. She clung to Yvaine's skirt so tightly that her knuckles went white.

Yvaine wasn't wearing a nun's robe today. For that, Cam was glad. The last thing he wanted was to be having lustful thoughts about a woman dressed like a nun, no matter if she really was one or not. Today, Yvaine wore her own clothes.

"Ye brought my daughter here? Into the catacombs?" asked Cam, shaking his head, not liking the idea in the least.

"I did," admitted Yvaine. "She wanted to see where ye and yer friends slept, and so did I." Yvaine balanced a platter of food on one hand, while smoothing back the little girl's hair with the other. "She's all right. There is no need to worry."

"I'm no' scared, if that's what ye think," said Avianca, trying to sound brave. Cam could hear the tremble of her voice and knew it was only bravado that made her say it.

"We missed you all at the morning prayers." Brother Gillies did not at all look pleased.

"Right. Sorry about that," said Cam, clearing his throat. "I guess we were a little tired this mornin'."

"Aye, we were," agreed Nash. "However, my brathair and I were tired for a whole different reason than Cam."

"What do ye mean?" asked the monk.

Cam threw his friends a daggered look. "They mean they were fishin' while I was helpin' yer sister set up shop."

"Sure, it does. If that's what ye want to call it," mumbled Nash.

Cam ignored him, and continued. "I never thought puttin' together a chandler's shop would be so much work."

"That's no' even half of it," explained Yvaine. "I only brought with me the things I could fit in the wagon. I'll have to make do with what I was able to take, but it willna be easy."

"What's that ye've got there?" asked Cam, smelling the food, stretching his neck to see it.

"I thought ye all might be hungry since ye missed the mornin' meal." Yvaine walked in and put down the tray on a nearby table.

"What kind of food do we have here?" asked Nash, anxiously pushing North aside to see the array of food being offered.

"There is a small loaf of bread for each of you, as well as some cheese and fruit," explained the monk.

"Thankfully, no grapes," commented Nash, picking up a loaf of bread and taking a big bite. "I never want to see another grape as long as I live."

"Or fish," added North.

"Give them the ale, Avianca," said Yvaine, nodding to the little girl. The girl took a bottle from the monk and handed it over to Cam.

"Here ye are, Da," she said with a big smile, holding the bottle carefully with two hands.

Nash and North both stopped eating and looked over in surprise at hearing her call him Da. Neither of them said a word about it.

"Thank ye, Avianca. Ye're a guid helper." Cam took the ale from her, not reprimanding her from calling him Da. Today, he kind of liked it. "Well, what do ye think of the room?" he asked Yvaine. "Impressive, isna it?" He stepped to the side and held out his arm.

"Very nice," she said, walking into the center of the room. Her foot hit something, and she looked down. "What's that?" After picking up a chess piece, she inspected it closer.

"Oh, my!" exclaimed the monk, his eyes opening wide. "What in heaven's name is Lord Rook's chess game doin' on the floor?"

"I knocked into the table in the dark and it fell over. I guess I neglected to pick it up," explained Cam.

"If you three can't take care of things in here, you'll have to sleep in the stable instead," the monk warned them, picking up piece after piece. "This game is special to Lord Rook. I wouldn't want anything to happen to it."

Cam thought it odd that the monk should say that, after he told them Rook didn't want to bring the game to his new castle. He figured there was more of a story behind it, but it wasn't for him to ask.

"We'll get that," said Cam, nodding to his friends. Together, they picked up every piece and put them back on the game board atop the table. "Now, there will be nothin' for Lord Rook to get angry about."

"Does Lord Rook have a nice faither like mine?" asked Avianca, making Cam feel awful now for ever having suggested that the monk find her a good home. Yvaine was right. The girl was his responsibility, no matter if he liked it or not.

"Lord Rook's father is the King of England," the monk explained. "Since the king ordered his triplet sons killed at birth, I wouldn't call him nice. I would say your father is much nicer than Lord Rook's, my dear."

Cam kept thinking of his situation with Avianca. Was it right to bring the little girl back to the clan, when Cam wasn't even married? After all, she wasn't just his child, but also the child of a common whore. Perhaps the clan wouldn't accept that. Or it would be too inconvenient for everyone to tend to her when he went out fighting. Since she'd already lost her mother, would Avianca be able to accept it if he died on the battlefield, protecting his clan? If so, she'd really be an orphan.

Confusion wracked his brain, and doubt crept back in. Mayhap he'd made his decision too quickly. Perhaps he still needed time to ponder things over. He didn't want to put anyone of his clan in an awkward position. Avianca deserved a good family with caring parents, after what she'd been through. Especially after losing her mother so early in her life. But would she really be happy with him, or would she regret it as soon as she got older? Mayhap she'd just run away like he did when he was a child.

"Thank ye for the kind words, Brathair Gillies," he said. "However, I dinna ken if I deserve them." His eyes fastened to the child, his heart about breaking for her as he started thinking that mayhap any parents would be better for her than him. "I'm no' exactly sure I am a nicer faither than King Edward at all."

"WHAT DID YE mean earlier when ye said ye might no' be a kinder faither than King Edward was with his bastard triplets?" Yvaine was melting beeswax in a bucket of hot water, preparing to make taper candles since her workshop was now set up and functional.

"It doesna matter," said Cam. "Show me how to make candles. It all seems so interestin'."

"All right," she said, eager to show the Highlander her skills. "I have only been doin' it for a year – that is, the time I was married to Dun. Still, I learned a lot by watchin' him."

"Then I'll learn by watchin' ye as well." He reached out and cupped her chin, softly stroking her bottom lip with his thumb. It made Yvaine feel special. For such a rugged Highlander, he was the gentlest, kindest man she'd ever met.

"I think the wax is just about ready," she told him.

"Do ye make candles from tallow, too? I think I ken more about makin' them from animal fat. Like, dinna use pig fat or it will really smell."

She giggled. "All tallow candles stink."

"Aye, but those made from cattle and sheep fat are no' quite so repugnant."

"I see that ye do ken a little about this skill, after all."

"That's everythin' I ken. That and how to light a fire." He flashed her a smile that made her feel warm inside.

"I would hope a Highlander would ken how to make a fire."

"Ye tell me." He dropped his hand from her chin, slowly running it down her chest. Then he took the tip of one finger and made lazy circles over her nipple until she could see it getting taut right through her clothes.

"That's enough." She pushed his hand away. "We keep that up, and I'll never get any candles made. Now watch out, because I am comin' through with hot wax. Ye'll have to move to the side. Unless ye want the hair pulled right off yer arms, I warn ye no' to splash any on yerself."

"I'll be careful," he said, stepping back and giving her a wide berth.

"First, I want to explain that there are two guilds for chandlers. Either the Tallow Chandlers' or the Wax Chandlers' guilds."

"I see. So, ye belong to the latter," he said with a nod.

"Aye, but it wasna always that way. Before I married Dun, he made tallow candles. I am the one who found the customers, especially with churches, that allowed us to start makin' wax candles instead."

"It's hard to believe all that wax comes from bees," said Cam, looking down at the bucket. "I suppose if ye run out, ye can just mix in a little tallow, right?"

"Wrong! Never," she exclaimed. "It is a serious offense, and one can go to prison for that. I found Dun doin' it more than once and was afraid that if it was discovered, we'd end up behind bars. I always dumped those batches."

"Guid thing," said Cam. "It would be terrible to go to prison. Especially for a bonnie lassie like ye."

If only he knew what he was saying. Yvaine looked over to a bruise on her arm. "Dun used to punish me for dumpin' the mixed wax, even though I was probably savin' his life."

"I wouldna have done anythin' to help him if I were ye," said

Cam. "Mayhap ye should have let the cur be arrested or thrown in prison. Or even be killed."

"Oh!" she gasped, wondering what Cam would say if she told him that she was glad the man was dead. He must have thought that his words upset her, because he ended up apologizing.

"I'm sorry, lass. It was wrong of me to speak that way about the dead. I only meant that he had no right to hit ye."

"I dinna want to talk about it anymore."


CAM DIDN'T WANT to upset Yvaine by talking about her dead husband, so he decided he would focus on the art of making candles instead.

"What kind of beeswax candles are we makin' today?" he asked, looking around the room at everything they'd set up. A tall wooden frame that she'd called the drying tree was set up right next to the long, deep trough that she poured the hot wax into.

"We are makin' hand dipped candles," she explained. "These are the favorites amongst the nobles and the clergy, and used the most."

"Is it hard to do?" he asked.

"No' once ye ken what ye're doin'." She handed him a piece of board about the length of his arm that had about six strings hanging over it.

"What is this for?" he asked curiously.

"These are the wicks we will use," she explained. "I've taken a guid, woven twine and cut the pieces to the right lengths. I have already primed the wicks, too."

"Primed? Like in the prayer service?" he asked, having the names of the canonical hours stuck in his head since he would be attending them several times a day.

"Nay," she said with a giggle. "I've hardened the wicks by dipping them in wax and then straightening them out with my fingers. This will ensure when we dip the candles, that the wicks dinna float."

"I have somethin' ye can make hard usin' yer fingers," he said in a sultry voice, leaning over and nibbling at her earlobe.

"No' now, Cam," she scolded him. "We have to work quickly before the trough of wax starts to cool." She took the board from him and dipped the hardened wicks into the hot wax and lifted it up again. "It is important to have the right rhythm, so the candles stay erect."

"Och, lass, ye are makin' me think of things that have nothin' to do with candles."

She ignored his lusty comment and kept talking. "After the first dip, the board is placed across the dipping tree for a few minutes to allow the wax to dry."

"That doesna look like candles. It looks more like waxy strings," he said, studying the wicks.

"No' yet it doesna. But after about five and twenty dips, ye'll see a taper emerge." She picked up a different board with more primed strings hanging over it and handed it to him. "Here, ye give it a try."

"All right," he said, carefully walking over to the hot wax and gently dipping the ends into it.

"Nay, ye need to submerge the whole wick in one motion so the candle will be smooth. Like this," she said taking hold of his hand to guide him. In a smooth movement, she helped him to dip the wicks and then gently and slowly lift them back out again.

"That's it?" he asked. "Do I put it on the dryin' tree now?"

"Aye. Ye learn fast."

"Or is it called a dippin' tree?"

"They are both the same, so it doesna matter what ye call it," she explained.

He placed the board with the dipped wicks hanging down over the tree and they continued the process.

"There is nothin' to it," he said, feeling confident now. "It is quite fun."

"Messy fun, but I agree," she said, smiling at him. Her face lit up with life, and her cheeks looked rosy. She seemed so much happier and healthier today.

To Cam's amazement, after a while, the dipped wicks started to look like actual tapered candles.

"I see it. I see the candles emergin'," he said excitedly, proud to have been a part of this amazing process.

"Now, the candles are the right size, but see these drips on the bottom?" She carefully palmed the bottom of a candle. "They need to come off, so the candles are smoother on the ends." She removed the drips, then took a pair of candles off the rack. Each wick made two tapered candles, one hanging on each side.

"So, it's finished?" he asked.

"No' quite." She laid the candles down on the table. "We need to trim the bottoms now with a knife."

"I'll do it," he said, eager to show her how much he'd learned. He took the knife from her, meaning to lop off the bottom ends of the candles, but she stopped him.

"Wait. Ye dinna want to slice it, ye need to gently roll the candle and let the blade do the work." She took his hand again to demonstrate. With the feel of her touch, the candle was the last thing on his mind. Her body was pressed up to him, causing him to become warm. Her sweet scent filled his senses, making him want to kiss her again.

"Now, we'll let them harden for a day, and then they'll be ready to ship to our customers." She held up the dual candles and smiled. "Before we bring them to market, or make a delivery, we'll cut the candles apart and trim the wicks on an angle. So, what do ye think?"

She was still smiling at the candles she dangled before him, but his eyes were on her.

"I think I want to kiss ye and make love with ye again." Slipping his arms around her waist, he pulled her to him and kissed her passionately. She held the candles out to the side.

"Cam," she said, breaking away. "I'm sorry, but this process is time sensitive. If the wax is too cold or too hot, it makes all the difference in the world. Plus, we need to be careful that the candles dry properly and dinna crack." She walked over to the drying rack and hung the tapers back up.

"Well, we wouldna want that to happen, would we?" Cam walked up behind her, putting his hands on her shoulders, kissing the side of her neck.

"Cam, didna ye hear the church bells ringin'?" Nash walked in with North, both of them stopping in their tracks when they saw him.

"No' this again," grumbled North.

"We're makin' candles," said Cam, over his shoulder. His hands were still on Yvaine.

"So, is that what ye're callin' it now?" Nash glared at him.

"What do ye two want?" asked Cam.

"Brathair Gillies said ye havena attended a single prayer ser-vice yet today. He wants ye to attend vespers and compline both," North announced.

Cam let out a sigh, tired of going to church. "I'll be glad when this punishment is over." He started for the door.

"It doesna look like much of a punishment to me," said Nash, his eyes still on Yvaine.

"Aye. Makin' candles and kissin' lassies sounds better than plowin' fields all day, which is what we've been doin," agreed his brother.

"Have ye two seen Avianca lately?" asked Yvaine, dipping some more candles. "She hasna been up here and I wonder what she is up to."

"She's with Sister Edna in the kitchen," said Nash. "The girl wanted to see how the monks made bread."

"Mayhap I'll stop by the kitchen after the prayers and check out the bread as well," said Cam.

"Cam, ye do ken that there are no more meals before mornin'," Yvaine reminded him.

"I'm hungry," he said, looking over his shoulder as he walked out the door. "Hungry for more than just bread and ale," he mumbled under his breath, taking one last look at Yvaine, not able to get the memories of their love making out of his mind.

$$\cdot\bullet\cdot\diamond\cdot\bullet\cdot$$

# Chapter Thirteen

"**C**AM, GET UP!"

Cam felt something hit his arm and woke up from his sleep to see North standing over him holding a lit candle. Nash looked on as well.

"Hmmm?" he asked, wondering why his friends were waking him up in the middle of the night.

"Brathair Gillies is at the door," Nash informed him.

"Now? What does he want?" Cam pushed up to one elbow.

Nash explained. "He said he's here to escort ye personally to matins and lauds, since ye conveniently didna show up for compline last night after he warned ye that ye needed to be there."

"What time is it?" asked Cam, rubbing one eye. "Isna it the middle of the night?"

"It is 3 a.m.," said Brother Gillies from the door. "Don't you hear the church bells ringing, Cam?"

"Three in the mornin'?" He groaned. "The only thing I hear is my pillow callin' me back to sleep." Cam dropped back down to the bed with his eyes closed.

"Come on, ye lazy dog." North handed the candle to Nash and pulled Cam out of the bed.

"Is this really necessary?" asked Cam with a yawn.

"It is if ye want me to give a good report to the lairds of Clan MacKeefe," the monk answered.

"Ye'd better go, Cam," Nash told him. "If no', somehow, we're all goin' to get punished for it in the end. I wouldna welcome that. I need a break from all the hard work."

"Me, too," agreed North.

"You boys have been very helpful around the monastery since you've arrived, and I thank you," said Gillies from the door. "I am going to send a missive to Lord Rook first thing in the morning and ask him if you can have a reprieve, and stay at Naward Castle for a few days."

"Och, I canna wait," said Cam, getting dressed. "This place has no whisky, and I'm sure Lord Rook has plenty of Mountain Magic. I swear the ale here is naught but weak, dirty water from the pond."

"Cam, ye are half-asleep or else ye'd realize that Brathair Gillies is no' talkin' to ye," spat North. "He means Nash and me."

"That's right," said the monk. "They've earned their reward, although I can't say the same for you, Cam. I haven't seen you do much of anything since you've been here."

"I do a lot," Cam protested.

"Riiiiiight," said North. "We saw him in the chandlery yesterday – makin' candles as he calls it. However, it looked like he was doin' a little more than that if ye ask me."

"What?" Gillies' eyes opened wide. "Cam, if I find out you are behaving improperly, especially around my sister, I promise you that my report to the Lairds MacKeefe will not be favorable at all."

Cam yawned before he answered. "I assure ye, I did nothin' to offend yer sister. Ask her yerself, if ye dinna believe me."

"Mayhap I will," said Gillies. "Now hurry up, because tonight I decided you will lead the chants as well as read the psalms from the Bible."

"Me?" Cam didn't like the sound of this at all. He wasn't a monk. Why was Brother Gillies wanting him to do this?

"Yes, you," answered Gillies. "Don't try to talk me out of it, because I won't change my mind."

"Wonderful." Cam let out a frustrated breath. "I canna wait." He reluctantly followed Gillies to the door. When he turned around to give his friends a piece of his mind for nearly telling the monk that he'd bedded Yvaine, he stopped at what he saw. Both men were diving for the bed once again. Shaking his head, he turned around and followed Brother Gillies out the door.

Since Yvaine couldn't sleep, she finally decided to get up. Her tossing and turning on the pallet was only going to wake up little Avianca, and she didn't want that.

To her dismay, Yvaine had been dreaming of making love with Cam. She would have welcomed the dream, had it not ended with Cam turning into Dun. The horror of her late husband's face staring at her with open eyes from the floor, almost caused her to scream aloud. Yvaine hadn't felt so unnerved since the night she'd killed her husband.

After dressing, she paced the floor, looking over at little Avianca's face that was lit up by the candlelight. This was Cam's daughter. Yvaine had started to care for the lass, even though she'd just met her. Avianca deserved a good home with parents who loved her and wanted her. Sadly, she wasn't sure that home should be with Cam.

Yvaine's hand went to her belly, her thoughts filled with the baby that was growing in her womb. Part of her wanted this baby more than anything. She longed to be a mother and to have a child to love as her very own. Still, another part of her knew that every time she looked at the child's face it would only remind her of her abusive husband who forced himself on her to conceive the baby in the first place.

Would she be haunted by the thoughts of the beatings she'd endured from him each time she looked at the child they'd conceived together? Even if she could push past this, what would happen when she held her baby or looked at its face? Would she be haunted by the fact it was she who took the life of the child's father? How was she ever going to explain what happened to the baby's father without lying?

The truth was something she would never be able to admit to her son or daughter. Therefore, she'd be living a lie. A lie that would only grow bigger and darker with each passing year as her baby grew.

Doubt flitted through her mind that she could even raise this child now, once it was born. Mayhap the bairn in her womb should never know her at all. She supposed she could ask her brother to find a family to take in her baby as well Cam's daughter. If so, would she end up regretting her decision some day?

It made her wonder if this was how Cam felt in regards to his daughter. Would Avianca only remind him of his tryst with a whore, not to mention his life as the bastard of a whore, having grown up in brothels? She thought he'd been acting irresponsible and selfish when he said he wanted Brother Gillies to find a home for the girl. But now . . . now she wasn't so sure he was doing the wrong thing. In a way, she understood exactly what Cam was going through, because she was having the same feelings and doubts as him.

The church bells rang out in the dark, signaling the nighttime prayer session of the monks. Feeling as if she needed to go to church to pray for guidance, Yvaine decided to attend the service. Avianca was tired, and would surely sleep until morning. She always did. The girl was a good sleeper. Leaving the candle burning so the wee lass wouldn't feel scared if she woke to find herself alone, Yvaine made sure to put the candle in a glass jar so nothing would catch on fire. Then she tucked in Avianca, giving her a kiss on the head. With a deep sigh, she turned and headed out the door to attend matins and lauds.

Yvaine was a few minutes late arriving at the church, and the prayer session had already started. Once she got settled, she realized Cam was there, too. He was sitting up front, which she thought was odd. The Highlander hated being here and always hid way in back whenever he actually attended the prayer sessions at all.

She was about to move and join him up front, when Cam stood up, and surprised her by walking up to the pulpit. What was he doing? Then he opened a Bible that Gillies handed him, and started to read psalms to the rest of the monks. She almost laughed aloud. As if that wasn't shocking enough, after the psalms, Cam started to chant. He clearly had no idea of how to do it, and it sounded more like groans, as if he had a stomachache. Cam was surely in misery, either way. In her opinion, it was the furthest thing from leading the monks in something that was highly spiritual.

After the session ended, Yvaine met Cam as he all but high-tailed it to the door, no doubt wanting to escape.

"Cam?" she called out, causing him to stop in his tracks and turn around.

"Yvaine?" His mouth fell open in surprise. "God's teeth, please dinna tell me ye just heard all that." His eyes darted to the pulpit and then back to her.

"Please refrain from using the Lord's name in vain, especially in church," scoffed Gillies, joining them with anger painting his face.

"Let us go outside to speak," whispered Yvaine, taking Cam's arm as they exited the church.

"I'm sorry ye had to witness that, but yer brathair forced me to do it." Cam sighed deeply and shook his head as if disgusted by his own actions. "He said if I didna, he was goin' to give a bad report about me to the lairds of my clan. I am so embarrassed, lassie."

"Nay, dinna be," she said, trying not to laugh by what had just happened. "I thought it was very . . . interestin'." She couldn't look at him with a straight face, so she focused elsewhere as they headed through the cloistered walkways. Thankfully, it was dark so he hopefully wouldn't see her face. "Actually, I was surprised to see ye awake at this time."

"Believe me, I wouldna have been if yer brathair hadna come to my door and my friends hadna dragged me out of bed."

She couldn't help but giggle, finding this all so amusing.

"Why are ye up at this ungodly hour?" he asked, curiously.

"I couldna sleep."

"Och, I hope Avianca didna keep ye awake."

"Nay. She is sleepin' like a bairn. I just had some bad dreams, that's all."

"About yer late husband?" he asked, almost causing Yvaine to gasp. How did he know?

"Mayhap," she said, holding on to his arm, but looking at the ground. "I – I dinna remember, exactly."

"It's all right to admit it, Yvaine. I understand completely."

"Y-ye do?" She started wondering if, somehow, he possibly knew the truth. Then again, how could he? She hadn't even told Gillies.

"It must have been horrible to watch yer husband die right there at yer feet."

"Ye have no idea." A shiver wracked her body, and Cam noticed.

"What's wrong, Yvaine? Ye're shakin'."

"I'm fine." She forced a smile. "I suppose it's just a chill from the night air, that's all."

"Then come closer, and I'll warm ye." He tried to put his arm around her, but her mind was confused. She didn't know right now if she wanted him close to her or if she should push him away.

"Nay," she said, deciding on the latter. Dropping her hold on his arm, she stepped away, looking around the courtyard. "I suppose it wouldna be guid if anyone saw us together. I dinna want my brathair to give a bad report about ye to yer lairds."

"I guess ye're right," he answered with a frown. "But at least let me walk ye back up to yer room."

"Nay." She shook her head, wanting to get far away from him right now. If she didn't, it would be too tempting to kiss him again, or to possibly do even more with him than just that. "I'll be fine."

"Yvaine, is somethin' the matter? If so, ye can talk to me about it. Ye can tell me anythin' at all. I've shared my secret with ye, and if anythin' is on yer mind, ye can do the same with me. I mean, after all, we are lovers now."

They may be lovers, but she couldn't share her thoughts. She still had secrets she hadn't shared with him, and was also feeling like she may have made a mistake by making love with Cam in the first place. She had only wanted the chance to feel elation – to experience what others did while coupling. Perhaps she'd been selfish. Yvaine longed to be happy. Cam made her feel that way, but now she felt guilty. She decided she didn't deserve to be happy. Not after what she had done. Nay, she didn't deserve someone as wonderful as Cam at all.

"I dinna think we should have made love, and we'd better no' do it again," she blurted out, saying the words even though she wasn't sure it was what she really felt in her heart.

"What?" He stepped out from the cloistered area into the moonlight. A soft glow bathed his handsome face. Her heart ached for him, but this was how it had to be. "I dinna understand, Yvaine. I thought ye wanted to make love with me."

"I might have wanted it, but now I realize I was wrong."

"How can ye say that when ye ken it isna the truth?"

"Are ye callin' me a liar?" She asked the question, if only to keep him from saying more about the situation.

"Why dinna ye tell me the real reason why ye suddenly changed yer mind? After all, ye begged me to bed ye, so I dinna believe ye are regrettin' it now."

Feeling shaken, and not wanting to have to answer, Yvaine did the only thing she could to stop the conversation. She slapped him across the face. "Stop makin' me sound like a whore, because I am no' one of yer usual trollops," she told him.

Cam's hand went to his cheek and his gaze interlocked with hers. The hurt in his eyes almost made her cry.

"I'm sorry, Yvaine. The last thing I ever wanted was to make ye feel like a whore," he said in a mere whisper.

Yvaine felt horrible now. "I ken," she answered, already regretting the slap.

"I also find it odd that ye, a woman who has been abused by her late husband, would dare strike out at me with a slap. This is the second time ye've done so."

He was right, and it shook her to the core. Was she no better than someone as horrible as Dun? "I – I'm sorry," she apologized, her lip trembling as she held back her tears. Her action frightened her, and she started to wonder just what she'd become. "I didna mean to do that. Honest, I didna want to hurt ye." She turned and ran back to her room, not stopping until she had closed the door behind her. With her head against the wood, she cried.

Cam had been nothing but nice to her, but she stuck out at him without giving him an explanation. What in the devil's name was the matter with her? She wasn't only a murderer now, but was turning into an abusive woman. How her life was taking a nasty turn.

Yvaine never meant to hurt Cam, but only wanted to stop him from finding out her secrets. Now, she could see how wrong she'd been. Had her heart really turned this cold, or was she only trying to douse the fires of passion within for this Highland warrior?

"Why are ye cryin'?" came Avianca's small voice as she appeared next to Yvaine, reaching out and taking her by the hand. "Did somethin' make ye sad?"

Yvaine dried her tears, taking the girl to her bosom in a hug. "I will be fine, Avianca," she told her. "I just had a little spat with yer faither, but now I wish I hadna."

"Please dinna fight with my da," said the girl. "He loves ye."

Yvaine's heart about stopped beating when she heard the little girl's words. She kneeled down next to her, looking her in the eyes. "Why would ye say such a thing?"

"I see the way he looks at ye. It is no' the same way he used to look at my mathair."

"Y-ye saw Cam with yer mathair?" Yvaine's heart felt wounded. No child should have to witness something like that.

"I saw him once with my mathair, but he didna look at her the same way as he does ye." Such wisdom from such a young child felt mystical, and yet frightening at the same time.

"What . . . what were they doin'? When ye saw them?" she asked, holding her breath as she waited for the answer. God, she hoped she wouldn't have to explain coupling to the child. Not here, not now.

"My da was at the tavern where my mathair worked."

"In her . . . bedroom?" Yvaine bit her bottom lip so hard she thought it would bleed.

"Nay," answered Avianca, looking at her curiously. "What would he be doin' in there?"

"Oh . . . I – I'm no' sure," she answered.

"They were in the kitchen. Cam was tryin' to get some food. My mathair didna want to share it. He was no' happy. No' like he smiles when he is around ye."

Yvaine laughed aloud, pulling the girl to her and kissing her atop the head. Thank the heavens, this wasn't as bad as she thought.

"Well, men do like to eat, and I am sure Cam is no different," she told the girl. Relief filled Yvaine that Avianca hadn't seen her mother and Cam coupling, after all. The child might have grown up in a brothel, but the lass was young, innocent, and still naïve. Yvaine hoped Avianca would stay that way for a long time to come.

# CHAPTER FOURTEEN

YVAINE HAD MANAGED to stay away from Cam all day yesterday, finding excuses not to have him at her side. Thankfully, since North and Nash had gone to spend a few days at Naward Castle with Lord Rook, Gillies had been making Cam do all the chores by himself. That alone, kept him very busy.

She'd even taken some time off from making candles to watch the monks illuminate manuscripts. Honestly, she didn't have the slightest interest in that at all, but it gave her an excuse to sit in the dark and have time to think. Not to mention, it put her safely far away from Cam. Sister Edna had been tending to Avianca lately, but in Cam's free time, the little girl wanted to be with him. Thankfully, by the time night fell, Cam had been so tired that he'd gone straight to bed, and Yvaine was by herself again.

This morning Yvaine spent time making candles in the chandlery. Yesterday, Gillies had told her that he was able to secure an order from the nobles. It came from Naward Castle, but at least it was a start. This work kept her mind off her troubles and, for that, she was glad.

The door to the chandlery opened, and as she suspected, it was Cam who came to see her.

"Good mornin'," she said, dipping the wicks, keeping focused on her work.

"Yvaine." Cam stepped into the room and closed the door

behind him. "It seems ye have been avoidin' me, and I dinna ken why."

"Have I?" She glanced over to him, and then hung the candles on the drying rack. Picking up another board with wicks, she took the next batch over to the hot wax. "After this candle order is finished, I hope to start makin' soap as well. Ye've been busy and so have I. That's all there is to it."

"No' too busy to spend a few minutes together at a meal, or even see each other at one of the prayer sessions."

"I have an important order to fill, and dinna have time for nonsense."

"Nonsense?" He made his way over to her, taking the board with the dipped candles from her, hanging it on the drying rack. "Since when is spendin' time together considered nonsense? Is that what ye really think?" After hanging up the candles, he turned around and reached out to cup her cheek.

Yvaine's eyes closed and her head tilted back. It felt so good to have him touch her again. She'd missed it, and wanted it more than anything. Then she felt his lips upon hers. For a mere moment, she accepted it. But it didn't last long when thoughts of Dun once again filled her head. Her eyes popped open and she broke the kiss, quickly turning away.

"What is the matter, Yvaine?" he asked, hurt resounding in his voice. "If I did somethin' to offend ye, then please tell me what it was."

"Nay. Ye did nothin'," she said, picking up a trimming knife, starting to cut the hardened drippings of wax off the bottom of the candles. "I'm sorry. I just canna kiss ye."

"That wasna how ye felt when ye all but begged me to make love to ye. What changed?"

Yvaine bit the inside of her cheek to keep from crying. How could she tell him that she'd been acting selfish, and that if he found out all the truths about her, he wouldn't want to ever touch or kiss her again. It was a heart-wrenching thought but, deep down, she knew it was true. If he was aware of the rest of her secrets, he would never want her in his life. That thought alone terrified her. She'd started having feelings for Cam. More than anything, she wanted him in her life. Or what was left of her life, anyway.

"I – I think I made a mistake, Cam. We never should have coupled."

"Coupled?" He looked at her in confusion. "Is that what ye're callin' it now? Was that all it was to ye, lass? Because to me, it was different than all the other lassies I've ever bedded."

"How so?" she asked. "After all, ye made a point to tell me ye were only doin' it in lust."

"That's what I thought, at first. This time – with ye – it felt special. I dinna ken why, but it felt right, for the first time in my life. I have started to have feelin's for ye, lass. Please dinna push me away."

"Everythin' is movin' too fast," she said, taking a deep breath and releasing it. "My life has changed in ways ye canna even imagine. It is so overwhelmin' that it makes my head spin. I need to slow down."

He nodded silently. "I understand. It's my fault," he said, taking a step away from her. "Ye've been through so much lately, and I had no right to push ye into . . . into what we did."

Her heart about broke to hear him say that. He thought he had done something wrong. "Nay, Cam, it is no' yer fault," she tried to convince him. "Ye are right that I wanted it as much as ye. I should have told ye –" She stopped in midsentence, not able to continue. She saw how much Cam truly admired her, and part of her didn't ever want that to change.

"Ye should have told me what?" asked Cam, waiting for her to continue.

Yvaine bit her lip and shook her head. She quickly looked in the other direction so she wouldn't have to look into his eyes. He came up behind her and gently laid his hand on her shoulder. Even when he was angry with her, his touch was soft and caring.

"It's all right," he said in a mere whisper. "Take yer time,

Yvaine. I didna mean to rush ye. I understand that ye need the proper time to mourn. Now, please, let me help ye with the candle order."

"Nay, that willna be necessary." She closed her eyes and shook her head, trying to ward off the feelings she held in her heart for this wonderful man.

His hands snaked around her waist, causing a shiver of delight to surge through her. She couldn't have this. It felt too good! Once again, the thought invaded her mind that she didn't deserve happiness – the happiness that she now knew Cam could give her.

"Please, dinna push me away, lass," he whispered in her ear, trying once again to convince her, although he said he'd wait. He nuzzled the back of her neck with his mouth. Damn, this felt good and she wanted his touches and caresses more than anything right now. But she couldn't. She almost gave in but, thankfully, the door opened, and Cam quickly stepped away from her.

"Sister," said Gillies, looking at them oddly. "Why are your cheeks flushed? Are you not feeling well?"

"I'm just hot from the wax, that's all," she told her brother, wiping her hands on her work apron. "What is it ye wanted?"

"I came to tell you that you have visitors. Actually, I was looking for you as well, Cam."

"Me?" Cam had the look on his face like he wanted to hide away rather than to do whatever it was the monk was going to ask him to carry out.

"Visitors?" Yvaine hurried over to the door. "Who even kens I'm here?"

"It's Cam's friend, Gavin, and his new wife," said Gillies.

"Gavin is here?" Cam hurried to the door and looked out. "I wonder if somethin' is wrong. He shouldna be here."

"Davita is here as well?" asked Yvaine. "I wonder why she would risk takin' the trip over the border."

"Ye ken Davita?" Cam asked her.

"Of course, I do," she answered. "Davita is my friend from the village."

"Och, aye, that's right. I should have remembered." Cam swiped his hand through the air. "I'm sure cordwainers and chandlers have a lot in common."

Cam guided Yvaine down to the courtyard where they met his good friend, Gavin. Davita was at his side.

"Gavin. What a surprise," said Cam. "What the hell are ye doin' here? I thought ye'd be back in the Highlands by now."

Brother Gillies cleared his throat in a subtle reminder that Cam was cursing inside the holy walls once again.

"Cam," said Gavin, shaking his hand and giving him a hearty slap on the back. "I highly expected to see North and Nash here, beggin' me to take them back to Hermitage with me. Where are they?" He scanned the courtyard for his friends.

"They're no' here right now. They are havin' a respite at Naward Castle while I slave away doing the chores for three in their absence," grumbled Cam.

"They earned a break, you didn't," Brother Gillies reminded him.

"Davita? Why are ye here?" asked Yvaine, rushing over to hug her friend.

"Yvaine, I had to come. I felt so bad for ye, with losin' yer husband and all," said Davita.

"That's right, she did feel a need to be with ye," explained Gavin. "We may be newly married, but Davita wouldna let me rest until I brought her to ye."

"I still dinna understand," said Yvaine. "Why would ye risk the trip here just to be with me?"

"I figured ye might need a friend right now." Davita put her hand on Yvaine's arm. "Was I wrong?"

Tears filled Yvaine's eyes but she quickly blinked them away. A friend was exactly what she needed at the moment. She felt honored and thankful that Davita would come all this way to be with her instead of spending her precious time alone with her new husband.

"I suppose it would be nice to have the company of another woman – besides Sister Edna that is," said Yvaine with a smile.

"Where's the girl?" Gavin asked Cam. "Did ye already find a family to take her?"

Yvaine's eyes darted over to Cam as she waited for his answer. She wasn't at all sure if he meant to keep or get rid of poor little Avianca. It seemed his decision wavered back and forth each day.

"Nay, she is still here," Cam informed him. "Right now, Avianca is with Sister Edna. I was about to collect her to have a bite to eat together. The wee lass has taken a likin' to me for some reason, and wants to spend time at my side."

Gavin chuckled. "Well, mayhap it's because ye are her faither. Now, where is this food ye speak of? I worked up an appetite on the trip here."

The men headed away, leaving Yvaine standing alone with Davita.

"I still canna believe ye and Gavin traveled here by yerselves to see me." Yvaine walked slowly with Davita as they headed over to the infirmary for the morning meal.

Davita smiled. "I have to admit, we were assisted. Gavin wanted to travel alone, but after the latest happenin' with the English when ye came here, I begged him to ask for an escort. Some of the MacKeefes rode along with us, but turned around and headed back to Hermitage Castle as we approached the priory. Dinna let Gavin ken that I told ye. He doesna want to look weak in front of his friends."

"Well, what do ye expect from men?" asked Yvaine, and both of the women giggled.

"What about ye?" asked Davita. "Are ye tryin' to look strong by no' tellin' them everythin'?"

Yvaine stopped walking. "What do ye mean?"

"Yvaine, I must admit that the real reason I am here is because I ken yer secret."

Yvaine's body froze and she could barely speak. "What secret?"

"Dinna play the dolt with me," Davita scolded.

"Wh-who told ye?"

"My little brathair, Archy, filled me in. He works for yer brathair, Keithen, takin' care of the henhouse. He overheard Keithen speakin' about yer secret to one of the whores in the tavern."

"God's eyes, nay," whispered Yvaine, putting her hand to her mouth. If her secret was out, then she would be arrested and probably hanged for her crime. Her body started to shake.

"Ye look so frightened, but ye needna be," Davita assured her, taking Yvaine's hand in hers. "I am here to help ye get through it. Have ye told yer brathair, Gillies, or Cam and his friends about it yet?"

"Nay! Oh, please tell me that ye havena told anyone."

Davita's expression revealed to Yvaine that the woman thought she was being silly. "Just Gavin, but he willna say a word. It is yer secret to tell."

"This is awful," said Yvaine, feeling like she was going to faint. "It's the worst thing that could have ever happened to me. My life is over. I didna want anyone to ever ken about it."

"Yvaine, really! I think ye're overreactin'. This is a time for celebration, but ye dinna seem very happy at all."

"I dinna think Dun would agree with ye about me celebratin'," she mumbled, feeling sick to her stomach now.

"Aye. It's a shame that Dun willna ever get to see his bairn. Still, ye need to carry on without him now. I ken it is hard, but I am here to help ye cope."

"M-my bairn?" Yvaine blinked twice in surprise and her hand went to her belly. "Ye are talkin' about me being pregnant."

Davita giggled. "Of course I am. What did ye think I meant?"

Relief washed through her, but Yvaine still needed to know how much Davita's brother overheard from Keithen. "Did Archy hear Keithen say anythin' else? About me?" She looked cautiously at Davita from the corners of her eyes.

"Just that ye were bairned," said Davita. "Why? Do ye have another deep, dark secret ye're hidin' from everyone?" Davita said it in a playful manner, making Yvaine realize that her secret of killing Dun was still safe after all.

Yvaine laughed, too. "I suppose I was just shaken, and didna want anyone to ken about me bein' bairned until I was sure I wouldna lose the baby."

"How far along are ye?"

"No' quite four months now."

"Well, I'm sure once Cam finds out, he'll stop sniffin' after ye like ye were a dog in heat."

"What do ye mean?"

"Gavin told me how Cam only wants one thing from women, and it is no' marriage, that's for sure."

"Of course," she said, feeling sad about the entire situation. She had felt that Cam really cared for her, but perhaps it was all just a story to get her into bed, after all. Mayhap she'd been more of a fool than she'd thought.

"When are ye goin' to tell him?"

"I – I'm no' sure."

They continued to walk to the infirmary. "Well, what are ye waitin' for? Ye are goin' to start showin' soon. Ye canna really think ye can keep this a secret much longer."

"I suppose no'."

"Ye probably should let the others ken as well."

"I will. Eventually," said Yvaine, feeling now as if she should have told Cam before they ever got intimate together that she was carrying a baby. He wasn't going to be happy that she kept this important information from him. Then again, she was sure his reaction to the news would be a lot less severe than if he ever found out her other deep and dark secret.

"So, how are things goin' for ye here at the priory?" Gavin asked as he and Cam headed into the infirmary. "Tired of it yet?"

"I was tired of it before I even got here," said Cam. "I dinna like all the prayer sessions, the unbearable silence, and also all the hard work. However, I am gettin' to ken Yvaine, and I think I am startin' to have feelin's for the lass. Although, I am no' sure she returns those feelin's for me."

"How well are ye gettin' to ken her?" asked Gavin with a lifted brow.

"We've made love, if that's what ye're askin'."

"Blethers, Cam, I canna believe ye." Gavin chuckled and shook his head.

"What do ye mean?"

"I canna believe ye'd go to bed with someone like her."

"She might be a new widow but, honestly, I think I am startin' to fall in love with her. This has never happened to me before."

"Really." Gavin looked at him like Cam had two heads.

"Why are ye givin' me that look?"

"I just find it amusin' that the first lass ye ever start to fall for is a bairned one."

"Bairned?" This took Cam by surprise that his good friend should say this. "Nay, Gavin, ye're wrong. She's no' pregnant. I mean, I dinna think so. We just made love, and it is too soon to even ken for sure what our union might have brought about. Why would ye even say that?"

"I'm no' talkin' about ye, ye fool. I'm talkin' about Yvaine bein' pregnant with her late husband's bairn."

"Oh?" Cam's heart raced. "Why do ye say such things?"

"I dinna say anythin' that isna true."

"How do ye ken this?"

"Davita told me. Her little brathair overheard Yvaine's brathair and one of the tavern whores talkin' about it. It's the whole reason why Davita wanted to be here for Yvaine. She thought a pregnant widow in a priory would need a friend. Or at least need another woman who isna a nun to talk to about her condition."

"Bid the devil," whispered Cam, staring off into space. "I suspected she might be pregnant at first, but she denied it."

"She did? Are ye sure? Why would she do such a thing?"

The more Cam thought about it, the more he realized she hadn't denied it, just never gave him an answer. It was just like her little secret of not really becoming a nun.

Everything started to make sense now to Cam. This was the reason she had been pushing him away lately. She must have felt guilty for making love when she was pregnant with another man's child. A man who she'd yet to get over mourning for.

"Och, she didna tell ye?" asked Gavin.

"Nay. She must have forgotten that bit of information before she lured me to her bed."

"Lured ye?" Gavin chuckled again. "Come, now, Cam. Ye are the one who always does the lurin' where the lassies are concerned."

"No' in this case. I might have lusted after her, but couplin' was her idea. Mostly, anyway."

"Why would she do that? I mean, before tellin' ye about her condition?" asked Gavin.

Cam looked over to see Yvaine and Davita enter the infirmary along with a line of monks.

"I dinna ken her reason, but I intend to find out. Dinna tell her or Davita that I have knowledge that she is bairned."

"Whatever ye want," said Gavin with a shrug.

"Excuse me," said Cam. "I see Sister Edna and Avianca. I will bring the girl over." Cam ignored Yvaine, walking right past her as he approached and lifted up his daughter. If Yvaine wanted to play silly games with him by keeping secrets after he'd been so open about his life to her, then mayhap he should play a few games of his own.

"CAM, SHOULD WE all sit together for the meal?" asked Yvaine, but

Cam didn't answer. Instead, he purposely ignored her.

"Come, Avianca, let me get ye some food," Cam spoke to the little girl in his arms before walking away.

Yvaine's heart lodged in her throat. Cam had snubbed her, and it wasn't because he didn't see or hear her standing right there.

"Why did he do that?" Yvaine asked Davita.

"I dinna ken," answered Davita. "Men often act in odd ways that are just too hard to decipher. I wouldna worry about it. Shall we get some food?"

"Aye," said Yvaine, heading to a table where Gavin was waving them down. She sat next to Davita, right across from Cam who had yet to even look at her.

"Why dinna the monks talk?" Avianca asked her father.

"It's silly, I agree," said Cam, taking a bowl of food from a monk, laying it in front of his daughter. "It is because they have taken a vow no' to speak, and so they remain quiet. However, no' everyone at Lanercost Priory has taken vows of silence, even if they act like it." He accepted another bowl of food for himself and looked over at Yvaine when he spoke, making no secret that he meant her.

Yvaine accepted her food, and then leaned over to whisper to Davita. "I think he kens. Gavin must have told him."

"If ye have somethin' to say, please speak loud enough so we can all hear," said Cam. "Unless, ye purposely dinna want me to ken things."

"Nay, it's no' like that, Cam," she tried to explain, but his anger was up and he didn't want to listen.

"Shhh," he told her, giving her a nasty glare. "Canna ye see that Brathair Gillies is about to say prayers over the food?"

"Can I talk with ye?" she whispered across the table. "Later?"

"I dinna ken if I'll have time," he whispered back. "After all, just like ye said, we are both too busy for nonsense."

"Please, no talkin' at the meal," Brother Gillies called out, stopping their conversation.

Yvaine ate in silence, watching how Cam helped to cut up Avianca's food. He also poured a drink for her, and put his arm around her when she wiggled so much that she almost fell off the bench. She'd changed her mind about him now. He'd make a good father someday, she was sure.

Her hand went to her belly hidden under the table, and she wondered what kind of mother she'd be. Dun would have been a horrible father, and would have probably spanked their child or hurt it in the end. But what about her? Would she be a terrible mother, too? Davita told her she should be happy to be pregnant, but with everything going on in her life, it only scared her instead. If she had her choice, she'd rather be pregnant with Cam's child than with Dun's.

Her eyes fell upon Avianca again, and her heart swelled. The little girl was so sweet. What if she had a daughter just like her? Could Yvaine leave her past behind her and start a new life again? Or was bringing a child into her tangled life the worst idea of all right now?

⇥⇥⇥⫻⇤⇤⇤

"WHAT DO YE mean ye are all goin' to Naward Castle but I have to stay here?" Cam asked Gavin later that day.

"Brathair Gillies asked if I'd escort Yvaine to the castle with the candle order tomorrow," said Gavin.

"I'll take her there," Cam offered, eager to get away from his surroundings.

"Nay, you have to stay here at the monastery," said Gillies, walking up with Yvaine and Davita. Little Avianca skipped along, following them. He and Yvaine hadn't spoken at the meal and didn't even see each other for most of the day.

"My friends are already there," said Cam. "Surely, a short trip to the castle to deliver a candle order isna against the rules. After all, the castle is so close, I can see it from here." Cam pointed to

Naward Castle that could be seen in the distance.

"I'm sorry," said the monk. "I have my orders."

"I want to go to the castle, too," said Avianca. "Can I go? Can I, can I?"

"I dinna see why no'," said Yvaine. "Gillies, will it be all right for her to come with us? Davita will be along to help watch over her."

"I suppose so," said the monk, speaking to Cam next before he could object again to not going with them. "Cam, you will help the lay brothers scrub the floors in the church. Afterwards, there are peas to be shucked and fences to be mended. I will write down everything on a list. In the morning, you'll be expected to muck out the stables as well."

"Mayhap some of these chores can wait until Nash and North return," Cam suggested, but the monk wouldn't hear of it.

"Nay. These are things that need to be done right away."

"It figures," mumbled Cam, not liking the sound of this at all. "My friends willna ever want to come back now. No' when they are drinkin' Mountain Magic and dancin' with all the bonnie lassies." Cam started feeling sorry for himself.

"If ye didna have a sentence to serve, ye'd be comin' with us," Yvaine reminded him. He wasn't sure if she said it to hurt him or not, but her words rubbed him the wrong way. He probably should have kept his mouth shut, but he couldn't remain silent after a comment like that.

"Hell, if I didna have a damned sentence to serve in the first place, I'd never be in this godforsaken place at all."

He didn't need to look over to Brother Gillies to know the monk was shooting daggers at him from his eyes right now.

# Chapter Fifteen

"I THINK THAT'S it," Yvaine told Avianca, closing the last box of the candle order the next morning. Avianca had been helping her – actually slowing her down and breaking candles, but still, Yvaine didn't complain. She enjoyed spending time with the little girl. It made her wonder what it would be like when she had a child of her own. Mayhap it wouldn't be as frightening as she thought earlier. She supposed she had been jumping to conclusions, and having her own child wouldn't remind her of Dun that much, after all. Or, at least she hoped not.

"So, we're goin' to the castle like Cam's friends?" asked Avianca.

"Aye. We'll only be gone for a day, but will be back on the morrow."

"Yay!" shouted the little girl with excitement.

The door to the room burst open and Cam stood there, dirty from head to toe. His breathing was labored, as if he'd run up the stairs.

"Cam?" Yvaine looked at him and laughed. "What have ye been doin' to get so dirty?"

"Cam!" cried Avianca, running to him, but he held out his hands to stop her from hugging him.

"Dinna touch me, Avianca. I am covered with horse dung."

"Eew," said the little girl, wrinkling her nose. "Ye stink."

"She's right," said Yvaine, waving her hand in front of her

nose. "Ye'd better stay in the doorway, Cam. I canna risk my candle order smellin' like . . . like that."

"I was muckin' out the stables like yer brathair insisted, so what do ye expect?" A muscle ticked in his jaw. "One of the horses decided it didna like me and I ended up in a pile of sh–"

"We get the idea," said Yvaine, stopping him from swearing in front of his daughter. "Did ye want somethin'?" Yvaine busied herself with the boxes.

"Aye. I want to ken why ye have been avoidin' me."

"Me?" That statement surprised Yvaine, since Cam had been going out of his way to steer clear of her all day yesterday. "It seems as if ye are the one avoidin' me instead."

"Cam, I canna wait to go to the castle with Yvaine," said Avianca.

"Call me Da," he told her, managing to surprise Yvaine yet again. "Avianca, ye arena goin' anywhere."

"Yes, she is," said Yvaine. "Avianca is comin' with us. Dinna worry, we will be back tomorrow mornin'."

"So, it seems everyone is goin' to Naward Castle but me," complained Cam.

"I'm sorry, but ye are no' allowed to come."

"Da, I want to go with her," said Avianca excitedly.

"Nay," he said again, causing the little girl to frown.

"Why no'?" asked Yvaine.

"Because I said so."


CAM DIDN'T LIKE the fact that Yvaine was planning on taking his child with her. He felt left out, and it only made him despise his punishment even more. Mayhap having his daughter here with him would make him feel better and not so alone. Avianca seemed to like being with him, and he was getting used to the idea of having a daughter. He wanted to get to know her better. This would be the perfect chance to do so, without all the others around.

"I dinna think ye're bein' fair to the lass," Yvaine told him.

"I dinna think ye were bein' fair to me, by no' tellin' me ye are bairned."

Her head snapped up and her eyes popped open wide. "Avianca, sweetheart, can ye wait down in the courtyard for us?" asked Yvaine.

"All right," said the little girl, leaving the room.

Once she was gone, Yvaine continued.

"I'm sorry, I didna tell ye, Cam. I had planned on doin' it, but ye've been avoidin' me. I didna have the chance."

"Didna have the chance?" He shook his head in disgust. "Ye should have told me before we ever got intimate."

"I ken, ye're right." She truly did look sorry, but he didn't care. He wanted her to know how badly it hurt him and that it wasn't all right to keep secrets from him. Not when he'd already opened up and told her his.

"Why didna ye think to mention it before?"

"I – I suppose I was scared."

"Of what?" he asked, entering the room, dragging dirt all over the floor. "Was it me ye were afraid of? I dinna understand. Lass, what have I ever done to hurt ye?"

"Nothin'," she replied. "Ye have been ever so kind to me. I was wrong in no' tellin' ye about it. It's just that . . . I mean . . . I have been havin' thoughts lately, wonderin' if I even want to keep my baby. I've been very confused."

"What?" That took Cam by surprise. "Do ye mean ye'd consider givin' up yer baby?"

"I – I dinna ken, Cam. Ye see, I am no' sure that I willna always think of my abusive husband every time I look at the face of my child."

"Oh. I see," he said, starting to understand her now. "Even so, Yvaine, it's no' right. It isna the bairn's fault. Ye canna give away yer child. What is the matter with ye?"

"Me?" she asked, becoming defensive. "Isna that exactly what ye're doin' with Avianca? Givin' her up to another family, rather than to raise her yerself?"

"That's different," he said, shaking his head.

"Is it really?"

"Aye, it is. My child had a mathair that was a whore."

"Just like ye did," said Yvaine, raising her chin. "So, are ye afraid she's goin' to turn out like ye? Is that what puts doubt in yer head?"

"Nay. I mean . . . mayhap. A little, I suppose. Yvaine, I am a man who isna married. I'm a warrior, for God's sake. I still dinna ken if I'd ever really make a guid faither to any child – especially Avianca."

"Avianca has no one else, Cam. I dinna even see how ye could have ever considered no' takin' her to live with ye."

"Yer bairn-to-be doesna have anyone else either."

Her eyes interlocked with his, and neither of them knew what to say. They'd each made their point, and met their match. Finally, Cam broke the infernal silence.

"I havena told anyone yet, but I've decided to keep Avianca."

"Really?" Her features softened. "That's wonderful."

"I have grown very fond of her lately. Even though it will be hard, I plan on bein' the faither to her that she deserves. I decided I need to take responsibility for my actions. I canna let her go to another family, because if I do, someday I will regret it."

"Oh, Cam, that's the right decision!" She ran over to him, attempting to give him a hug, but he stopped her.

"Ye really dinna want to touch me right now, I assure ye."

"Ye're right," she said with a smile. "I am truly impressed by yer decision, and ken ye are doin' the right thing. Avianca will be so happy when she finds out. I ken how hard this is for someone like ye, bein' a Highland warrior and all. Especially, since ye arena married."

Cam felt nervous by what he was about to say, but knew it needed to be done. "Yvaine, I must admit that I had planned to ask ye to be the mathair of my daughter. However, I am no' sure that ye would want to do it. No' now that ye arena even sure ye want to keep the bairn in yer womb."

"Y-ye want me? To be Avianca's mathair?" she asked. "Cam, does this mean ye are askin' me to marry ye?"

"I – I guess so," he said, scratching the back of his neck and looking the other way.

Her smile dissipated. "Why do ye look in the opposite direction, and make it sound as if ye're no' sure about it, after all. That isna much of a proposal."

"I suppose no', but ye need to realize that things have changed."

"Things? What things?"

"I was sure it is what I wanted. Now I am havin' my doubts, since I heard from Gavin that ye are bairned and ye never told me."

"I said I was sorry."

"Yvaine, I poured my heart and soul out to ye, tellin' ye my secrets. Still, ye kept somethin' so important as this from me. Dinna ye realize how much that hurt me? It makes me wonder now if I can ever trust ye again."

"I see." Now it was her turn to look the other way. "For yer information, I think I want to keep my baby, too, Cam."

"Think?"

She turned to face him. "I ken I do," she answered. "I realize now that it was only bein' selfish of me to even consider findin' my bairn another family once it's born. I was wrong, and I admit it."

"It is a wise decision to keep it."

"I'm sorry I didna tell ye about bein' bairned, but there are a lot of things hauntin' me right now, and I'm confused."

"Hauntin' ye?" He looked at her quizzically, wondering just what she meant. "That is an odd word to use. It makes it sound like there is somethin' else ye arena tellin' me. Is there?"

It took a moment before she answered and, honestly, he didn't think she would. "Aye," she said in a soft whisper. "There is somethin' else, Cam."

"Well? What is it?" he asked, giving her every opportunity to tell him.

"Before I answer, I want ye to ken that I would love to be yer wife."

"Ye would?" Mixed emotions ran through him. Cam felt elated, but cautious and confused. Hell, he wasn't sure how to feel right now. He needed to hear more.

"Aye. I think we could give Avianca as well as my bairn a guid home together." She put her hand on her belly as she spoke, taking a step closer to him. "However, I canna marry ye without first bein' totally honest with ye. I dinna want to start our marriage when I still have a secret I've kept from ye. From just about everyone, really."

"Go on," he said, coaxing her, needing to know exactly what she meant.

"Cam, I'm afraid once ye hear what I have to say, ye'll no longer want me as yer wife. Ye may no' even want to admit that ye ken me at all."

"What does that mean? Of course, I will," he said. Her words made him wonder what else the woman could possibly be keeping from him. "Yvaine, no matter what it is, ye can tell me. Please. Dinna be afraid."

"I am afraid," she whispered, looking at the ground. Her body trembled. "I'm scared of no' only what will happen to me, but also that ye'll despise me if ye ken the truth of what I've done."

"Nay, lass. I could never despise ye. Ye are sweet and carin' and it touches me deeply the way ye've taken care of my daughter. Ye have nothin' but love in yer heart."

"I'm glad ye think so, but I'm afraid that is far from the truth."

"Please, Yvaine. Tell me what it is that's troublin' ye so much that it makes yer body quake."

"We're just about packed and ready to leave," said Gavin, appearing at the door at the worst moment possible. Cam was finally going to find out what was haunting Yvaine, but now she'd never do it with Gavin there, he was sure. "Brathair Gillies sent me up here to help ye carry down the last of the boxes that are goin' to Naward," Gavin continued, not even knowing he was interrupting an important conversation. "Davita is already waitin' in the wagon."

"Aye, thank ye," said Yvaine, quickly turning back to the candles that were part of the shipment. "These boxes are all goin' to Naward," said Yvaine, turning and pointing to them. Cam knew she was trying to hide the tears she was holding back. His window of opportunity had just closed. He'd been so close, but now he'd never find out what Yvaine was hiding from him.

"I'll load them at once." Gavin took the boxes, and stopped for a second to talk to Cam before leaving the room. "Egads, Cam, ye're never goin' to get Yvaine to like ye, smellin' like that. Go take a jump in the pond and wash off that wretched stench."

"Thanks for yer suggestion, but I dinna need it," said Cam. He had hoped to get back to his conversation with Yvaine, but right when Gavin left, Brother Gillies walked in, making matters worse.

"Yvaine, I have just heard something from the child that I can't believe," he said to her.

"That Cam refused to let her go to Naward Castle?" asked Yvaine.

"Nay," said the monk. "Avianca said you are having a baby."

"Oh, that." Yvaine let out a deep sigh. "Aye, it's true. I am pregnant with Dun's child," she said, turning to face her brother.

"Why didn't you or Keithen mention this to me earlier?" The monk was obviously not happy at all to hear this.

"What does it matter?" she asked him. "Are ye goin' to turn me away now that ye ken the truth?"

"I never said that." The monk fidgeted. "However, this changes everything, Yvaine. Once you start showing, I'm afraid I am going to have to ask you to leave Lanercost Priory."

"Leave?" she asked in surprise. Terror filled her eyes. "Where would I go?"

"I don't know, but I can't have a pregnant woman waddling

around the priory," snapped the monk. "It's bad enough I let you stay when you are not planning on joining the Order. There seems to be no real reason for you to be here. Perhaps you should go home. Back to Hermitage where you belong."

"Hermitage is no longer my home," she told him in a shaky voice. "Gillies, I canna believe ye'd kick out yer own sister, after everythin' I've been through."

Gavin appeared back at the door. "Yvaine, we need to leave now, or we'll risk runnin' into trouble. It'll be gettin' dark soon, and I'm no' so sure how safe we'll be travelin' after sunset."

"Go," said the monk. "We'll talk about this when you return." Brother Gillies turned and left the room.

"I'll be right there," said Yvaine, starting to leave, then stopping in the doorway, talking over her shoulder. "I'm sorry, Cam. I promise ye I will tell ye everythin' once I return."

✳✳✳✳✳

BY THE TIME the sun set, Cam felt exhausted and wanted nothing more than to go to bed. He'd finished all his chores and taken a bath in the lavitorium since Brother Gillies forbid him to jump into the pond to wash off. Thankfully, he no longer stunk like dung. Unfortunately, as much as he'd wanted special time to spend alone with his daughter, it never happened. Avianca was upset with him for not letting her go to the castle. She had stayed with Sister Edna instead of wanting to be with him at all.

This is not how he wanted things to be. Cam realized now that he'd been wrong in telling the little girl she couldn't go to Naward Castle. He was upset at the time, and never should have spoken in haste. Even if he had to be doomed to live this life of hell, his daughter didn't deserve it. She'd been through such hard times lately, losing her mother. What the wee lass needed was love and happiness – something it seemed he was failing to give her.

If he could take her to the castle right now to make up for his mistake, he would do it in an instant. That, of course, was never going to happen. Brother Gillies made sure he knew he wasn't allowed to leave. The monks watched him carefully, and expected him to show his face at the services. Now, he wondered if he should have stolen a horse from the barn and risked it all, just to make his daughter smile.

"Avianca," he called out, seeing Sister Edna heading to the upstairs tower room to put the little girl to bed. "Wait up." He ran across the courtyard, meaning to stop them.

Brother Gillies looked up from the cloistered area, hurrying over, probably to reprimand him for shouting once again.

"Didna ye want to spend time with me?" Cam asked the little girl, reaching out for her. Avianca hid behind the nun, gripping on to her skirt. It felt like a dagger to his heart. He'd never be able to undo the damage he had done.

"You seem to have scared the child," said the nun, pulling the little girl closer to her. "I think it would be best if you left her alone."

"Nay, she's no' scared of me. I'm her faither. She's fine," said Cam, reaching out for Avianca once again. This time, the little girl started crying very loudly.

"What is going on here?" growled Brother Gillies in a stern voice, looking as upset as Cam felt right now.

"The Highlander is frightening the child," said the nun. "She doesn't want him near her, and I can't blame her." She looked at Cam in disgust, making him feel even worse than he already did.

"What have you done, Cam?" asked Brother Gillies.

"Nothin'," said Cam with a shrug of his shoulders. "She's just upset that I wouldna allow her to go to the castle, but she'll get over it."

Avianca cried even louder, reminding Cam of those first few days with her. He wished more than anything that Yvaine was here right now to calm the child down. Yvaine had a magical way with the girl that he had yet to learn. Yvaine would make a good mother someday. He had no doubt about it.

"This is unacceptable," spat the monk. "First, I find out I have a pregnant woman within these holy walls, and now I have a violent, shouting Highlander and a screaming child. This has to stop immediately, and I plan on putting an end to it."

"Guid. Please do," said Cam, tired of being reprimanded by the monk. "Send me back to Hermitage Castle, and put both of us out of our misery."

"Take the girl up to bed immediately," Gillies commanded the nun. As soon as they left, he turned to Cam. "I suggest you go to bed as well. Ever since you arrived, this priory has been in utter chaos."

"Then do somethin' about it," Cam challenged him, not caring anymore if he got a bad report from Gillies, or even if he had to start his punishment all over again somewhere else. "I'll be more than glad when this is all over." He turned and headed back to the catacombs. All Cam wanted to do was sleep, and forget about Yvaine and her secrets, his crying daughter, and the monk who was out to make his life a living hell. Mayhap with some rest, things would all look better in the morning.

✦◦◇◦✦

# CHAPTER SIXTEEN

CAM AWOKE TO sunshine streaming in the vents, lighting up his face. Rolling over on the bed, he heard the church bells ringing. He highly expected Brother Gillies to be pounding on his door throughout the night, forcing him to attend each of the canonical hours since the monk had been so angry with him last night.

Oddly, no one had disturbed him, and he couldn't imagine why. He'd just finished dressing when there came a knock on his crypt room door.

"I think ye're a little late, Brathair Gillies," he said with a chuckle, pulling open the door to see Yvaine standing there with Nash and North. She wrung her hands and looked so upset, that it made him think something had happened.

"About time ye two got back," he said to his friends. "Mayhap now I can get a wee break from doin' all yer chores."

His friends weren't smiling.

"Why all the gloom this mornin'?" asked Cam, tying back his hair. "I was the one trapped here while ye three spent a guid time at the castle. I hope ye brought me back some Mountain Magic."

"Cam, somethin' is wrong," said Yvaine, still wringing her hands in worry.

"I'll say." He stretched his neck, looking at his friends. "I dinna see a bottle or flask in yer hands at all."

"Haud yer wheesht, ye fool and listen to the lass," spat North, surprising Cam since his good friend never spoke to him in such a harsh manner.

"What is it?" he asked, feeling like he needed to know. "Has Brathair Gillies given a bad report about me to our lairds? Do I need to start a new punishment somewhere else?"

"It's no' always about ye, Cam," said North. "This has to do with yer daughter."

"Avianca? What about her?" His head snapped up and he stopped jesting with them. "Where is she? God's eyes, dinna tell me she is ill. Has somethin' happened to her? Has she fallen down those steep stairs?"

"If ye'd shut yer mouth for a second, we'll tell ye," said Nash.

"I'm sorry," he said, feeling his heart racing like crazy. "Please, tell me what has happened."

"She's gone, Cam," said Yvaine, looking like she was about to cry.

"What do ye mean gone? Is she . . . dead?" He closed his eyes, not wanting to believe that the poor, young girl's life could possibly already be over.

"No' dead, ye dolt." Nash shook his head. "She's missin'."

"Och, is that all?" said Cam, letting out a breath of relief. "She's probably still upset with me, and is hidin' in the kitchen or mayhap in the orchards. We'll find her. She canna have gone far."

He started to take a step out the door, when Yvaine's hand on his arm stopped him. He looked down into worried, sad eyes.

"What is it, lass?" he asked.

"My brathair has been missin' all mornin' as well," said Yvaine.

"So that's why he didna wake me."

"Davita was able to get Sister Edna to tell her that the monk took the wee lass in the early hours of the mornin' atop his horse and rode out the gates," she continued.

"Gillies took her somewhere?" asked Cam, not understanding this at all. "Do ye think he took her to Naward Castle, after all? Mayhap he did it to stop her cryin'."

"Nay," said North. "We just came from there, and we would have seen them on the road."

"I dinna like anyone takin' my daughter from me without askin'." With his hand on the hilt of his sword, Cam ran through the catacombs and out into the courtyard with the others right on his heels. When he got out into the open he saw Brother Gillies riding back into the courtyard, but the girl wasn't with him. Gavin and Davita stood there talking with Sister Edna.

"What the hell is goin' on? Where is my daughter?" Cam ground out, meeting the others and the monk as he dismounted.

"The child kept crying loudly all night long and I couldn't calm her," said Sister Edna, seeming very upset.

"Damn it," said Cam. "I should have insisted on stayin' with her."

"Nay. I should have stayed here with her," said Yvaine. "I'm the only one who can really calm her."

"I asked Brother Gillies for help. I'm sorry, but I was awake all night and didn't know what to do," continued the nun.

"Where is Avianca now?" Cam demanded to know. "Gillies, ye were seen ridin' out of the priory with her." Cam felt panic for the child rushing through his veins.

"It's Brother Gillies to you," said the monk with a stone-like face. "Sister Edna asked for my help, and that is exactly what I did."

"Gillies, where is she?" asked Yvaine. "Please tell me that she isna harmed."

"The lass isn't harmed, and is in good hands," said Gillies.

That made Cam feel a little more at ease, but he still needed to know where the man took his daughter.

"Why isna she with ye?" asked Cam, becoming very suspicious.

"She isn't here because she now resides with her new family," stated the monk, causing a gasp from Yvaine, and a wave of silence from the rest of them.

"New family?" asked Gavin. "I dinna understand. Cam is her

faither."

"He is, but he didn't want her," said the monk. "He told me when he arrived here that I was to find a good home for the girl, and so I did."

"Nay, Brathair, ye're wrong," cried Yvaine. "Cam may have wanted that at first, but he changed his mind. He was goin' to take his daughter back with him to his clan. I'm sure he told ye that." Yvaine looked over at Cam, and he felt like hiding under a rock.

"I'm afraid, I might have forgotten to mention it to Brathair Gillies with all the prayer services and chores I had to do," Cam said in a low voice feeling like this was all his fault.

"Egads, Cam, how could ye?" asked Nash.

"Now ye've lost yer daughter for guid, and it's no one's fault but yer own," added North.

"Damn it, Monk, why did ye take her without sayin' somethin' to me first?" Cam's hand itched and the warrior blood within him wanted a fight. If Gillies hadn't been a monk, Cam would have stuck his blade through the man's heart for what he'd just done.

Gillies fought Cam with his words, just as sharp as any blade. "Excuse me, but if I remember correctly, you were the one who told me last night to do something about the girl's crying."

"I never meant for ye to take her away, and ye ken it," Cam shouted.

"Well, how was I to know that?" said the monk in a huff. He looked over to the nun. "Sister Edna was here. She will vouch for me that you told me to put you out of your misery."

"He did say that," agreed the nun with a nod.

"Cam? How could ye?" gasped Yvaine, looking at him in horror, as if she thought he was some sort of monster.

"Nay, it wasna like that. I was talkin' about him sendin' me back to Hermitage, no' about him takin' away my daughter."

"You also said you couldn't wait for this all to be over. Isn't that right, Sister Edna?" asked Gillies.

The nun looked as if she felt uncomfortable. She wrung her hands now much in the same manner that Yvaine had done earlier.

"Sister Edna?" Gillies asked again, coaxing her to answer.

"Aye, Brathair Gillies, he did say that." Her voice was soft and she stared at the ground. "Now, may I be excused?" she asked. "I need to tend to the sisters."

"Of course. Thank you," said the monk, stepping aside to let her leave.

"Brathair Gillies, when I said I wanted it all to be over with, I was speakin' of carryin' out my sentence," Cam tried to explain. "I never spoke a word to ye about the girl at all. I'm sorry, but ye are mistaken."

"It's for the best that she has a loving family to live with now," the monk answered, not seeming upset by the situation at all. "I'm sorry, Cam, but you are a Highlander with a quick temper and no experience in raising children. It would never have worked. Besides, Avianca was afraid of you."

"She wasna afraid of me!" Cam exploded, not wanting to think that his own daughter feared him. Then his thoughts drifted to how Avianca had hid behind the nun rather than to go with him. Mayhap his own daughter really didn't want to be with him, after all.

"You didn't want her, just admit it," snapped the monk. "It's absurd to even think you could care for her by yourself. You don't even have a wife."

"Mayhap no' now, but someday I will," Cam answered, feeling defeated.

"I am goin' to marry him," Yvaine spoke up. "We had planned to raise Avianca and my bairn as our family." She put her hand on her belly and rubbed it when she spoke.

"What? Cam is gettin' married?" asked Nash in surprise.

"To Yvaine?" Gavin looked just as surprised and confused.

"How much did we miss while we've been away?" asked North, scratching his head.

"It's true we were talkin' about marriage, but nothin' was determined for sure," Cam told his friends, glancing nervously over at Yvaine. Part of him was happy she'd come to his rescue. Another part of him despised that she said this aloud when they'd never finished their conversation regarding her deep, dark secret. For all he knew, she might be right. Once he knew her hidden truth, he might not want her as his wife, after all.

"Sister, you are not marrying this barbaric Highlander," warned Gillies, angry with Yvaine now.

"Why no'?" she asked. "Because he is a Scot? Dinna forget that we are Scottish, too, even if ye speak and act like a Sassenach now. I will do whatever I please and ye canna stop me, Brathair."

"I might not be able to stop you two from getting married, but this is my priory and I insist you both leave at once." He looked up at Cam's friends. "All of you. I want you all gone by tomorrow."

"But where will I go? Please dinna make me leave," pleaded Yvaine. "Gillies, I am yer sister. Let me stay here. For now, at least."

"I never should have agreed to let any of you stay here. Now once again, I expect you all gone by the end of the day tomorrow." He turned to walk away, but Cam reached out, gripping his arm tightly.

"We are no' goin' anywhere until ye tell me where ye took my daughter."

"Let go of me," the monk commanded, gaining the attention of the rest of the monks now who came hurrying over to see what all the commotion was about. "I found a good family for the girl, and I'll never tell you where I took her. She is so much better off without you." He shook out of Cam's hold and glared at Yvaine. "She's better off without any of you."

Gillies walked off with the rest of the monks. Cam took a step to follow, but Gavin stopped him, holding him back.

"Nay, Cam, dinna do it. Ye've already made the monk angry and he'll most likely tell our lairds things that will keep ye from bein' accepted back into the clan."

"I dinna care anymore," Cam retorted, struggling out of Gavin's grip. "That bastard took my daughter away from me, and I will no' stop until I find her and bring her back where she belongs."

"Nay. Cam, he's right," said Yvaine with a sad sigh. "Being angry isna goin' to do anythin' to help the situation, or to find Avianca."

Cam was ready to explode. "I willna let him get away with this. I swear, I will kill the man if need be, but no one takes away my daughter and gets away with it. Ever."

"Dinna talk that way," said Yvaine, seeming to become so upset with him all of a sudden. "Ye dinna want to kill anyone."

"I'm a Highland warrior, Yvaine," he told her through gritted teeth. "I've killed many men, and will kill many more in my lifetime. One more doesna matter at all to me. Even if the man is yer brathair, I swear I will make him pay for what he's done."

"Nay!" she shouted, crying now, and getting the attention of all Cam's friends. "Ye dinna mean what ye say. I ken it."

"How could ye even ken what I'm feelin'?"

"I ken, because I killed a man and wish every day that I could go back and change what I've done."

"What did ye say?" asked Cam, thinking he'd misheard her.

"I am a murderer, Cam. I am evil and now I'm goin' to hell," she cried.

"Nay, lass." Cam tried to calm her down. "Dinna say that. Ye couldna hurt a fly."

"I'm serious," she said, her voice shaking as well as her body. "I killed a man, and it's true. Now ye all know my deep, dark secret that I tried so hard to forget and no' to tell anyone.'"

"Really?" asked Davita, her eyes darting back and forth. "What do ye mean? What are ye sayin'?"

"Aye, lass. Explain," said Nash. "Who could ye have possibly killed?"

"It was my husband, Dun," she said, raising her chin and

getting a crazy look in her eyes that made Cam a little worried. "He was drunk as usual the night of yer weddin', Davita. He wouldna let me leave the house and that is why I wasna there to help ye celebrate. Dun grabbed me, wantin' to have his way with me like he always did. He always forced himself on me, and it hurt." Tears filled Yvaine's eyes as she explained. "He hit me. He always hit me. He hurt me and didna care about me at all."

"Oh, Yvaine," whispered Davita. Everyone stood silent, in shock and not sure what to say since none of them could believe what they were hearing.

"I put up with him so long, but I didna want him to hurt the bairn. I fought with him and tried to run, but I couldna get away," explained Yvaine. "So then, I did what I had to do. No' only to keep from bein' hurt, but to protect my unborn child. I didna mean to kill him, I swear. I just wanted him to stop. So I grabbed the closest thing which was a heavy candle holder and hit him over the head." She cried and her body shook as she continued to speak. "That's when Dun fell at my feet. When he didna move, I realized he was dead." She whimpered and clasped a hand over her mouth, shaking her head. Then she slowly lowered her hand, biting at her bottom lip. Her hand went to her belly, and she looked down as she finished her story in naught more than a whisper. "I am a murderer. I killed my unborn child's faither. How will I ever tell this to my bairn someday?"

Davita gasped and held her hand to her mouth as well, moving closer to Gavin.

"Well . . . ye only did it in self-defense," said Gavin, obviously not knowing what to say to that.

"Aye. Self-defense. From a man who beat ye," added Cam.

"How could any man treat his pregnant wife like that?" asked Davita. "It is no' right."

"Dun never kent I was pregnant," she told them. "I was too afraid to tell him."

"Afraid to tell him?" asked Cam. "Why?"

"I'd think my bruises would answer that," she replied. "He

never wanted children, and if he kent, I was sure he would do somethin' to try to make me lose the bairn. I couldna take that chance. And if the child had been born, I'm sure in his drunken stupor, he would have beat and killed it someday. I had to stop him. I had to protect my bairn."

"Och, lass." Cam went to her and put his arm around her as she continued to cry. "Ye are no' a murder and no one thinks ye are. Please dinna say that."

"It doesna matter." Yvaine looked as if she were being drained of life. "All that matters is that I am goin' to hang for what I did. My life is over now. My bairn might be killed, too, if I am no' allowed to birth it first. Oh, what have I done?"

"Nay. Dinna even think that," Cam told her. "I would never let that happen, I promise. After all, ye didna really mean to kill Dun."

"That's what I used to think," said Yvaine. "But lately, I am no' so sure anymore." She looked directly into Cam's eyes with a cold stare that about froze his heart solid. "I wished many times Dun was dead, and now my wish has come true." It was frightening to hear her speak this way. He didn't like to see the woman he loved looking and acting so evil. It was like he didn't even know who she was anymore.

"Yvaine, stop it," he whispered. "Ye are no' a bad person. Ye didna really want him to die. It's no' true and ye ken it."

"I killed him, Cam, and I'm glad of it. It might have been done in self-defense, or it might have been on purpose. I no longer ken the answer. Still, it doesna really matter. I will die now for what I did, and my only regret is that my bairn will lose its life as well." She looked down to her belly. "I killed a man and I feel . . . nothin'." Her words came out in a raspy whisper. "I dinna deserve to live. I dinna deserve to be happy. I am evil, since I feel no remorse at all for takin' a man's life."

"Stop it!" commanded Cam, but she kept on going. His arm slipped off from around her shoulders.

"I am glad the bastard is dead, because now he canna ever

hurt anyone again."

Yvaine turned and hurried toward the catacombs, leaving Cam, Davita, Gavin, North, and Nash standing there silently, not saying a word. So, Cam finally knew the secret Yvaine was keeping from him, just like he'd wanted. The only trouble is, now he wished more than anything that she had never told him at all.

# CHAPTER SEVENTEEN

Yvaine rushed into the catacombs, wanting to hide away from everyone. She'd just admitted her dark secret aloud, and there was no going back from that! She had boldly told Cam and his friends that she was a murderer and because of it, she would hang for her crime now. That troubled her immensely. Still, in a way, it was also a relief to have that secret out in the open. It had weighed heavily upon her conscience as well as her soul. No longer would she have to carry the burden on her shoulders of pretending to be someone she no longer was.

She'd made a mistake, and would now pay for it with her life. But mistake or not, it still didn't change the fact that she was happy that Dun was dead.

"Yvaine! Yvaine," called out Cam from behind her as she hurried into the underground mazes, not caring where she was going or if she'd ever be found again. Her life was as good as over now anyway, so she might as well get used to being amongst the dead. Without a torch, it was impossible to see where she was going. Her foot hit something and she fell to the ground. Feeling around, her hand settled atop something round. When she picked it up, trying to decipher what it was, she realized it was a skull.

She screamed, throwing it down and getting to her feet.

"Yvaine, dinna move. I'm comin' to get ye," called out Cam, his voice getting closer. She thought she saw a torch burning up ahead, and hurried toward it, not wanting to talk to Cam right now. When she followed the light, it led her to the door of the underground room where Cam had been staying. She frantically felt around for the lever to open the door, but could not find it.

"Lass, slow down before ye hurt yerself." Cam came up behind her, grabbing the torch from the wall, and putting his arm around her, pulling her to him.

Yvaine could hold back her emotions no longer. She burst out crying, hiding her face against Cam's plaid.

"Calm down, sweetheart. It's goin' to be all right," he told her, using his foot to find and move the lever attached to the secret room's door. The stone slid aside, and he pushed the wooden door open, motioning for her to go inside. He brought the torch with them and closed the door behind them.

"Oh, Cam, now ye ken my secret and ye have every right to hate me."

"Hush," he told her, placing the torch in a holder on the wall and lighting several beeswax candles before extinguishing the flame of the main torch. "I dinna hate ye, and neither do I condemn ye for what ye did."

"But I killed a man," she cried. Every time she said it, she felt worse and worse.

"In self-defense," Cam added. "No one is goin' to blame ye for tryin' to protect yerself."

"That's no' true and ye ken it. While men have the right to beat their wives, women canna do anythin' to harm their husbands. If they do, they pay for it with their lives."

"Come here." Cam reached out and put his arms around her. He held her tightly, kissing the top of her head. "I'm goin' to help ye, I promise."

"There is nothin' ye can do. Dinna get involved. This is no' yer problem, it's mine. Cam, ye need to go find Avianca and bring her back. That is what's really important. We both ken she belongs with ye. My brathair had no right to take her away from ye."

"I'm afraid it is partially my fault for no' tellin' him sooner that I'd changed my mind and wanted to raise her on my own." He kicked off his boots and removed his weapon belt, sitting on the edge of the bed. Then he reached over and pulled her atop his lap. "I will get Avianca back, if it's the last thing I ever do," he promised.

"But how?" she asked with a sniffle, wiping away a stray tear with the back of her hand. "Ye dinna even ken where to look for her."

"I'll find out. Dinna worry about that. I'll also help clear yer name so we can get married and raise our family together just like we planned." He gently laid his hand on her belly.

"Blethers, how can ye even say that after what I told ye? Ye dinna want a murderer as the mathair of yer children."

"Mayhap no', but I do want a strong lass who can protect my children from harm. That, my dear, is none other than ye."

"I'm no' strong." She whimpered. "I cry more than anyone I ken."

"Cryin' doesna make a person weak, Yvaine. All it does is show that the person has feelin's. Emotions are a guid thing because it proves that the person has the ability to be compassionate . . . to care . . . to love." He picked up her hand and kissed each finger as he rattled off his list.

"Then ye dinna hate me?" she asked, seeming like she still needed confirmation.

"I dinna hate ye, lass. However I think ye may hate yerself."

"I'm no' a guid person, Cam! I killed a man and I am glad he is dead. That makes me a horrible sinner."

"I'd be glad, too, if I had been the one to kill the bastard. Dun didna deserve to live. No man should ever hit and hurt a woman, especially no' his own wife . . . or bairn," he said, reaching down and kissing her on her belly.

"I've gone and ruined everythin'," she told him with a pout.

"On the contrary, ye escaped yer prison. For standin' up to the man, I admire ye."

"A lot of guid it does to admire a woman who will soon be

swingin' from a rope around her neck."

"Stop that kind of talk! I told ye, I'd help ye to clear yer name, and I will." He reached over and kissed her gently on the mouth.

"What are we goin' to do about savin' yer daughter?"

"Our daughter," he said, stressing the word *our*.

"How can ye say that? Ye canna possibly still want me as yer wife after what I just told ye."

"Actually, I do."

"Really? Ye're no' just sayin' that because I'm about to be condemned to death?"

"I've had enough talk about that, and I think it's time we think about somethin' else."

"Like what?" she asked.

"Like how much we're both goin' to enjoy makin' love in this nice, private, big bed."

"Ye canna mean it."

"I do. If ye do." He looked at her with a crooked smile, making her laugh.

"The last time we made love, I did it because I wanted to ken how other women felt. This time, I will do it because I remember how guid I felt. Also, at least I'll be able to spend one last time with the man I love."

"Love?" he asked, looking up in surprise.

"Aye. I believe I am fallin' in love with ye, Cam. Just like ye said ye were fallin' in love with me."

"I suppose we're both bein' daft by sayin' it aloud," he said. "After all, we've only just met. It might only be lust in disguise."

"Whatever it is, I dinna care right now. All I care about is ye and me, feelin' happy and sated. Bein' together."

"I'll agree to that," he said, pulling her down on the bed, straddling her and kissing her with passion. "Promise me that until we've finished, ye'll only think happy thoughts, Yvaine."

"I promise," she said, feeling relaxed now that she'd been honest with Cam and he still seemed to love her anyway.

His hands gently slipped down her breasts, and then he was

pushing up the hem of her skirt. Little by little, his fingers moved higher, until he had removed her underclothes and was bringing her to heights she'd never known, just using his hand. He played with her womanly folds as he kissed her, making her squirm with delight at his touch. Then he reached up and undid her bodice, fondling her breasts, and bringing her nipples to peaks with his mouth.

"Ooooh, Cam, this feels so guid."

"Enjoy it, lass."

"But I want to pleasure ye as well. Tell me what ye like."

He pulled back and looked at her, his eyes twinkling. "Do ye really mean that?"

"Of course, I do."

"Ye do realize that the things that pleasure me the most are what I've experienced with whores."

"Oh. I see. Well, I'm no' sure I can do that, but if ye instruct me how, I can try."

He flipped down on his back and removed his trews, then pulled her atop him.

"What are ye doin'?" she asked. "I am a woman. I canna be on top."

"Who says?" he asked, using his hand to spread her legs until she was straddling him much in the same manner that he'd been doing to her. "I want ye on top. I dinna want to hurt the bairn." He reached out and ran a finger down her chest and to her stomach, swirling his fingertip around her navel, making her giggle.

"Tell me what to do, Cam. I want to learn."

"Touch me," he said, waggling his brows as he looked down to his erection.

"Oh!" she said, swearing it moved on its own. "All right." She slowly reached out and closed her fingers around his hardened form.

"Now squeeze. Gently."

She followed his instructions, making him moan. "What's

next?" she asked, eager to please him.

"Kiss me . . . there.""

"There?" Her heart skipped and she felt scared. "I – I . . . I will try." She moved her head down and kissed him. Before she knew it, he guided her to take him into her mouth. His hips moved beneath her and he moaned louder and louder as she sucked him, and then let him go. The action was making her feel randy, and she wanted to make love the usual way. She straddled her legs around him, taking his manhood into her body, doing the dance of love.

His hands closed around her hips and he helped her as he entered her slowly, and pulled back out in a smooth manner. The motion became faster and faster, exciting her and bringing her to life.

"Ride me, lass," he told her. "Ride me astride like ye are commandin' a stallion."

"Oooh, Cam, I canna believe I am doin' this," she said, as he slid in and out and then used his fingers to arouse her even more at the same time.

"Let yerself go, love. Release all those pent-up emotions."

"Yes, yes, yeeeeesss," she cried, throwing back her head, arching her back as she rode her man like a stallion. Excitement grew stronger and stronger and she felt the warmth from her core travel up to every part of her body. She wasn't sure she wouldn't burn up from the passion between them.

"Are ye almost there, love?" he asked, through ragged breathing. "I am no' sure how much longer I can wait."

Something about those words set her off. She squealed and moaned, leaning toward him so he could play with her taut nipples as she reached the precipice and shouted out with passion as she reached her peak.

His actions followed hers quickly. He grunted and growled, sounding much like an animal until he shouted out at the top of his voice.

"Och, lass! This is guid!" he exclaimed as he reached his peak, releasing his seed into her. She couldn't get pregnant since she already was, but still the thought of Cam's seed within her made her so excited that she reached her peak a second time, just that fast.

"I – my heart is racin' so fast I think I might collapse," she said with a giggle.

"Then let me hold ye so ye willna fall to the floor."

Cam wrapped his arms around her and held her closely. With her ear up against his chest she could hear the rapid pounding of his heart.

"Do ye really think ye can help me, so I willna be condemned to death?" she asked.

"I dinna make promises I canna carry out."

"Then, I want to help ye, too," she said, pushing up on one elbow to look him in the eyes.

"What do ye mean?"

"I will help ye to find Avianca and, together, we will collect her and bring her back before we have to leave the priory tomorrow."

He chuckled, the deep rumble of his laugh vibrating against her cheek as she once again placed her head on his chest. "How, pray tell, do ye plan on doin' that? We dinna even ken where the monk took her."

Yvaine smiled, feeling confident now. "I can find out easy enough," she told him.

"Even so. Ye ken Brathair Gillies will never let us leave tonight to look for the girl. He closes the gate of the priory at sunset. We will be trapped inside until mornin' and then it will be too late to get her."

"No' necessarily," she told him. "I learned a few things from Lord Rook's wife, Lady Calliope, durin' my visit at Naward Castle."

"I dinna understand."

"Just trust me, Cam. As soon as I find out for sure who has Avianca, I'll get us out of the monastery without anyone's knowledge. We'll be back with yer daughter before anyone even wakes for the day. They'll have no idea that we even left."

"Well, that does sound like a fable since the monks get up in the middle of the night," he said with a chuckle.

"Ye ken what I meant," she said, already devising her plan in her head. "Are ye up for the challenge?"

"I'd never turn down the opportunity to get Avianca back, so yes. Just tell me what to do, and let's save *our* daughter."

# Chapter Eighteen

"Here she comes," said Davita, peeking out the door of the chandlery, seeing Sister Edna heading up the stairs toward her. "I hope she cooperates," whispered Davita, talking to Yvaine who was in the room.

"She will," said Yvaine. "Just give me a few minutes alone with her and be sure to distract anyone who might interrupt us. Cam is already keepin' my brathair busy."

"How is he doin' that?" whispered Davita.

"He is makin' sure Gillies stays in church, by bein' there with him. He is apologizin' to him."

"Oh, now that I'd love to see," said Davita with a giggle. "Sister Edna," she said, throwing the door wide open. "It's so nice of ye to come help Yvaine pack up her candles."

"I'll do what I can to help," said the nun. "But I don't understand why Cam and his friends don't help her."

"Cam and I had a little spat, and I didna want to ask him," said Yvaine, already feeling guilty for lying to a nun. It didn't matter, she told herself. She had to do whatever it took to help Cam get his daughter back. "Oh, Davita, I seem to have forgotten some of my packin' material down in the wagon. Would ye be kind enough to fetch it for me?"

"I'll do it," said the nun, but Davita was already halfway out the door.

"I've got it," said Davita, closing the door behind her.

"What is it you want me to do?" asked Sister Edna, seeming very uncomfortable. "I'm afraid Brother Gillies won't be happy if he finds me up here with you."

"We'll be finished before the prayers are over, dinna worry about that. Now, if ye can hand me those candles, I need to wrap them all and stack them safely together in a box."

The nun turned to do so.

"Avianca usually helps me, but now that she's gone . . ." Yvaine sniffled and turned around, pretending to wipe her eyes.

"I can see ye miss the lass. She was cute," said the nun.

"I wish I could have at least told her guidbye. She must be so frightened." Yvaine took the candles from the nun and wrapped them carefully together.

"Yes, she did seem scared when Brother Gillies took her from me. I really didn't want to see her go either.'"

"It's probably for the best," said Yvaine, just to throw the nun off the track. "It just amazes me how my brathair was able to find a guid family for her so quickly."

"Humph," snorted the nun, picking up more candles. "If you can call them good."

"So, ye dinna approve of Avianca's new family?" asked Yvaine, fishing for information.

"They are peasants, and I don't even know why they'd want another child when they already have six of their own to feed."

"Peasants?" asked Yvaine. "Nay, I'm sure ye're mistaken. I ken my brathair. He wouldna bring the lass to anyone unless they were noble. They must be nobles, I'm sure of it."

"Nobles? If Elenor and Abe Woods are nobles, then I'm the Queen of England."

Now Yvaine was getting somewhere. She smiled inwardly. "Well, I'm sure they work for nobles then, and are very respectable."

"I wish that were true." The nun ran her fingers along the tapered candle in thought. "I hate to say anything bad about anyone, but they've been stealing wood from Lord Rook's forest for quite some time now. I know, because they tried selling me some the last time I went to Naward's market. It was cold and I was covered in a cloak and they didn't know I was a nun."

"Oh, that's no' guid. And yet, Lord Rook lets them live in the village?" She thought they might live there, and was just guessing at it.

"Lord Rook only lets them stay because Abe's late grandmother was somehow related to Lord Clifton."

"Lord Clifton? Who is he?" asked Yvaine, taking the candles from her and wrapping paper around them. "I've never heard of him before."

"I don't know much about him, but I think his wife died young and he never remarried."

"Where is he from?" asked Yvaine curiously.

"He's a border lord nearby is all I know. He travels to Scotland fairly often. He has stayed at Lanercost Priory several times, but that was many, many years ago. I was just a young girl the last time I saw him, and a novice here. He passed through, and that was at least a good twenty-five years ago, I'd say."

"So, is that where my brathair took Avianca? To Lord Rook's village then?"

The nun looked up with wide eyes, realizing what she'd revealed.

"I've already said too much. I must go now," she told Yvaine, hurrying to the door.

"Brathair Gillies, how nice to see ye," came Davita's voice almost shouting from outside the door as she tried to warn Yvaine. The door banged open and Gillies stood there with his fists on his waist.

"Sister Edna, what are you doing up here?"

"I – I –" stuttered the nun.

"She was only helpin' me pack so I can leave," Yvaine interrupted.

"Get down to the kitchens. Now," ordered the monk.

As the nun left, Yvaine looked over to see Davita holding up her palms, apologizing for letting Gillies pass.

"Leave us," the monk instructed Davita over his shoulder.

Yvaine looked over to her friend and nodded slightly for her to go. Once the door closed, Yvaine continued to pack her things.

"Can I assume ye are here to help me pack then, since ye just ran off Sister Edna?"

"I don't know what kind of game you're playing, Sister, but I warn you, it's a dangerous one."

"I have no idea what ye mean."

"I heard you killed your husband."

Her hands stopped and her heart pounded. "Who told ye?" she asked, not looking up at her brother when she spoke.

"These walls have ears. Nothing is beyond my knowledge."

"Hah! Ye sound as if ye're my enemy, instead of my family."

"Yvaine, the monks don't speak, so anyone talking is heard all the way from one end of the priory to the other. I heard every word you told Cam and your friends. Why didn't you or Keithen tell me that's why you're here? To hide."

"I'm no' here to hide. No' really."

"Don't lie to a man of the cloth."

"All right," she said, thumping down a heavy candle holder, facing her brother now. "Keithen didna think ye'd take me in if ye kent the truth."

"He's right. I wouldn't have. You are a murderer, and I will not harbor fugitives in my priory."

"God's eyes, Gillies, I am yer sister!"

"Now you're starting to sound like that stupid Highlander with your cursing."

"Cam is no' stupid, and I love him. We are goin' to get married."

"Not if I can help it, you're not." Gillies hurried to the door.

"Where are ye goin'? What are ye goin' to do?"

"I'm going to do what I should have done long ago. I am sending a missive to Hermitage Castle, telling the Lairds MacKeefe that Cam did not cooperate. And you are going to have to leave at once, Sister. I can't have you here."

"What if I willna go?"

"Don't tempt me to include what you did in that letter to the MacKeefe lairds."

"Ye wouldna! I am of yer own bluid, Gillies. Please, dinna do it. Ye'll ruin both my and Cam's lives. Just let us go in peace."

"You have both put me at great risk. If the bishop finds out what is going on here, I'll lose my position at the priory. I worked so hard to get where I am. I will not have it all taken away."

"So, what if ye do? Is that really so bad?" she asked him.

"This is all I've ever wanted, Yvaine. No one is going to take it from me."

"Oh, ye mean the way ye took Cam's daughter away from him?"

"Don't get involved," Gillies warned her.

"I am involved, because this includes me. I want to be Cam's wife, and raise Avianca and my bairn as our children together. We will be a family. A real family."

"Forget about the girl. There is someone else who wants Avianca more than Cam, and she is with them now."

"The peasants named Wood? They have enough children of their own. Why did ye let them have her? Avianca is Cam's only child."

His head snapped around at hearing her mention the Woods. "I'll have Sister Edna saying penance forever for telling you that. What else did she say?"

Yvaine felt terrible for speaking up now. She didn't want the nun to get into trouble. Still, she didn't want her own brother to tell the MacKeefe lairds her secret and send her to prison either.

"Please, Gillies. Keep this to yerself, and dinna send a missive to Hermitage Castle, I beg ye. Please, dinna tell them I killed Dun."

"Don't tell me what to do." He stormed out the door and Yvaine ran after him.

"Gillies, nay! Dinna do it." She reached out to grab him as he started down the steep, stone stairs. He was angry, and jerked his arm away from her. Yvaine's sleeve got caught on him, and his motion set her off balance. "Gillies! Help me," she cried, reaching out for her brother.

His hand went out to her but it was too late. Her sleeve ripped. Yvaine fell, tumbling down the stairs, until she landed sprawled out in a heap at the bottom. Pain seared through her, and she felt warm liquid gush from between her legs. Her head dizzied and she looked up to see Gillies running down the stairs after her. As if in a dream, she heard Davita's voice, and then Cam's from afar. The sound of thundering footsteps over the ground rumbled in her ears as they all came running toward her.

"Yvaine, I'm so sorry," cried Gillies, kneeling down next to her. "Oh, God, nay," he said, his face becoming pale. He quickly blessed himself and started to pray.

"I – I'm all right," she said, then followed his gaze. That's when she noticed blood staining her gown. The pain in her belly became unbearable, and she realized just what had happened. "Oh, nay. Nay!" she cried. "Gillies, please help me," she begged her brother. "I dinna want to lose my baby."

## CHAPTER NINETEEN

C AM SHOT ACROSS the courtyard at a run as soon as he saw Yvaine take a tumble down the stairs. His friends were right behind him.

"Yvaine!" shouted Cam, throwing his body on the ground next to her, cradling her head in his arms. "God's eyes, what happened?"

"She fell down the stairs. It's my fault, I'm sorry," said Brother Gillies. "I never meant to hurt her."

"I should run my damned blade through yer heart right now," Cam ground out.

"Cam, stop it," said Nash. "We need to concern ourselves with Yvaine."

"I've lost my baby, Cam." Yvaine looked up to him with sad eyes. "I ken I did."

"Everyone, get back," said Davita, pushing the men away with her words. "Someone, fetch the healer, quickly."

"Sister Edna is a healer," said Gillies.

"I'll get her." North turned and ran toward a group of nuns standing just outside the church.

"Dammit, how did this happen?" asked Cam, angrier than all hell. He'd been keeping a close eye on Gillies during the prayer session, but the man was too smart for his own good. He must have known something was up, because he managed to dodge Cam and his friends and leave the church without them knowing it. "I canna believe ye, her own brathair, is responsible for somethin' like this."

"Oh, Cam. I'm so frightened. Ow! I am in so much pain." Tears streamed down Yvaine's cheeks making Cam feel helpless right now.

"If you all hadn't been up to something, I wouldn't have become suspicious and followed Sister Edna up here in the first place," spat Gillies.

"Stop it! All of ye," shouted Davita, holding Yvaine's hand. "Canna ye see ye are just upsettin' her more? We need to move her to a bed."

"Take her up to her room," instructed Gillies, standing up.

"Nay. No more stairs." Cam scooped up Yvaine, holding her securely in his arms. He could see the big bloodstain on the front of her gown. It didn't look good at all. He wanted to remain positive, but he felt it in his heart that she had already lost her baby, just like she'd told him.

"Let me through, let me through," said Sister Edna, pushing her way to the front of the crowd. She gasped and held her hand to her mouth. "I was just with her. Oh, how did this happen?"

"Dinna ask," growled Cam.

"Someone, fetch my medicine bag. Quickly." Sister Edna waved a hand through the air.

"I'll get it," offered Nash. "Where is it?"

"I'll show you," said another nun, leading him away.

"I'm bringing her to my room." Cam didn't wait for anyone to object. He headed to the catacombs with Yvaine in his arms. It didn't feel right, since this was the place of the dead. But he wanted her to be comfortable and away from everyone else. At least here, he could keep a good eye on her.

"I'll light torches so we can see in the catacombs." Gavin ran ahead of them.

"I'll help him." North followed.

"Cam, this wasna supposed to happen," said Yvaine in a soft voice. "I'm so sorry. I've ruined all our plans."

"Here is yer bag, Sister." Nash ran up and handed it to her.

The group entered the catacombs. Cam was careful not to drop Yvaine as he made his way to the secret room. North got there first and opened the door. Sister Edna and Davita entered, lighting candles. Cam followed, stopping and turning to talk to the others. "I think it's best if the rest of ye wait outside the room for now," he said in a soft voice.

"I agree," said Gavin. His other friends nodded.

"I want to enter. This is my priory and she's my sister," objected Gillies.

"Even more reason for ye to stay behind right now," Cam answered. "That is, unless ye feel like riskin' yer life by enterin'. I'm very angry with ye, as we ken, and I canna promise I'll be able to control my temper."

"Gillies, please, just listen to Cam. Oooooh," cried out Yvaine with her hand on her belly.

"Come on, Brathair." Gavin's big body blocked the monk's way to keep him from entering the room.

"Close the door when ye leave," Cam called over his shoulder. As he gently laid Yvaine down on the bed, he heard the stone sliding back into place behind him.

"I'll need privacy," said the nun, pulling the long purple curtains closed around the bed.

"I'll help ye," offered Davita, quickly looking back at Cam, then disappearing behind the curtains as well. "Cam, we'll need some rags and a basin of water," she called out after several minutes.

"I've got some fresh water right here." He handed the basin and some rags through the curtain. His heart almost broke when he got a glimpse of Yvaine lying in a puddle of blood.

"Oh, my. I'm goin' to need more rags and some buckets to haul away the soiled ones," called out the nun.

"I'll get them," said Cam, hurrying to the door.

"More fresh water, too," called out Davita as he left the room.

When Cam returned, he met Davita at the door.

"I'll take those. Thank ye." She reached out for them.

"Is she . . . is she all right?" asked Cam, stretching his neck, trying to see Yvaine.

Davita looked up at him and nodded slowly. "Yvaine will be fine after some rest, but it seems she's lost the baby."

"Damn," said Cam, running a hand through his hair. "Let me in. I want to see her." He started to take a step into the room, but Davita's hand on his chest stopped him.

"Sister Edna has asked that ye send a few of the nuns here to help clean up and change the beddin'. She has also asked that ye and the others stay out for at least a few hours to give Yvaine time to rest and accept what has happened."

"But I should be there with her." Cam looked up and once again tried to enter.

"Cam, please," said Davita. "Yvaine has gone through a lot and needs a little time alone."

"Of course," he said, taking a step back out of the room. "Please let me know as soon as I can enter."

Cam turned and left the catacombs, feeling as if life were crashing down around him more than anything right now.

⤜⤛⤛⤜⤜

"LET HIM IN," said Yvaine later that day, after having rested and accepted the fact that she'd lost her child. Sister Edna and Davita had tended to her, and even the rest of the nuns had helped in cleaning up the mess.

"I will be going now," said the nun, following Davita to the door of the secret room so Cam could enter. She held on to her healing bag and looked over her shoulder. "I really am sorry that you lost your baby. I'm also sorry about Avianca," she told Yvaine. "I wish there was something I could do to help you find her."

"Thank ye. Do ye mean that?" asked Yvaine. "Because if ye do, I will involve ye, but ye ken that Brathair Gillies will no' approve, and canna ken anythin' about our plans."

"Do you mean to go out to look for the girl?" asked the nun.

Yvaine and Davita looked at each other but didn't answer.

"I promise not to tell him."

"Guid," said Yvaine. "Then be back here at sunset to help. Come by yerself and dinna mention this to anyone since the walls seem to have ears."

"Very good," said the nun with a nod, leaving the room as Cam entered.

"Yvaine!" Cam rushed over to the bed. "How are ye?"

Cam's friends started to enter the room as well, but Davita blocked their way.

"It's all right, Davita. Tell them to enter, and close the door behind them. I want to talk to everyone at once," said Yvaine from the bed.

"All right." Davita stepped aside. Gavin, Nash, and North entered the room. Then North pulled the lever to close the door behind them.

"I wanted ye all to ken that I lost the baby." Yvaine had spent hours crying, but decided to finally accept it.

"I'm so sorry, lass." Cam looked at her with such sad eyes that it almost made her want to cry again.

Yvaine cradled a mug of hot cider in her hands, and slowly took a sip before continuing.

"It's all right, and I dinna want anyone to feel sorry for me."

"I'll kill Gillies for this, I swear I will," Cam ground out.

"Nay, ye willna, and I dinna want to hear talk like that again. This wasna his, or anyone's fault." She handed Cam the cup of cider and he placed it on the bedside table.

"Ye certainly are takin' this well," said Nash, sitting down at the table with the chessboard.

"Aye. I canna believe ye dinna even blame yer brathair." North sat across from his twin to play a game of chess.

"It was an accident. Besides, I had time to think, and I realize that everythin' happens for a reason," she answered.

"Lass, what reason can there possibly be for losin' a bairn?" asked Cam under his breath.

"It was a message from God," she told Cam.

"Nay," he said, shaking his head. "Ye are no' bein' punished for killin' Dun, if that is what ye are goin' to say."

"I did think of that, but I dinna believe it's true," she answered. "I decided it was a gift from God instead."

"Now, I'm really confused," said Gavin, pouring himself a cup of hot cider from a pitcher on a table near the door.

"Yvaine told me that she has accepted the loss, and that it will actually be for the best," said Davita, taking the cup from her husband and taking a sip.

"For the best?" Cam looked up, confused. "That is insanity talkin'."

"Nay, it's no'." Yvaine reached out and took Cam's hand in hers. "I think the child didna want to be born. No' yet. That is, mayhap my child shouldna ever have to ken their faither was abusive and its mathair killed him."

"But it isna the child's fault," said Cam.

"Nay, but I believe when my name is cleared and we start a family of our own, that child will come back . . . but as our child instead," she told him with a smile.

"Ye are stronger than I could ever be," mumbled Cam. "I'm glad ye have a positive outlook."

"Why shouldna I have one?" she asked. "After all, it is ye who promised ye'd help me clear my name, so I willna go to prison. I have nothin' to worry about, do I?"

Yvaine almost laughed aloud when she saw Cam squirm in his chair.

"I'll do what I can," he said, looking at the floor, not sounding as confident as he was earlier.

"Enough talk about me," said Yvaine. "I wanted ye all in here so we could discuss our plan for savin' Avianca."

"Savin' here?" asked Nash, moving his knight on the chess-board. "I thought she was already gone and given to another family."

"She is," said Yvaine. "However, I found out from Sister Edna where Brathair Gillies took the wee lass. So tonight, we're goin' to get her and bring her back."

"We?" Cam looked at her and raised a brow.

"Well, no' me, I'm sad to say." Yvaine sighed. "Sister Edna said I needed to rest and stay in bed for a few days. I would only slow ye down. However, she offered to help, so she will be takin' my place."

"A nun is goin' to help us?" asked Gavin in surprise. "I dinna like this."

"Yvaine, I hope ye didna tell her anythin'," said Cam.

"She'll run right back to the monk and report everythin'," agreed North.

Yvaine had doubts as well, but decided she needed to trust Sister Edna. "I believe she is genuine and feels bad that the girl is gone. I think she will really help us."

"What if she is lyin'?" asked Cam.

"Nuns dinna lie." Yvaine tried to reposition herself in bed. Cam quickly jumped up to help her, and to fluff her pillows. "It's the chance we're goin' to have to take. That is, unless one of ye kens the way through the catacombs in the dark."

"The catacombs? What are ye sayin'?" asked Nash.

"I'm sayin', we – ye can sneak out tonight through the cata-combs. Lady Calliope, Lord Rook's wife, told me that they lead underground all the way to Naward in one direction. In the other, they go all the way back to Hermitage Castle."

"What?" Gavin made a face. "The tunnels lead back to Her-mitage? Across the border? That far?"

"I guess so," said Yvaine. "Lady Calliope kens them like the back of her hand."

"I'd rather take a horse, thank ye," muttered Nash.

"That's all fine and guid," said North. "But Lady Calliope isna here to help us."

"Nay, and that is why I asked Sister Edna to join us," Yvaine explained. "I am guessin' that since she's been here so many years that she at least can lead ye through the tunnels back to Naward to find Avianca."

"I dinna ken about this," said Nash. "The whole thing sounds . . . dangerous and unbelievable that we even think we can pull it off." He captured North's pawn.

"Aye," agreed Gavin. "What makes ye think we'll even be able to find the girl once we get there?"

"My brathair left her with peasants of Naward that live in the village. They are the Woods family. I'm sure Sister Edna will ken them."

"Mayhap there's another way," said Davita. "I mean . . . it will be dark in the tunnels . . . and scary."

"Ye'll stay here to tend to Yvaine," Gavin told his wife. "I dinna want ye in the catacombs at night."

"I willna object," said Davita, looking very relieved.

"I still dinna agree with this plan," said Nash.

"Then stay here if ye want, but I will be goin' to find my daughter." Cam jumped up, looking like he was ready to leave.

"What will we do with her when we get her here?" asked North. He moved his bishop and captured Nash's queen.

"Damn," spat Nash under his breath.

"He does have a point," agreed Davita. "As soon as Brathair Gillies finds out what we've done, he'll be takin' the girl right back to Naward."

"Over my dead body," spat Cam.

"Well, since I'm here instead of spendin' time back at Hermitage Castle with my new wife like I should be, I guess I'll help ye," said Gavin with a shrug.

"I willna let ye down, Cam. I will go, too." North got to his feet.

They all looked over to Nash.

"What?" asked Nash, looking up, his hand wavering above his

chess pieces. "Oh, all right." He got to his feet as well. "I suppose fightin' off rats in the catacombs at night is still better than all the chores the crazy monk has been makin' us do."

"Then it's settled," said Yvaine, feeling confident. "Tonight, we put the plan into action, and by mornin', Avianca will be back with us for guid."

They heard a small scratching noise from the vents that led to the catacombs.

"What was that?" asked Gavin, looking toward the door.

"Probably rats," complained Nash. "Get used to it. These tunnels are goin' to be filled with rats, and they're all goin' to be hungry for a little human flesh."

✦◦◇◦✦

# CHAPTER TWENTY

"**I**S EVERYONE READY?" asked Yvaine later that night as Cam paced the floor of the secret room.

"We're all here, but there is no sign of the nun," complained Nash.

"Davita filled her in on our plans an hour ago, and she was still willin' to help us," said Yvaine.

"She's no' comin'. I told ye that. She probably betrayed us already to that stupid monk." Cam grew more and more impatient and just wanted to go find his daughter and bring her back quickly.

"I am here, and I heard what you called Brother Gillies. It wasn't nice." Sister Edna walked into the room. She held a basket over one arm, and was covered from head to toe with a long, hooded robe.

"I suppose Brathair Gillies is right behind ye?" asked Cam.

"Nay. Why would he be? He doesn't know anything about this. I didn't tell him," said Edna.

"Well, that's a surprise." Cam stormed across the room. "What's in the basket?" He started to reach for it, but she quickly moved it away.

"I have brought some food and ale for the trip."

"Guid. I'm starvin'," said Nash, hurrying over to her. "I'll have somethin' to eat right now."

"It's for Avianca," said the nun. "I'm not sure if she'll even have been fed since the Woods family is poor and has so many mouths to feed."

"I still dinna understand why Brathair Gillies would take the lass to such a poor family," said Gavin.

"He probably got tired of her cryin' and gave her to the first family he saw," Cam answered, pacing back and forth.

"I'm sure that isn't what it was," Edna replied. "Brother Gillies has his reasons for doing things, although he rarely explains to anyone what they are."

"Enough of this clishmaclaver. I'm ready to leave," said Cam. "How long will it take to get to Naward?"

"It's only a half-hour on foot, but since we'll have to travel slowly through the catacombs, it might take longer," answered the nun.

"Gavin, get the torches. Let's get a move on," instructed Cam. He walked back to the bed, leaning over to give Yvaine a quick kiss. "I promise ye, everythin' is goin' to work out. Dinna worry," he told her in a low voice.

"I'm no' worried," she said. "Now get on!"

"I hope ye ken the way through these catacombs," Cam grumbled as he passed up the nun.

"Of course, I know the way. I've lived here for twenty-five years. Just follow me, and I'll get you to Naward quickly to collect the child."

Cam followed the nun through the catacombs, holding the torch high to ward off the rats.

"Ow, somethin' bit me," cried Nash from the end of the line as he jumped around and used his sword, swiping it at the ground. "Someone give me a torch to hold so I can see the rats to kill them."

"Stop yer complainin', Nash, and put that blade away before ye hurt someone." Cam could see the exit up ahead and stepped in front of Sister Edna to lead the way. "We're here, Nash, so ye can stop cryin' about rats now."

Once they all exited the catacombs, Cam looked over to the

nun. "Where do we find the Woods family?"

"Their cottage is just up ahead. However, it is late and they will be sleeping I'm afraid."

"No' if they have rats, they willna," mumbled Nash, following them through the streets, still holding his sword in case a stray one followed them.

"Mayhap I'll just sneak in and grab Avianca and leave," suggested Cam. "That way, no one will even ken she is missin' until mornin'. By then, we'll be on the road and on our way home."

When they approached the cottage, Cam signaled for the rest to be quiet while he snuck into the house. He saw the lights on in the main room, and figured they mustn't all have gone to bed yet, after all.

He climbed in a window, seeing the sleeping children. "Avianca?" he whispered, not able to see well in the darkened room. When he reached out for a girl who he thought was his daughter, the child sat up and screamed.

"Shhh," he told her, holding a finger to his lips, but it was too late. The door to the bedroom was flung open, and the room filled with light from a lantern being held by a man.

"Who's there? What's going on?" called out the father.

"I'm no' goin' to hurt yer children, I promise." Cam lifted his hands above his head. "I'm only here to get my daughter, Avianca, and then I will leave. Where is she?"

"You're too late, Cam. She's no longer here." Another man stepped into the light of the lantern, and to Cam's dismay, it was none other than Brother Gillies.

"Nay! No' ye," said Cam as the front door smashed open and North and Nash ran in with their swords drawn.

"We heard a scream," said Nash, holding his sword in two hands.

Now, the peasant's wife screamed, running to the bedroom, gathering up her children. "Please, don't kill us," she cried.

"Put away the swords, boys," growled Cam, thinking his friends were making matters worse.

Then the back door was flung open and Gavin ran in with his sword drawn as well. Sister Edna was right behind him.

"Stop!" yelled Cam, pushing his way into the main room. "Lower yer weapons, ye fools. These people are unarmed."

"Brathair Gillies?" Gavin saw the monk and lowered his sword. "What are ye doin' here?"

"Me? What are all of you doing here? Especially you, Sister Edna?" asked the monk.

"She told him our plan," shouted Nash, glaring at the nun.

"It was a set up all along. We shouldna have trusted them," said North.

"I didn't tell him, honest I didn't." Sister Edna looked very upset.

"She speaks the truth," said Gillies. "I overheard your plans through the vents, standing right outside your door." He chuckled.

"Where is Avianca?" Cam demanded to know. "What did ye do with my daughter?"

"Your daughter?" asked the male peasant, looking over to the monk. "I don't understand. You told us she was an orphan."

"So, she's here?" asked North. "Just give her to us and we'll leave."

"Nay, you're too late," said the monk. "I got here before you and the girl has been moved to a different place. You see, this family was just holding on to Avianca until the arrangements could be made for her to go to her permanent home."

"With whom?" asked Gavin.

"I'm sorry, but I've been sworn to secrecy and can't tell you that," said Gillies.

Cam reached out and grabbed the monk by the front of his robe, pulling him close and growling in his face. "Dinna test me, Monk. I'm still no' certain that I shouldna kill ye, after all."

"Nay, no killing, please," said the man, holding out his palms. "I was told my family would be safe."

"Don't worry, he's not going to kill anyone," said Gillies. "If so, that would make him no better than my murdering sister."

The woman gasped from the other room, and her children cried now.

Cam released the monk, still feeling like he wanted to kill him. "Yer walls with ears are goin' to get ye in deep trouble someday, Brathair. Now, I willna ask again. Where is my daughter?"

"Do what you want, you'll never find her." Gillies headed for the door. "And don't bother to threaten this nice family because they have no idea where I took the child either. Now, I suggest you all get back to the priory and continue packing since you're leaving on the morrow."

Brother Gillies left, taking his horse that was tied to a tree.

"I'm sorry about this," Cam told the family. "We were never goin' to hurt any of ye. I am just desperate to find my daughter."

Cam led the way out the door, and the others followed. They were getting ready to leave when the man ran out of the house to stop them.

"What is it?" asked Cam.

"I'm sorry," said the peasant named Abe. "I can't even imagine what my wife and I would do if someone took away one of our children."

"It wasna yer fault. Thank ye for sayin' that though. Let's start back," Cam told the others.

"I don't know exactly where he took the girl, but I do know who probably has her."

"What?" Cam spun around on his heel. "Then tell me, please."

"There is a man, a border lord, Lord Robert Clifton, who comes through Naward often. I've heard talk that he's been wanting a Scottish child for a long time now."

"Why?" asked North.

"I'm not sure. I am guessing that since the lass was Scottish, Brother Gillies might have taken her there."

"Where is this man's castle?" asked Cam.

"I don't know. All I know is that it's on the border."

"Well, thanks anyway," said Cam, turning to go.

"They won't be there yet. Brother Gillies just met with the man not fifteen minutes ago. You might still be able to catch them on the road if you hurry."

"Which way are they headed?" asked Gavin, causing the man to point in the right direction.

"Do ye have horses we can borrow?" asked Cam. "We'll never catch them on foot."

"I only have the one, and it is a plow horse, but you're welcome to use it."

"Well, a lot of guid that does," spat Gavin. "Mayhap we can steal some horses from another family down the road."

"Not many peasants have horses," said Sister Edna. "And I don't want to be a part of stealing anything."

"Of course, no'," said Cam. "Neither should ye have to. We're already so grateful for all yer help, Sister.

"I agree," said Gavin. "Nash and North will escort ye back to the priory through the catacombs. I'll ride double with Cam on the horse to get the girl."

"Nay, I'll go alone," said Cam. "Ridin' double will only slow us down. I might miss the chance to save Avianca."

"Then, if ye're sure, I'll go back with them," said Gavin. "Mayhap I can help keep the peace since Brathair Gillies is bound to be upset with Sister Edna for helpin' us."

"Aye," said the nun. "Thank you."

"Well, since the nun has the food, I willna complain." Nash smiled and looked at the basket. "Mayhap a little snack on the way back is just what we need."

"If you don't mind, I'd like to leave the basket of food with the Woods family for their children." Edna handed the basket to the father.

"Thank you. We appreciate your generosity," said the man, nodding and heading back to the house. "I'll get the horse saddled for you right away."

Not five minutes later, Cam sat atop the horse as his friends and Sister Edna headed back to the catacombs.

"Thank ye, once again," said Cam. "I'm sorry if we scared yer wife and children."

"Good luck," called his wife from the door, holding the youngest of their children in her arms. "I hope you find your daughter."

"Thank ye." Cam turned the horse, and looked down at the father of the family once more. "Tell me, why did ye help the monk to begin with?"

"He offered us money to hold the girl until he could set up the meeting with the permanent family," the man replied. "I feel ashamed to have done it now. I didn't know the child was anything but an orphan. I only agreed for the money to feed my family. I'm sorry."

"Dinna be," Cam replied with a smile. "If I had children to feed, I would have done the same thing. Thank ye, and guidbye." Cam nodded and headed down the road to try to catch Lord Clifton, and to find his daughter. He missed Avianca with all his heart. After seeing the Woods family and how close they were although they had very little, it made him think what a fool he'd been. All he wanted to do was to hold Avianca once more and, this time, he'd never have another doubt about wanting to be her father again.

# CHAPTER TWENTY-ONE

C AM RODE LIKE the wind, finally managing to catch up to the traveling party that had his daughter. He stayed hidden in the dark, wondering the best way to take her back. He could see little Avianca riding in the back of a horse-drawn wagon. She was with a handmaid and looked very frightened.

He could ride right in and demand they give her up. Nay, that would probably never work. This was an English border lord and he was a Highlander on the wrong side of the border. He'd be killed before he even had a chance to say a word.

Mayhap he could sneak in and pluck her from the wagon and ride away quickly before they knew what happened. Nay, he decided. He was riding a plow horse and he'd never be able to outrun knights. Then, to his luck, they decided to stop and camp for the night. This would be his big chance. Once they were all sleeping, he'd sneak in and take back what was his. Now, all he had to do was wait.

"WHERE IS HE? Cam should be back by now." Yvaine was going crazy waiting for Cam, envisioning things in her head like his lifeless, headless body lying on the side of the road somewhere.

"He'll be back. Stop worryin'." Nash continued his game of

chess with his brother. Both of them didn't seem to have a care in the world.

"Aye, Cam has survived many battles, and I hardly think he'll be taken down just by tryin' to save a wee lass." North's hand wavered above the chess pieces until he finally selected one and moved it.

"Ye've all been back for hours now," said Yvaine. "Why didna at least one of ye stay with him?"

"Gavin tried that," said Nash, moving his rook. "Cam told him to go back with us and the nun."

Gavin and Davita weren't here right now. Neither was Sister Edna. After hearing what happened, Yvaine sent Gavin and Davita to look after the nun so Gillies wouldn't do something nasty to the woman for helping them.

The church bells started ringing, and Yvaine could hear something else through the vents in the ceiling. "What's that?" she asked, looking upward.

"Probably just another prayer session." North captured Nash's bishop, causing Nash to swear.

"Nay, it's no' time for another prayer session for hours. Listen," she told them. "I think I hear shoutin'."

"That's just North cryin' since I'm about to capture his last knight." Nash chuckled and took the piece, causing his brother to frown.

"That wasna fair. Ye tricked me into movin' that piece when I didna want to," spat North.

"Shhhh," said Yvaine, putting her feet on the floor. "I could have sworn I heard Cam's voice. I am goin' out to the courtyard to see what is goin' on."

"Nay!" Nash jumped up and held out his hand. "Ye are no' supposed to leave the bed."

"I'm fine. I need to make sure Cam is all right, if that was him I heard."

"North will go. I'll stay here with ye, and he'll report back to us."

"Hmm?" North looked up to see Nash nodding his head, pointing to the door. "Oh, right. I'll be right back."

After he left, Yvaine decided that she didn't want to just sit there and not know what was happening out in the courtyard. "I'm goin', too," she said, getting up and putting on her cloak and shoes. Her body was sore, but she'd stopped bleeding. She was sure she would be fine.

"Are ye sure ye should be doin' this?" asked Nash, jumping up next to her. "I was told that ye were to stay in bed no matter what."

"Dinna try to stop me, Nash. I am goin' with or without ye to the courtyard. I hear the bells and now shoutin'. I am sure somethin' is wrong. Now, are ye goin' to help me or no'?"

"Cam is goin' to kill me," said Nash with a sigh, walking to her side and holding out his arm. "All right. Let's go."

✦✦✦

CAM NOW REALIZED that he should have thought out his plan a little more thoroughly before attempting to save his daughter. He'd been able to sneak up to the wagon, but when he tried to lift her out, Avianca woke up and started crying, giving away his presence.

Now, he was a prisoner of Lord Robert Clifton and would probably be dead right now if Avianca hadn't told them that his story about the priory was true. So, back to Lanercost they went, but Cam didn't expect this would go well for him at all. After all, Brother Gillies was in charge and the deciding factor. Cam was sure the monk wasn't about to say anything to help him get off the hook.

"What's this?" asked Gillies, walking out of the cloisters to join them.

"This man says the girl you gave me is his daughter," answered Lord Clifton. He was a big man with blond hair that had streaks of gray running through it. He was about twenty years older than Cam. His long beard made him look even older. "Is this true, Brother Gillies?"

"Well, if you can believe a Scot," said the monk, not surprising Cam at all that he would twist the truth.

"He'd be dead right now if the girl hadn't confirmed his story."

"Mayhap she is his daughter . . . or mayhap she isn't. Who really knows? The fact is, you wanted a Scottish child, and now you have one, Lord Clifton." Gillies wasn't acting very nice for a monk.

"Not to mention, your pockets are full of my coin," grumbled the man. "I asked for an orphan. I never meant for you to find me a child who has a living parent."

"My mistake, my lord," said Brother Gillies bowing his head. "Then, are you returning the girl?"

"Keep the coin, if that's what you're really asking," snapped Robert. He surveyed Cam in the firelight, then looked back to the little girl. "Tell me, Highlander. Why are you even here?"

"He's here to work off a punishment," the monk blurted out before Cam could say a word.

"Is this true? What did you do?" asked Robert.

"I assure ye it was nothin' as deceitful or disrespectful as givin' away someone's child." Cam glared at the monk when he spoke.

"My lord, the Highlander expressed to me as soon as he got here that he wanted me to find a home for the child," explained the monk. "I only did what he asked."

"Is this true?" The border lord looked down from atop his horse, waiting for Cam's answer.

"Aye, I'm afraid it is," Cam sadly admitted. "However, since then I have changed my mind. I've had a change of heart. I want my daughter to live with me." Cam looked over to Avianca who was being held back by the handmaid. "Avianca, I'm sorry. I hope ye can forgive me for bein' such a fool."

"Da, I want to go home," said the girl. "Back to Scotland."

"Cam!" came a voice from behind him. Cam turned to see Yvaine hurrying across the courtyard holding on to Nash's arm for support.

"Yvaine? What the hell are ye doin' out here? Ye are supposed to stay in bed," Cam scolded her.

"I heard the bells and then voices and I was worried." Yvaine spotted Avianca and a smile pursed her lips. "Avianca! Ye're back." She held out her arms and the little girl broke free, running to her. "I am so glad ye are all right." She hugged her, going down on one knee to do it.

"Who is this? Are you the mother of the child?" asked the border lord.

"Nay, she's not. This is my sister," said Gillies. "The child is not hers, and the Highlander is not her husband."

"No' yet, but soon to be," she told them.

"I don't understand," said the man.

"I am Yvaine, my lord." She stood back up with Nash's help. "I have just had a miscarriage, plus I am mournin' the death of my husband."

"I'm sorry to hear it."

"Hah! She's not in mourning. That's a lie," blurted out the monk, making Cam want to strangle the man.

"How did your husband die? Was it in war?" asked Lord Clifton.

"Nay, my lord," she answered, her eyes darting back and forth. "My husband was a chandler, no' a warrior like Cam."

"Then he died from an illness?" the man persisted with his questions.

Yvaine's gaze locked with Cam's. When he shook his head warning her not to reveal the truth, she let out a deep sigh. Of course, she didn't heed his warning.

"I killed him, my lord," she answered softly. "It was in self-defense, when he tried to hurt me and my unborn child." She freely admitted her guilt in front of everyone, making Cam groan softly. That was the last thing he wanted her to say.

"Really?" The border lord stared at her with interest and then started laughing. "Brother Gillies, it seems you not only shelter barbaric Highlanders and orphans, but murderers as well."

"She's no' a murderer and my daughter isna an orphan." Cam broke free from the guard and joined Yvaine, putting his arm around her. He placed his other hand protectively on the shoulder of his daughter.

"I'd hate to think what the king will do, once he hears from me what is really going on at this priory. Or the bishop. I am friends with them both, you do realize." Lord Clifton's words were an obvious threat.

"Nay, please don't," begged the monk. "I didn't know all this when I agreed to let them stay here. Please, don't say a thing."

Lord Clifton dismounted his steed and walked over to Cam. "I suppose I could be persuaded. That is, if the girl is returned to me without any trouble."

"Nay!" shouted Cam and Yvaine together, holding on tightly to Avianca. The little girl started crying, gripping on to Yvaine's leg.

"Who is the mother of the child, anyway?" asked the lord.

"Her mother was a whore who died," the monk told him.

"A whore?" The border lord took great interest in this story. "Scottish or English?"

"Scottish, of course," answered Cam in a low voice. "I wouldna be caught dead lyin' with a Sassenach."

"I don't blame you." Lord Clifton actually smiled. "I've always taken a liking to the Scottish over the English as well. They make the best lovers."

"You can have the girl," said Brother Gillies. "Take her. Just don't say a word about any of this to anyone or it will ruin me. Please."

"Brathair!" snapped Yvaine. "What has happened to ye since ye've been here? I hardly ken ye anymore."

"Why do ye even want the child?" asked Cam. "Excuse me

for sayin', but ye are too old to raise such a young daughter."

"True," said the man. "However, I made a mistake many years ago that I still regret to this very day. I think this will help me ease my weary mind. Come with me, Child."

When he motioned for his guard to collect Avianca, Cam's eyes settled on the man's ring he wore on his index finger. It was a gold ring with circles and a boar in the middle. It had a bright blue, square stone. He knew this ring. He knew it well. His heart skipped a beat, and it felt as if he were reliving his past.

"Cam, dinna let him take her," begged Yvaine, trying to hold the girl back.

Cam released his daughter, letting the guards take her. He stood silent as they loaded the crying girl into the wagon. He was unable to even move to do anything to stop it.

"God's eyes, Cam, what's the matter with ye?" growled Gavin, hurrying to his side with Nash and North on his heels.

"Do ye need us to stop him?" Nash went for his sword.

"Nay!" said Cam, holding up his hand. "Dinna draw yer weapons. I dinna want any further trouble. I will handle this by myself."

"Then for God's sake, do somethin' quickly," begged Yvaine. "They are about to ride away with her. We canna lose Avianca again."

Cam walked over to the border lord who had just mounted his horse. "Ye had a bastard son once. A son born from a Scottish whore, didna ye?" he asked the man.

Lord Clifton froze, looking down at him from atop the horse. "Why would you say such a thing?"

"I ask ye, because I believe it to be true."

"Who told you this?" asked the man suspiciously.

"No one had to tell me. I know it because I recognize yer ring, my lord. I've seen it before. When I was naught but a child." He heard Yvaine gasp from behind him, knowing what he meant.

"I don't understand. What are you saying?" Lord Clifton sat with his back as straight as a board, looking very uncomfortable now.

"Ye see, I am a bastard. My mathair was a Scottish whore," Cam told him. "I was raised in brothels."

"So, then you've probably seen me in the Scottish brothels. It's no secret. I told you I've been there before. Still, your accusation of me siring a whore's bastard is false and has nothing to do with me."

"On the contrary, my lord, I think it has everythin' to do with ye." Cam's whole life was about to change, and a little voice inside him urged him to stay quiet. But he couldn't. His daughter was about to be taken from him and he would say anything right now if he thought it would help him to keep her. "Ye want a Scottish orphan birthed from a whore because ye once had a child from the same, isna that right? Ye regret leavin' him behind, and ye think this will ease yer guilt."

"Is this right, my lord?" asked Brother Gillies, shaking his head. "You have a Scottish bastard?"

"What is he saying my lord?" asked one of his guards.

"It can't be true," said another.

"Nay," answered Lord Clifton with no emotion at all on his face. "You are mistaken. I never had a child with a Scottish whore. I am an English lord, and have two daughters, but no son at all, I am sorry to say."

The man denied it, but something told Cam that he just didn't want to admit it in front of everyone. Cam knew that ring, because he'd once worn it himself. He no longer cared what anyone thought. He would take any measure to save his daughter. Besides, if Yvaine could tell her secret to a courtyard filled with people, then his secret would be told to all as well.

"I dinna think I'm wrong, my lord," said Cam. "As a matter of fact, I ken I am right."

"Nay. You are mistaken." Lord Clifton turned a full circle on his horse. "Besides, I just met you. How could you possibly think you know anything about my past?"

"I ken, because my faither once had a ring just like yers before he walked out of my mathair's life forever. I am his son, the child he never kent. I am yer bastard son, my lord. The one ye abandoned when ye left my mathair, after promisin' to marry her."

The border lord didn't say a word. He and Cam stood there staring at each other.

Cam finally spoke. "Why dinna ye get off the horse and we can discuss this matter further?"

# CHAPTER TWENTY-TWO

YVAINE WATCHED WITH wide eyes, not able to believe that after all these years, Cam had finally come face to face with his true father. Could it be real? Emotions surged through her, as she felt excited, yet frightened for Cam at the same time. If Lord Clifton truly was Cam's father, it could mean a happy reunion. However, if the man didn't want to acknowledge him, he could end up causing a lot of trouble for Cam. If he wanted to, Lord Clifton could get Cam imprisoned for making such an accusation of a nobleman.

"Oh, Cam, I hope ye ken what ye're doin'," she said to herself, feeling her heart beating against her ribs. She waited for the worst to happen, but thankfully the tides finally turned in Cam's favor.

"All right," said the border lord with a slight nod of his head. "I will talk with you, but it must be in private." He dismounted his horse, handing the reins to one of the monks.

"We can use the charter house to talk if you'd like, my lord," offered Brother Gillies, ready and eager to lead the way. The man obviously meant to be included.

"I said I want this to be a private conversation," he replied, getting a scowl from Gillies.

"I have just the place," Cam told him. "However, I'd like Yvaine to be present when we speak, if ye dinna mind. She is soon to be my wife, and I'd like to include her."

"If that's what you wish, then so be it," he answered. "Where are we going?"

"It's this way," Cam told him, taking Yvaine's arm and leading the border lord to the catacombs.

"You're taking me to the catacombs?" asked the man in surprise, stopping before they entered. "That is an odd place to go. Mayhap we should stay in the open." Yvaine saw his hand waver above his sword.

"I assure ye, there will be no trouble," Cam promised. "We're only passin' through the catacombs to get to a secret room. Ye'll soon see. Gavin, I'd like ye to keep everyone, especially Brathair Gillies, far away."

"Aye," said Gavin, understanding that Cam didn't want the monk listening through the vents again.

"I want my guards stationed outside as well," said Robert, not trusting Cam.

"If it'll make ye feel better, I'll leave my weapons, but yer guards will no' enter the catacombs, my lord."

"Your man must leave his sword behind as well," said the border lord, nodding at Gavin.

"He will," said Cam, getting a grumble of protest from Gavin. Cam threw down his weapons one by one, then nodded to Gavin who did the same. It finally seemed to satisfy the English lord so they continued.

Cam lit a torch and led the way through the underground mazes. When they got to the secret room and Cam pulled the lever causing the stone door to slide open, the border lord chuckled in delight.

"I am impressed," he said in amusement, entering the room right behind them.

After lighting a few candles, Cam handed the torch to Gavin who was standing just outside the room. Then he pulled the lever, closing them privately inside.

"This is some room." Robert's eyes roamed from floor to ceiling and then back again. "It looks more like the space of a noble, then belonging in a priory filled with monks."

"It once belonged to the king's bastard, Lord Rook," Yvaine told him.

"The Demon Thief?" The man's brows raised.

"Yes, he's the one. Would ye care to take a seat?" Cam offered him a chair at the table.

"All right." The man unsheathed his sword, and out of the corners of her eyes, Yvaine saw Cam's hand reaching for his sword that was no longer there.

"Ye can place yer sword on the table with the chess game, my lord," she said, reaching back and stilling Cam's hand.

"So, this must be one of the famous chess games that the bastard triplets played while plotting to kill their father." Robert placed his sword on the table and then sat down, picking up a chess piece to examine it.

"It is my understandin' that the Legendary Bastard Triplets of the king were stealin' from him, but werena tryin' to kill him," said Cam. Then he added under his breath, "Although, I wouldna have blamed them for wantin' him dead."

"That sounds like malice in your voice," said the border lord. "Am I the only one to sit?" He nodded to the chair.

"Sit down across from him, Cam," Yvaine told him. "I'll use the bed."

Once they were all settled, the conversation continued.

"I ken ye dinna want to admit it, but ye are my faither. I'm sure of it," said Cam. He looked more angry than happy to have found the man after so many years.

"I never admit anything before I know all the facts," said Lord Clifton, twirling the chess piece of the queen around in his fingers. "What was your mother's name?"

"Ye ken damned well that her name was Elspeth."

"Elspeth?" He put the piece down on the board. "Nay, I don't know anyone by that name. I'm sorry. That proves I am not your father." He started to stand, but stopped halfway up when he heard what Cam had to say next.

"She didna use her real name at work. Instead, she called herself Libby."

"Libby," whispered Robert, slowly sitting back down. From where Yvaine sat, she swore the man's eyes seemed to become glassy. "Are you Libby's son?"

"I am. Now do ye believe me when I say ye are my da?" asked Cam.

Lord Clifton slowly shook his head. "It can't be. My son is dead. I heard the story from the Scottish monks when they sold my ring back to me. This ring," he said, holding up his hand. "It is the one I let Libby steal from me the last time I was with her. It is also the one she found on my son's remains."

"Let her steal?" asked Yvaine from the bed.

"Yes," he answered over his shoulder. "I purposely left it on the nightstand, knowing she'd take it. I wanted her to have it. To pay for raising a child, should one have been conceived that night."

"Ye told her ye wanted to marry her," spat Cam. "She was in love with ye!"

"I know."

"Why did ye lead her on that way?" asked Yvaine. "That was cruel."

"It wasn't cruel, and I didn't lead her on. I fell in love with Libby and, in the moment, I told her I'd marry her. I'd just lost my wife at a young age, and that is really what I wanted to do. But the next morning, I realized my mistake. I was a nobleman. I couldn't marry a whore, no matter how much I thought I loved her. I figured I was just lonely, and that was all there was to it. It just . . . wasn't going to work. I knew then I could never see her again."

"That ring," Cam nodded to the man's hand, "was the one my mathair gave me before she decided to send me to live with another family. I gave it away to a young lad, and that is who the bear mauled."

"I see," said Robert, looking down at his ring.

"Excuse me, Lord Clifton," said Yvaine, standing up and walking over to the table. "But if ye bought back the ring from the monks, and kent the whole story, why didna ye go to Libby? Ye must have kent where she was."

"In my heart I wanted to," he said. "I never remarried after my wife died. But I do have two daughters, and I didn't want to disgrace them by marrying a whore. I don't want them to ever know I have a bastard son either. I'm sorry. I am a noble, and this cannot be. Sometimes I feel I made a mistake with Libby, but I had to leave it all behind. I only hope you can understand."

"I'm no' sure I ever will," said Cam. "Ye see, family is so important to me that I would never want to hide behind a title instead of bein' true to my heart."

"I'm sorry, Cam. I believe you now. I am thrilled to have found you after all these years, but at the same time, I curse it."

"What the hell does that mean?" asked Cam with a grunt.

"Cam, I think I understand." Yvaine placed her hand on Cam's. "It means he has another life now, just like ye do. If he was to acknowledge ye are his son, he might lose his other family, or his land and title. I'm sure his family means a lot to him. Both his families, as well as who he is and what he's earned."

"I see," said Cam in a soft voice, no longer looking at the man. "At least do me the favor of lettin' me raise my daughter. Please, dinna take Avianca away from me. Ye have two daughters, but she is my only child."

"I will not take her away," said the man, standing up, sheathing his sword. "However, only under one condition."

"What's that?" Cam stood as well.

"That you let me visit my granddaughter, as well as you on occasion. I will come to Scotland to see you, but it will be in secret, of course."

"Then ye willna be tellin' everyone out in the courtyard that I am yer son?" he asked.

The man shook his head. "I can't. I will say it was all a misunderstanding, and that your accusation was not true. You will agree that you made a mistake."

"Oh, Cam," said Yvaine, her heart breaking for him.

"Will ye tell the monks that Avianca is to live with me in Scotland, so I will no' have trouble takin' her with me?"

"Yes. I will tell them that I am convinced she is your daughter and that the girl should live with you and not me."

"Then I agree," said Cam, holding out his hand for Lord Clifton to shake it.

The border lord shook Cam's hand and then pulled him into his arms and hugged him, making Yvaine's mouth drop open in surprise.

"I am so glad to have found you, Son. Libby will live on through you."

Cam remained speechless, and did not return the hug.

"Now, tell me where I'll be able to find you." Cam's father released him and straightened out his clothes.

"He's with the MacKeefe Clan now," Yvaine told him, when Cam didn't answer. "He'll either be at Hermitage Castle or at the MacKeefe camp in the Highlands."

Robert chuckled. "Well, I don't think an Englishman traveling to the Highlands is a good idea. However, if you'd be kind enough to send me a missive at Castle Clifton in Brampton when you're at Hermitage, I'll make the trip up to see you. And to see my granddaughter, Avianca, as well."

"What do ye say, Cam?" asked Yvaine, when Cam seemed hesitant to answer. "I ken it isna the ideal situation, but at least ye'll be with yer faither, and Avianca will have a grandfaither now."

"I dinna ken," said Cam, holding his jaw firm. "It's a lot to ask, after what I've been through."

"I'm giving you your daughter back, MacKeefe. At least do me this small favor. I may have caused you and your mother heartaches, and for that I am truly sorry. But it is in the past, and I can't change it. Libby is gone now, and I feel the least I can do to make it up to her is to spend time with her son and granddaughter."

"It's no' right," said Cam. "Ye have another family that ye'll be lyin' to. I think it's best if we forget the past and both move forward instead."

"Cam," whispered Yvaine, not wanting things to end this way.

"Nay. He's right," said Robert, looking over at Yvaine. "I don't deserve to spend time with you or Avianca. I know it is not right to live a secret life and keep this from my daughters. But you have to understand that it isn't fair to them either. So, I guess this will be hello and goodbye all at the same time. Even still, I am happy to know you are alive, Cam. I feel at peace just to have met you. In time, I hope you'll tell Avianca who I was, but if not, I can't blame you. I will be leaving now." He turned and headed to the door.

"Thank ye," said Cam, causing the man to stop and turn around.

"For what?" he asked.

"Thank ye for no' takin' my daughter from me. I have held anger in my heart my entire life for ye. I hated ye for what ye did to my mathair, but now I think I can see things from both sides."

"So, does that mean you forgive me?"

"Nay. No' yet. But in time . . . mayhap. Just no' yet."

"I understand," said Lord Clifton with a nod. "Time heals many wounds, Son, although the wounds I've inflicted on you might take longer to heal than the time I have left on this earth." He knocked on the wooden door, and Gavin opened it from the other side. "Goodbye, Cam. I wish you a good life. Take care of Avianca."

"I will," Cam answered. "Gavin, please escort Lord Clifton back through the catacombs."

Once they left, Yvaine slipped her arms around Cam, giving him a big hug. "I ken how hard that must have been for ye. But do ye think ye were too hard on him? It wouldna have hurt to let him visit ye and Avianca once in a while, would it?"

"I've had enough heartache in my life, and I feel I need to protect Avianca from livin' a life of hell."

"Does that mean ye're never goin' to tell her that Lord Clifton is her grandfaither?"

He shook his head slowly. "I think if she kent the truth, it would only be harder for her. The wee lass thinks he's the villain right now, since she almost had to live with him. He was about to take her away from me forever."

"Dinna let her think that about him the rest of her life."

"Please, Yvaine, dinna tell me what to do."

"I'm sorry," she said, dropping the conversation, since she could see how upset it made him. He obviously wasn't ready to forgive his father. Not yet, but hopefully in time he would.

CAM HELD HIS sleeping daughter on his lap as he directed the wagon through the gates of Hermitage Castle just as the sun set on the horizon. Yvaine sat on the wagon bench next to him. The wagon was filled with Yvaine's belongings. They hadn't spoken much on the trip home, and neither had Cam's friends and Davita who rode their horses in front and behind them.

"Well, we're home," he said softly, not wanting to wake the wee lass.

"Aye. We're back to Hermitage." Yvaine didn't look happy at all.

"I wish yer brathair wouldna have sent the lairds the missive sayin' I didna cooperate. Now, I'll have to start my sentence all over. All I wanted was to be welcomed back into the clan." Cam sighed. "It doesna matter. I would serve a hundred sentences to get my daughter back."

"That's wonderful that Avianca was returned to ye," she said, flashing a smile that didn't last.

"What's the matter, Yvaine? What's botherin' ye?"

"Cam, this is yer home, but no' mine. I have a wagon filled with my things, but nowhere to put them. I'm sure the chandler's shop has been rented out by now. But even if it isn't, I would never go back. There are too many bad memories there."

"Dinna worry about that, Yvaine. We are gettin' married. Ye'll live with me and MacKeefe Clan now. Well, as soon as I finish my sentence, that is."

"I suppose." She looked off in the other direction.

"Did I do somethin' wrong?" he asked, suddenly feeling self-conscious.

"Nay, Cam." She reached out and gently touched him on the arm. "I am just havin' a hard time, that's all."

"If ye're concerned about . . . about what happened to Dun, dinna be. Yer secret is safe with me and my friends. Ye need no' worry."

"That's just it. I dinna want to live a life of secrets."

"What are ye sayin'? Surely, ye dinna plan on tellin' everyone what happened."

"Ye are the one who said I did nothin' wrong." Yvaine looked at him with hopeful eyes.

"In my opinion, ye didna, but I am no' so sure everyone will see things that way," Cam answered. "Yvaine, please, just remain silent. We'll marry soon and move to the Highlands and ye'll never have to be worried again. We just have to wait a little longer."

"I suppose ye're right," she said, leaning over and giving him a quick hug. "I look forward to marryin' ye and bein' Avianca's mathair." Her hand went to her belly, and her smile disappeared. That told Cam what else was bothering her.

"Ye're feelin' blue because ye lost yer bairn. Am I right?"

She nodded, biting her lip, looking like she wanted to cry. "Even though I ken it is for the best, I still canna wonder if my bairn was a lad or a lassie and what they would have looked like."

"We'll have plenty of babies together, and then ye'll have no doubt in yer head."

"Cam, ye're back!"

Cam looked to the side of the wagon to see Red and Violet running alongside them. He wondered what the whores were even doing here at the castle.

"Red? Violet?" he asked. "What is it?"

"Cam, ye've got to help us," cried Violet. "Somethin' horrible has happened."

"What?" asked Yvaine."

"Keithen has been locked away in the castle's dungeon, and he goin' to be sentenced to death," Red cried.

"What? My brathair is in the dungeon?" asked Yvaine as Cam stopped the wagon. "Why? What happened?"

"It was my fault, I'm afraid," said Red, crying hysterically now. "I was careless. When Dun's brathair paid me a visit, he was askin' about his brathair's death. He was ruthless and sneaky, and must have kent I had information about it. I sort of . . . told him what really happened to Dun."

"Nay!" cried Yvaine, jumping out of the wagon. "How could ye?"

"Gavin, can ye take Avianca?" asked Cam, getting to the ground and handing the child over to him.

"Of course. I'll have Davita put her to bed inside the castle," said Gavin, looking over at the whore. "What's goin' on here? Is somethin' wrong?"

"I'm no' sure yet. Tell Nash and North there might be trouble. Then all of ye, meet me in the great hall in fifteen minutes."

"Aye." Gavin hurried away while Cam pulled Red and Violet over to the side. Yvaine was with them.

"Stop cryin' and tell me how the hell Keithen ended up in the dungeon," said Cam.

Yvaine didn't give her a chance to answer. "If ye told Dun's brathair, Bart, the truth, then I should be imprisoned, no' Keithen."

"Aye, I agree," said Red. "But I didna say who hit Dun and caused his death. I did, however, tell him who was in the room when we hauled away his body."

"Keithen didna want anythin' to happen to ye, Yvaine," explained Violet. "That is why he took the blame. He said he and Dun had a spat and he hit him over the head, but never meant to kill him."

"Nay!" cried Yvaine, gripping tightly to Cam's arm. "I willna let my brathair die for somethin' I did."'

"Calm down, Yvaine, no one is goin' to die." Cam looked back at the whores. "Is there a trial scheduled?"

"Aye," said Violet. "First thing tomorrow mornin'."

"Cam, please do somethin' to help Keithen. Ye've got to help him," begged Red.

"I will. Now, everyone stop all the shoutin'. Violet, ye and Red go back to the tavern, and dinna say a word about anythin' to anyone. Understand? I am goin' to the dungeon to talk to Keithen."

"I'm comin' with ye," said Yvaine. "I will no' let my brathair die, no matter what I have to do to stop it."

Cam didn't like the sound of that. "Dinna do anythin' stupid, Yvaine. Please, just let me and my friends handle this. Just stay quiet." Cam headed to the castle with Yvaine at a brisk pace, getting a sinking sensation in his chest. This wasn't going to end well, he just knew it. What he didn't know was what he could do to save both Yvaine and Keithen's lives.

# CHAPTER TWENTY-THREE

C AM WALKED INTO the dungeon with Yvaine at his side. It hadn't been easy to convince the guard to let them enter, since Ian MacKeefe had given strict orders that no one was to see the prisoner.

"Ye've got two minutes, so make it fast," grumbled the guard. "If the laird finds out I've let ye in, he'll have my head. There's been a lot of chaos in the castle the last few days."

"We'll be fast. Thank ye," said Cam, taking Yvaine's hand as the guard unlocked the door. He headed into the dark, looking in each cell, but they were empty. Finally, he found Keithen in the very last cell.

"Keithen!" cried Yvaine, running up and gripping the bars to the cell.

"Yvaine?" Keithen was on the ground, his back against the wall. His head popped up when he heard his sister's voice. "What the hell are ye doin' here?" He jumped up and ran over to the door.

"Why are ye in here?" asked Cam.

"Bart, Dun's brathair, came to town askin' a lot of questions once he heard about his brathair's death."

"Why did ye say ye killed Dun?" whispered Yvaine. "Ye will hang for it now."

Keithen looked up with forlorn eyes. "I ken I will, Sister. But at least it willna be ye. I'd do anythin' to protect ye."

"That's honorable of ye," said Cam, thinking about Yvaine's other brother, the monk. He wouldn't lift a finger to help Yvaine if she were drowning right in front of him.

"It's stupid is what it is," spat Yvaine. "Keithen, I willna let ye take the blame."

"Ye can and ye will," said Keithen in a gruff voice. "It's bad enough that Violet and Red are involved in this. If Bart has his way, they'll be hangin' from the gallows with me before this is over."

"Time is up!" yelled the guard from the door. "Out! Now."

"All right, we're comin'." Cam leaned forward, talking to Keithen in a soft voice. "Where is Dun's body buried?" he asked.

"Under the biggest apple tree behind the tavern by the henhouse. Why?" asked Keithen.

"Never mind," he said, taking Yvaine by the hand. "Dinna worry. I will do all I can to clear everyone, I swear."

"Why did ye want to ken where Dun is buried?" Yvaine asked Cam as they headed to the door.

"Dinna fash yerself about it, lass. Tonight, ye will stay at the castle, and I want ye to watch Avianca."

"But what about ye, Cam? What will ye be doin'?"

"I'm no' sure yet, but I ken I willna be sleepin' at all tonight. I need to talk to my friends and come up with a plan for how to stop all this nonsense. There must be somethin' we're missin' in regards to Dun, and I am goin' to find it."

"Nay, Cam. Leave the dead alone," said Yvaine, but that wasn't going to happen. If Cam had to dig up dirt on Bart to shut him up and drop the charges, then that is exactly what he was going to do.

"ALL RIGHT, NOW remember, Nash. Tell Violet and Red to keep Bart in their rooms for the rest of the night," said Cam as he and his friends stood in the dark of the night, seeing Dun's brother, Bart, leaving the chandler shop and heading over to the tavern.

"All right, I will," said Nash. "But I still dinna understand what we're goin' to do to help Keithen."

"I'm no' sure yet, but North and I will have a look inside the chandler's shop. Mayhap we can find somethin' that will help clear Keithen's name. Gavin, ye see if ye can find the town's healer and ask information about Dun's health before he died."

"That willna work," said Gavin. "Ye're forgettin' the healer died months ago and the town still doesna have a new one."

"Then find anyone who might have heard about any ailments or physical problems Dun might have had."

"I will," he said, heading away as Cam opened the door to the chandlery and headed inside.

"I dinna like this," said North, following him and closing the door. "We are breakin' in. Canna we end up in prison for this?"

"No' if we dinna get caught. If Red and Violet do their jobs, we willna have to worry about it. Now find a candle and light it so we can see what the hell we're lookin' at."

"Where am I supposed to find a candle?" asked North, feeling around in the dark.

"We're in a candle shop, ye fool. It shouldna be that hard."

"Ah, here's one," said North, lighting a candle, giving them enough light to see things in the room. "There's no' a lot in here."

"Well, remember, Yvaine took a good amount of her things to the priory, and it is all still in the back of the wagon at the castle."

"What are we lookin' for?" asked North, shuffling things around.

"I'm no' exactly sure. Just look for anythin' that might seem out of place."

After looking around for a while, Cam was starting to think this was a dead end. He was about to suggest they leave when he saw the shadow of someone outside the door.

"Damn, someone's comin'. Blow out the candle and hide.

Quick!" Cam hid behind the front door. North blew out the candle and hid behind a trunk.

Cam heard the bells above the door jangle as someone entered. He figured it might be Bart. He picked up a board used in candle making, ready to bring it down over his head. He stepped out to do so, but stopped when he smelled the scent of roses, just like the rose soap Yvaine made and used.

"Yvaine?" he asked, hearing her scream. "North, hurry, light the candle."

Yvaine screamed again and hit him with her fists. He dropped the board and grabbed her, holding her tightly against him. "It's me, love. Cam. Dinna be afraid."

"Cam?" she asked, as North lit a candle and they could see each other's faces at last. "What are ye doin' here?"

"Me?" he growled. "I thought I told ye to stay at the castle and watch Avianca."

"Davita is watchin' her. Besides, did ye really think I would stay there and do nothin' as my brathair is about to be condemned to death for somethin' I did?"

"All right," said Cam, letting out a sigh. "Since ye're here, mayhap ye can help us."

"How?" she asked.

"Show me where Dun fell. When he died."

"That's why I came back," she told him. "I wanted to see it again, too. It was right over here. I didna take anythin' with me from this area, so nothin' has been disturbed. I hit him with this candle holder, and he fell against that table." She bent down and picked up the iron candle holder, handing it to Cam.

"Are ye sure ye hit him with this? I dinna see any blood on it," said Cam, turning it over in his hand to inspect it.

"Aye, that's the one," she said, looking over his shoulder.

"Perhaps there's another one and ye're mistaken," said North as he looked over the table. "Although, I see the wood splintered from where he hit the table when he fell."

"Nay, I'm positive, that is the one I used," she told him. "It is an odd one that doesna have a pair."

"Hmm," said Cam, handing it back to her. "And ye said his head was bleedin'?"

"Aye, there was a lot of blood. I mean, I think it was his head. I'm no' sure. I was very upset. All I remember was that he was lyin' in a big puddle of blood."

"Did the undertaker bury him?" asked Cam. "I'd like to talk to him."

"Aye," said Yvaine. "He was buried right away the next mornin'."

"What's this?" asked North, bending down and prying something from under the leg of the table. The table had drawers in it, and went all the way to the ground. He picked up a knife and held it up in the firelight. It was covered in dried blood.

"That's Dun's personal knife!" Yvaine blinked and cocked her head to see it better. "He was very particular about it, and never let me or anyone touch it."

"What did he use it for?" asked Cam.

"He used it to open packages, and cut twine, but mainly just for cleanin' the dirt out from under his nails, which always bothered me."

"It wasna used in candle makin' then?" asked Cam.

"Nay. Never. Cam, I have no idea why it is covered in blood."

"Was anyone else here when Dun died?" asked Cam.

"Nay. It was just me and him. What is this all about?"

"I'm no' sure," he said. "North, take the knife back to the castle, and keep it safe. It might be evidence to help us to clear Keithen's name as well as Yvaine's."

"All right, but what do ye mean?" asked North.

"I mean, Yvaine might no' have killed Dun after all."

"Cam, I ken what I did," protested Yvaine. "I hit him with this, and he fell against the table and hit the floor and died." She waved the candle holder around.

"If ye hit him with that and there was so much blood, then why isna there blood on it as well?" asked Cam.

"I – I'm no' sure," she said.

"I think that Dun was angry at ye, Yvaine."

"He was. He always was," she said in a shaky voice.

"Instead of beatin' ye this time, I am guessin' he planned on stabbin' ye with his knife."

Yvaine gasped, holding her hand to her mouth. "Ye might be right, Cam. The reason he was angry with me was because I complained that he was cleanin' his fingernails instead of cleanin' up the mess in the shop. He'd been drinkin' heavily, too."

"Och, I found two empty bottles of whisky behind the trunk when I hid there right before ye came in," said North.

"Whisky?" she asked. "We havena had whisky in the house for months. However, I saw him hidin' somethin' under his cloak earlier that day after he came back from the tavern. I bet it was whisky."

"North, take Yvaine back to the castle and make sure she stays there this time," instructed Cam. "Be sure to take the candle holder and the empty whisky bottles as well. I dinna want Bart comin' back and tryin' to hide any evidence."

"Are ye stayin' here?" asked Yvaine, as they collected the items and headed toward the door.

"Nay. I'm goin' to the tavern," Cam answered.

"Cam, this is no time for a drink, and I hope ye arena plannin' to spend time with the whores." Yvaine scowled at him.

"Actually, I think a drink is exactly what I need," said Cam. "Dinna worry, Yvaine," he told her, reaching out to stroke her cheek, giving her a quick kiss on the lips. "My days of beddin' whores is over now that I have ye. All I am goin' to do is talk to them, and figure out a way to prove that Dun died by his own hand, and no' yers or Keithen's."

# CHAPTER TWENTY-FOUR

C AM SAT AT the drink board in Keithen's tavern, drinking with Nash and Gavin, questioning the patrons about Dun.

"Damn, this whisky tastes guid, but Davita willna like it if she finds out where I've been," said Gavin.

"Then dinna tell her." Nash took a deep draw of his drink. "Is this what happens when a man marries? If so, I never want to get married."

"It is gettin' late, and we havena gotten any information that can help us yet," said Gavin. "I'm goin' back to the castle."

"Fine, then go." Cam waved a hand through the air. "I am no' leavin' until I have proof that will clear both Keithen and Yvaine. I just ken I will find out somethin' here if I wait long enough. If nothin' else, the undertaker is out of town but supposed to return tonight. I want to talk to him, too."

"Guid luck," said Gavin, leaving Cam and Nash still sitting there.

"Another drink, please," said Cam to the barkeep although he'd probably already had more than enough.

"I'm no' sure this is a guid idea," said the man. "Havena ye had enough?"

"I am no' leavin' yet." Cam felt frustrated. "Who are ye anyway? I dinna ken ye. Where is Keithen?"

"Cam, Keithen's in the dungeon, ye ken that," said Nash. "I agree ye had too much to drink."

"Och, I'm so tired, I canna think straight." Cam ran a hand over his face.

"My name is Farlan. I'm the proprietor of a tavern in the next town," said the man. "I came tonight because Red sent a missive saying Keithen was in the dungeon. I've been waitin' on ye all evenin' in case ye havena noticed."

"How often are ye here?" asked Cam.

"I only fill in when Keithen needs me. I dinna ken him well, but we barkeeps help each other out if need be. But I swear, if I'm goin' to have to keep servin' drunks like ye and that dead man, I'm no' comin' here anymore."

"Ye serve dead men whisky?" Cam laughed aloud. He was so overtired right now, after traveling all day and now drinking all night, that anything sounded funny to him.

"Nay, ye fool. I was talkin' about that no guid wife beater, Dun." He poured Cam another drink and was about to walk away when Cam stopped him.

"Wait. How did ye ken Dun was a wife beater? Who told ye that?"

"I didna ken until he told me, the night he died."

"Ye were workin' here then?" asked Nash.

"Aye. Keithen was up at the castle at some weddin' and I was here tendin' to his customers."

"That's right," said Nash. "It was Gavin's weddin'. We were all there."

"What did Dun say? And how drunk was he?" asked Cam.

"I thought he was just spoutin' nonsense at first, since he ordered two bottles of whisky and nearly drank them both while he was here. He even took the empty bottles with him."

"The bottles behind the trunk," whispered Cam to himself. "Did he say anythin' about Yvaine?"

"Who?" asked the man, squinting.

"His wife," said Cam, hating to have to say that aloud since Yvaine would soon be his wife.

"I'm no' sure he ever mentioned his wife's name. He just

bragged how he often beat her. He kept playin' with a knife, cleanin' his nails," said Farlan. "He seemed angry with her for some reason. He kept stabbin' the knife into the drink board, sayin' he wanted to kill her. Look, the marks are still there, right where ye're sittin'."

Cam looked down and ran his hand over the knife marks in the wood. A sick feeling coiled in his stomach, thinking how close Yvaine came to being killed that night. It could have been her lying in a puddle of blood instead of Dun.

"Would ye be willin' to tell Laird MacKeefe what ye just told me? At Keithen's trial tomorrow?" asked Cam.

"If it'll help out my friend, sure," said the man. "But who is goin' to believe me? I'm no' even from this town."

"He's right," said Nash. "We need more proof."

Cam thought of the items North had taken back to the castle. Those were not going to prove that Yvaine's hit over Dun's head wasn't what killed him, after all. "Do ye have a couple shovels we can borrow?" he asked the man.

"I suppose Keithen has some in the shed. But why?"

"There is only one way we're goin' to clear Keithen and his sister, and we need to move quickly since it is almost dawn."

"Cam, Violet wants to ken how much longer we need to keep that cur up in our room," said Red, coming down the stairs looking exhausted.

"Keep Bart there just a little longer," said Cam, sliding off the stool. "Red, do me a favor."

"Anythin'," said Red.

"Go see if the undertaker got back into town yet. Bring him here along with the butcher, the tanner, and the baker. Tell them all to meet me behind the tavern by the henhouse."

"The henhouse?" she asked. "Why?"

"Just go, and be fast about it."

"All right, I'm goin'."

"Can ye meet us out back as well?" Cam asked Farlan.

"Is this the whisky talkin'?" asked the man. "Or will it really help Keithen?"

"Nay, I'm serious. This is very important if we're goin' to help Keithen."

"All right then," said the man.

"Come on, Nash." Cam left with Nash right behind him. He stopped in the shed and found two shovels, handing one to his friend.

"Cam, ye're drunk," spat Nash. "What the hell are we doin' with shovels?"

"Nay, I'm no' drunk. I need ye to help me." Cam walked out to the biggest apple tree by the henhouse, seeing the wooden cross that marked Dun's grave.

"What are we doin' here?" asked Nash. "Isna that . . . Dun's grave?"

"It is," said Cam with a smile.

"Cam, I'm no' likin' the sound of this," said Nash, his face becoming pale.

"Haud yer wheesht and get diggin'," said Cam. "We're about to have a show ye willna forget. I hope to hell I'm right about what I suspect, because whatever we find is goin' to seal Yvaine's fate one way or the other."

CHAPTER TWENTY-FIVE

YVAINE PACED BACK and forth in the great hall the next morning, waiting for Cam to arrive. Everyone gathered there for Keithen's trial. Storm MacKeefe and his father, Ian, were both lairds of the clan and sitting atop the dais, getting ready to start since they would be the judges. The lairds resided over any problems that happened in the town.

"Here is the accused, my lairds," said the dungeon guard, bringing Keithen, with his hands tied behind his back, up to the front of the dais.

"There's the murderer who killed my brathair," called out Dun's brother, Bart, pushing his way up to the front. "Hang him now."

Yvaine couldn't stand it anymore. Her brother was not guilty, and she would not let him take the blame and lose his life because of her. If she didn't say something, she'd never be able to live with herself.

"He didna kill Dun, I did," she said, hearing the crowd gasp.

"Yvaine, nay!" shouted her brother.

"God's eyes, why did ye have to say that?" asked North, standing next to her. "Och, Cam is goin' to kill me for no' stoppin' ye."

"It's the truth," said Yvaine, pushing her way to the front. "I hit my husband over the head with a candle holder, and he fell dead at my feet."

"Yvaine, hush," said Keithen.

"I willna let my brathair lose his life tryin' to protect me," she added.

"Is this right?" asked Storm MacKeefe. "Keithen, did ye confess to the murder of Dun the chandler just to protect yer sister?"

Keithen looked over with angst in his eyes. He shook his head slightly.

"It's all right, Keithen," said Yvaine, walking up and putting her hand on his arm. "I have to tell the truth. I canna live a lie any longer."

"Yvaine, I dinna want to lose ye," said Keithen.

"I dinna want to lose ye either," she replied.

"Release Keithen," commanded Ian. "Instead, tie up the girl's hands."

"Da, is that really necessary?" she heard Storm ask his father.

"We have to upkeep the law, Son. No matter who has done wrong. It is our job, as lairds of the clan, to see to the town's trials."

Cam interrupted. "Mayhap so, but ye canna condemn anyone without first hearin' from a witness, and seein' the evidence I have to present." Cam walked through the great hall, followed by a group of people from the village.

"What is this all about?" griped Old Callum MacKeefe, Storm's grandfather, who had sentenced Cam and his friends. "These people shouldna be in here. Send them out."

"Wait," said Storm, standing up and holding up his hand. "I want to hear what Cam has to say. Go ahead."

"I have proof that Dun beat his wife," said Cam, walking up to Yvaine. "Look at these bruises that are still here." He pulled up the sleeve of Yvaine's gown to show him.

"Cam, nay," said Yvaine, feeling very embarrassed at this point.

"Yvaine, work with me," he pleaded. "I assure ye, this is all crucial to prove yer innocence."

"But Cam –"

"Please, Yvaine," he whispered, looking like he was so tired he was about to fall over. His hair was disheveled and his clothes were covered with dirt. "Trust me."

"I do trust ye, Cam," she said, holding up her arm for the lairds to see.

"Beatin' a woman is no crime," shouted one of the men in the hall.

"Mayhap no', but I am workin' up to my point," said Cam.

"She probably deserved the beatin'," yelled Bart. "She was always givin' my brathair trouble."

The crowd started talking and shouting now.

"Quiet!" shouted Storm in a deep voice. "Go ahead, Cam. I want to hear everythin'."

"Before that, I want to ken why this woman hit her husband over the head," interrupted Ian.

"Dun was drunk that night, and I was pregnant," said Yvaine. "I did it in self-defense, my laird. I didna want him to hurt my baby."

"Ye're pregnant?" asked Ian MacKeefe.

"Well, no' anymore. I lost the baby when I was stayin' at the priory," she answered.

"She's guilty or she wouldna have been hidin' in a priory," shouted Bart.

"Enough," snapped Storm. "Cam, ye'd better have a guid point, because this is gettin' out of hand quickly."

"I have a witness who no' only saw Dun drunk the night he died, but also swears he threatened to kill his wife – Yvaine," said Cam.

"Call him forward." Storm nodded.

"Farlan, please approach the dais and tell the lairds everythin' ye told me."


CAM LISTENED AS Farlan relayed his story, even telling about the knife marks in the drink board.

"That doesna prove anythin'," spat Bart.

"It proves the man wanted to kill Yvaine," Cam answered.

"Even if he did, the fact still holds that my brathair is dead and she killed him." Bart pointed an accusing finger at Yvaine.

"Show them the candle holder with no blood, as well as the whisky bottles and Dun's knife with the dried blood all over it," said Cam, calling Gavin and North forward with the evidence.

"The whore told me everythin'," said Bart. "She and her friend, the barkeep, and Dun's wife are all involved. I wouldna doubt that they secretly snuck his dead body out of the chandler shop and buried him before the undertaker even arrived," said Bart.

"That's no' true," Yvaine spoke up. "The undertaker was called, and he is the one who buried my husband the next mornin'."

"Will the undertaker step forward please?" Storm looked out at the crowd.

Cam looked over to Red but she was shaking her head. "The undertaker is out of town but should be back at any moment," Cam told him. "Half the town was at the funeral, so there are witnesses to that."

"All right. What's next?" grumbled Ian, looking tired and like he wanted this to be over.

"The whore also said my brathair was lyin' in a puddle of blood," shouted Bart. "If that is no' proof, I dinna ken what is."

"Which whore told ye this?" asked Storm.

"I did, my laird." Red shyly raised her hand.

"Is this true? Is this what happened?"

Red looked terrified, and as if she didn't know how to answer.

"It's all right, Red. Tell them the truth," said Yvaine calmly.

"It is as I remember it," said Red. "Violet and I as well as Keithen returned from the weddin' to find . . . Dun dead."

More noise arose from the crowd.

"It's no' lookin' guid," Nash whispered to Cam.

"Is there anythin' else ye have to say, Cam?" Storm looked over to him, almost as if he hoped there was. Storm was a fair man and didn't like to punish those who truly didn't deserve it.

"I have one more piece of evidence, and I think this will prove to ye and everyone that Dun fell on his own knife and that is what killed him."

"What do ye mean?" asked Bart. "How could ye possibly prove somethin' as ridiculous at that?"

"Bring in Dun, please," said Cam, really causing the crowd to go wild now.

"They're bringin' in a dead body?" cried one woman.

"Aye, that is exactly what I'm doin'," said Cam, waving his hand. The butcher, the tanner, the baker, and the undertaker who had just returned all carried in the covered body on a stretcher. Everyone moved aside to give them plenty of room.

"Cam, what is this all about?" growled Ian.

"I had a feelin' what I'd presented wasna goin' to be enough proof for some of ye. That is why Nash and I dug up Dun's body last night to prove it."

"God's eyes," said Storm, shaking his head and sitting back down.

"Dinna expose a decayin' body in this hall," shouted Callum.

Cam's hand was on the blanket that covered the body, as he was about to pull it away.

"Cam, nay. I canna bear to see him again." Yvaine turned her head and closed her eyes.

"Perhaps, it would be better if ye came down here?" Cam said to the lairds.

Ian and Storm walked down to the body, lifting the blanket to look beneath it.

"If ye'll notice, the man has a knife wound in the chest," said Cam. "There is a bump on the head, but that doesna seem to be the cause of his death."

"Nay, it's no'," said the undertaker. "I've seen plenty of deaths, and this one was due to the knife. His skull wasna cracked and neither was there a cut on his head anywhere."

"He's right," said Storm, inspecting the body.

"How do we ken that she didna thrust the blade through his chest?" Bart pointed an accusing finger at Yvaine. Cam saw Yvaine's body trembling, and wanted this to be over as fast as possible.

"I – I didna," said Yvaine. "I only hit him on the head. Dun never let anyone touch his knife, especially no' me. And he always had it on him."

"I have witnesses from town who attest that what she says is true," Cam told the lairds, nodding at the townsfolk.

"They dug up my brathair's body in the middle of the night and then stabbed it to make it look like this is true," Bart continued.

"I had a feelin' someone would say that, and that is why I made sure I had the same townsfolk as witnesses while Nash and I dug up the body. Ye can ask any of them, and they'll tell ye that the stab mark in the chest was already there, and we didna put it there at all."

"That's right," said the butcher. "I watched them the whole time."

"We all did," said the tanner.

"Dun told me he was goin' to kill his wife, and he had the knife on him at the time," said Farlan. "His knife marks are engraved in the drink board in the tavern. I will go and get the board and bring it here myself if ye want to see it."

"There's no need for that," said Storm, after speaking in hushed voices with his father. "Cover up the body and put it back in the ground, please."

"So, who is goin' to hang for killin' my brathair?" asked Bart, sounding bloodthirsty to Cam.

"It seems the one responsible for Dun's death is already dead," said Ian.

"That's right," agreed Storm. "Dun was a product of his own destruction, and no one here will be blamed."

"So, does that mean that Yvaine and Keithen are free to go?" asked Cam.

"Everyone is free to go. No one today is goin' to die, or goin' to the dungeon," said Storm, getting cheers from all but Bart.

"I insist someone pays for my brathair's death."

"If ye really want someone to pay, then I'll put ye in the dungeon for accusin' innocent people," bellowed Storm. "Now, leave Hermitage and never show yer face here again."

"What about the shop?" Bart wouldn't stop. "Now that my brathair is dead, I should get his shop and business."

"Are ye a chandler?" asked Ian.

"Well, nay," said Bart.

"Then I see no reason why ye should get it."

"Yvaine is his widow, and now owner of the business," said Cam. "Doesna the chandler's guild state that a widow can inherit her husband's place of business and run it herself after his death?"

"It's true," said the tanner. "Every guild has that rule."

"Yvaine is the owner of the chandler's shop now," said the butcher.

"We're happy to help her in any way we can until she gets back on her feet," added the butcher's wife.

"Then it's settled," said Storm. "The trial is over, and everyone can please leave."

"No' so fast," said Old Callum MacKeefe, getting to his feet. "I think it's time we address the issue of Cam MacKeefe and his conduct at the priory."

"What?" Cam was busy hugging Yvaine, but when he heard his name, he spun around. "I'm finished with my sentence."

"Cam, we've had a missive from Brathair Gillies, sayin' ye didna cooperate." Storm told him. "I'm afraid ye'll have to start over with yer sentence."

"It's no' true," said Cam. "I did everythin' the monk told me to do."

"We can assure ye it's true," said Nash. "That is, since we had to do chores as well."

"I'm sure ye did," said Storm. "Still, I'm sorry. Without confirmation from Brathair Gillies that ye carried out his orders, I'm afraid I canna let ye back into the clan, Cam."

"I'm here about that missive," came a voice from the back of the room. Cam turned around to see Brother Gillies standing there. He groaned.

"Brathair Gillies, how long have ye been here?" asked Storm.

"I wanted to be here to help clear my sister's name, but I see that it is thankfully no longer needed."

"Gillies?" said Keithen in surprise. "I canna remember the last time ye came to Scotland."

"Why did ye come?" asked Yvaine. "To cause more trouble for Cam? Havena ye done enough of that?"

"I'm sorry about that," apologized the monk. "Lairds MacKeefe, I give ye my word that Cam has carried out his sentence and has worked hard to accomplish any task I gave him, no matter how nasty it was. I only sent that missive in anger, and what I wrote isna true. The fact is, Cam's punishment is over and I hope ye will see it that way as well."

"Is he talkin' like a Scot?" asked Cam, not believing his ears.

"Brathair, it doesna sound like ye," said Yvaine.

"I am talkin' like a Scot because that is who I am," said Gillies. "I thought about everythin' that happened and realized I can replace things . . . but no' family. I was wrong, and I am sorry for any trouble I've caused ye, Yvaine and Cam. I willna worry about what the king and bishop think anymore because I have left Lanercost Priory."

"Ye did?" asked Yvaine.

"Aye. I havena had time to do it yet, but I am movin' to Scotland and I intend to find a new priory here."

"But ye said Lanercost was so important to ye," blurted out Cam.

"Nothin' is more important than family. Yvaine, I hope ye can forgive me for the way I acted toward ye."

"I forgive ye, Brathair," Yvaine told him. "However, I think it is Cam's forgiveness ye should be askin' for."

"Cam?" said the monk, holding out his hand. Cam looked

over to Yvaine and she was smiling and nodding.

"No hard feelin's." Cam shook the man's hand.

"Now, can I be the first to welcome ye into our family?" asked Gillies.

"What's this?" Storm looked up in surprise.

"Yvaine and I are gettin' married," said Cam. "We're goin' to raise my daughter, Avianca, together."

"Yay!" cried Avianca, breaking away from Davita, running and hugging both Cam and Yvaine. "I want Yvaine to be my new mathair."

"Will ye marry us, right here. Right now?" Cam asked Storm, unable to wait to start his new life with Yvaine.

"Slow down, Cam," laughed Yvaine. "If the MacKeefes are kind enough to let us get married here, I think we should post the banns for three days as is proper."

"Oh, I agree," said Storm's wife, breaking through the crowd. "We want this to be a special wedding and there are many plans to be made."

"Then in three days it is," said Storm, making it final. "But if this keeps up, I swear this castle is goin' to be called a church before long."

# CHAPTER TWENTY-SIX

*Hermitage Castle, three days later*

YVAINE NERVOUSLY GRIPPED the flowers in her hands so tightly that her whole body shook.

"Quit bein' so nervous," said Davita with a smile, fixing the veil on Yvaine's head. "Gettin' married is the best thing that ever happened to me, and it'll be a joy for ye as well, I am sure."

"I ken ye're right," said Yvaine, about ready to walk down the aisle. "However, remember, I've been married before and it was the worst experience I ever had."

"That's different. Ye're marryin' into the MacKeefe family now. Cam is a wonderful man, and ye dinna have a thing to worry about."

"I am sure that's true. I love him, and canna wait to be his wife."

"Have ye decided yet if ye're goin' to keep yer shop in town?" asked Davita.

"Cam told me I should, but I want to be rid of anythin' that reminds me of Dun. I am goin' to make candles for the MacKeefe Clan now. We will be livin' mostly in the Highlands, but just like ye, staying at Hermitage Castle at times as well."

"I am so happy that we will still be friends, and now also family." Davita gave her a big hug.

"Mathair, can I throw the flowers on the floor now?" asked

Avianca, standing there with a basket of petals in her hands.

"Yes, sweetheart. It's time," Yvaine told her, running a hand over the girl's head, and sending her down the aisle in front of her. "I'll never get tired of hearin' her call me Mathair," she whispered to Davita, as Davita followed the little girl.

"Yvaine, are ye ready?" Her brother, Keithen, stood there, waiting to take her down the aisle.

"I am more than ready, Brathair," she told him, wanting more than anything to become Cam MacKeefe's wife.


CAM WAITED WITH Gavin up at the dais in the great hall of Hermitage Castle. Today was a sunny day and the light shined in through the windows, brightening up the entire hall. The women had decorated the place with sprigs of heather and colorful ribbons. People from the town were there to celebrate with the clan. Gillies sat up in the front dressed in his monk's robe, smiling from ear to ear.

Cam's heart melted when he saw his daughter throwing flower petals in the air, and then jumping up, trying to catch them. Davita quickly grabbed her hand, and brought her over to Gillies before joining the wedding party. Keithen walked Yvaine up the aisle since her father was no longer alive. He gave her a quick kiss and then sat down in the front row with his brother.

Their vows went quickly, and before Cam knew it, he was married to Yvaine. Everyone was clapping and cheering.

"Kiss her," someone who sounded a lot like Nash shouted out for everyone to hear.

"Can I kiss ye, Yvaine?" he asked, feeling nervous for the first time to kiss a girl in front of people.

"Of course, Husband," she said, reaching over and kissing him. The kiss lingered and he heard Red talking to Violet in the background.

"He always was a guid kisser," she said. "But I never got one with that much passion."

"Congratulations," said Storm, shaking Cam's hand.

He was followed by the rest of the clan as they greeted Cam and Yvaine, one at a time.

"I will decide on a sentence for either North or Nash tomorrow," said Old Callum when he came to congratulate them. "Tonight, we're all drinkin' Mountain Magic."

The minstrels started up a lively tune, and everyone started dancing.

"May I have this dance?" Cam asked Yvaine. They twirled around the floor, laughing, especially when Avianca decided she wanted to dance with them.

"Ye have to wait, honey," said Yvaine, causing the little girl to pout.

"Why wait?" asked Cam, scooping up his daughter. "We can all dance together since we're a family now." He made Avianca laugh as the three of them danced together as a group.

"Cam?" came a voice from behind him. Cam turned around and froze. There stood his father with a small box in his hand.

"What are ye doin' here?" asked Cam, not sure how he felt about this.

"Cam, please dinna get angry at him," said Yvaine. "I asked Gillies to send Lord Clifton a missive, invitin' him to our weddin'."

"Ye should have asked me first, Yvaine." Cam scowled at her.

"I'm sorry," said the border lord, lowering his head. "I can see now that I shouldn't have come at all. I'll leave at once. I just wanted to give you this wedding present."

"I don't want anything from ye," growled Cam, but Yvaine took the box from him.

"Thank ye, Lord Clifton, for comin'," said Yvaine. "I'm sorry I put ye in such a position. I should have asked Cam's permission first."

"No harm done," said the man, smiling at Avianca in Cam's arms. "It was worth it just to be here for a few minutes. I'll leave now, and I won't bother you again. Congratulations on your wedding. I hope you two will be very happy together."

He turned to leave, and Yvaine leaned over and spoke softly to Cam.

"I'm sorry, Cam. I just wanted ye to have someone here on this special day that was from yer true family."

"I do," he told her. "I have Avianca." Cam stared at the back of his father as the man headed for the door.

"Och, Cam, look what he gave ye." Yvaine held up his father's ring that she plucked from the box.

Cam's eyes filled with tears, and he bit the inside of his cheek to keep his emotions contained.

"That's pretty," said Avianca, gently touching the ring. "Is the nice man who gave it to ye goin' to stay at the weddin'?"

"Nice man?" Cam looked down at his daughter. "I didna think ye liked Lord Clifton."

"I didna at first, but he smiled at me. And he let me live with ye, Da. I think I like him now." Cam's heart swelled to hear his daughter say this about the man that she didn't even know was her grandfather.

"Hold her for a minute, please, Yvaine." Cam gave the girl to Yvaine and ran to stop his father from leaving. He brought him back, taking Avianca into his arms once again.

"Avianca, this is Lord Clifton. Yer grandda," he told her.

"Yay! I have a grandda. Do ye want to dance with me, Grandda?" asked the little girl, reaching out her arms for him to take her.

"Would it be all right with you, Cam?" Cam's father didn't move, waiting for Cam's permission.

"Sure," said Cam, handing Avianca to him. At one time, he would never have done this. Before, he only wanted to pull his daughter away from the man. But this was his father, and Yvaine was right. Family was important, and he wanted him here on his special day, after all.

"You know, Libby would have loved to be here. I'm sure she'd be so proud of you, Cam," said his father.

Cam and Yvaine watched as the man smiled and laughed and

twirled around the floor with his granddaughter in his arms.

"That was guid of ye to call him back," said Yvaine. "For Avianca's sake, if no' yers."

"I only did it because ye took the time to think about me, invitin' him to the weddin' in the first place. No one has ever thought of me the way ye do, Yvaine. That makes me feel special."

"I love ye, Cam. Ye are special to me. I ken it is hard for ye to accept yer faither, but give it time. I'm sure it will become easier."

"I'm still no' sure it was the right thing to do, since he is harborin' the secret from his other family."

"He's the one who will have to live with the secret, no' us. I am glad we are goin' to start a new life together now."

"Are ye sure ye really want to leave town to live with the clan?" he asked her.

"I am more than sure, Cam."

"But willna ye be givin' up so much?"

"Nay, no' at all. I can still come back and visit my friends, but I willna be livin' in the shadow of Dun anymore."

"Willna makin' candles for the MacKeefe Clan make ye think of him?"

"Nay. No' if ye're the one makin' them with me." She smiled and reached over to kiss him.

"Och, I love yer kisses, lass," he told her.

"I'm a fast learner," she said with a wink. He knew she meant that he was the one who taught her how to enjoy making love.

"I may have taught ye a few things about . . . kissin'," he told her in a sultry voice. "However, ye are the chandler and taught me a few things about startin' fiery passion as well, my little *Highland Flame*."

# From the Author

I hope you enjoyed *Highland Flame* and will take the time to leave a review for me. It was fun to research medieval chandlers, and made me want to try making my own candles someday. I feel Cam and Yvaine were perfect for each other, since they both had hard lives to overcome before they found their happiness. Sometimes in life, things might not turn out for the best right away, but never give up hope. One can look at situations in their life as problems, or as opportunities to change, to make their life better. I hope to always choose the latter.

I like bringing in past characters from some of my other series, combining them with my new books.

If you want to know more about Lord Rook and his brothers, please be sure to read one of my favorite series ever, *Legendary Bastards of the Crown*.

The books in the series are:

*Destiny's Kiss* (prequel)
*Restless Sea Lord*
*Ruthless Knight* (Rook's story)
*Reckless Highlander*

Laird Storm MacKeefe and Lady Wren's story is *Lady Renegade* from my *Legacy of the Blade Series*.

The books in the series are:

*Legacy of the Blade Prequel*
*Lord of the Blade*
*Lady Renegade*
*Lord of Illusion*
*Lady of the Mist*

Nash MacKeefe's story is next in ***Highland Sky – Book 3*** of the ***Highland Outcasts Series.***
Happy Reading!

*Elizabeth Rose*

# About the Author

Elizabeth Rose is an Amazon All-Star, and bestselling, award-winning, author of nearly 100 books and counting! Her first book was published back in 2000, but she has been writing stories ever since high school.

She is the author of contemporary, western, paranormal, and her favorite – medieval romance. You'll find sexy, alpha heroes and strong, independent heroines in her books. Sometimes her heroines can even swing a sword. She loves adding humor to her work, because everyone needs to laugh more in life. Her ***Bad Boys of Sweetwater: Tarnished Saints Series,*** was inspired by people, places, and things in her own life. The location is the lake and small town of Michigan where she grew up visiting her grandparents.

Living in the suburbs of Chicago with her husband, she has two grown sons and one granddog – so far. A lover of nature, Elizabeth can be found in the summer swinging in her "writing hammock" in her secret garden, creating her next novel. Her secret garden is what inspired her series, ***Secrets of the Heart***, which of course centers around a secret garden too!

Elizabeth's current and upcoming books will be published by *Dragonblade Publishing* and independently too under *RoseScribe Media Inc.*